OPERATION BIKER

They make the Hell's Angels look like choirboys.

They beat the Mafia at its own grisly game.

They use a combination of old-fashioned violence and up-to-the-second computer technology to stay one step ahead of the law as they spread coast-to-coast.

They deal in drugs and guns and sex and death and demand that FBI special agent Walsh live up to their code of twisted honor and perverted manhood to prove himself worthy of wearing their colors.

Walsh proves himself, all right . . . maybe *too* well to come out of this deception alive. . . .

DEEP COVER

New from the #1 bestselling author of *Communion*—
a novel of psychological terror and demonic possession. . . .
"A triumph."—Peter Straub

UNHOLY FIRE
Whitley Strieber

Father John Rafferty is a dedicated priest with only one temptation—the beautiful young woman he has been counseling, and who is found brutally murdered in his Greenwich Village church. He is forced to face his greatest test of faith when the NYPD uncovers her sexually twisted hidden life, and the church becomes the site for increasingly violent acts. Father Rafferty knows he must overcome his personal horror to unmask a murderer who wears an angel's face. This chilling novel will hold you in thrall as it explores the powerful forces of evil lurking where we least expect them. "Gyrates with evil energy . . . fascinating church intrigue."—*Kirkus Reviews*

DEEP COVER

D. EDWARD BUNGERT

A SIGNET BOOK

SIGNET
Published by the Penguin Group
Penguin Books USA Inc., 375 Hudson Street,
New York, New York 10014, U.S.A.
Penguin Books Ltd, 27 Wrights Lane,
London W8 5TZ, England
Penguin Books Australia Ltd, Ringwood,
Victoria, Australia
Penguin Books Canada Ltd, 10 Alcorn Avenue,
Toronto, Ontario, Canada M4V 3B2
Penguin Books (N.Z.) Ltd, 182–190 Wairau Road,
Auckland 10, New Zealand

Penguin Books Ltd, Registered Offices:
Harmondsworth, Middlesex, England

First published by Signet, an imprint of New American Library,
a division of Penguin Books USA Inc.

First Printing, January, 1993
10 9 8 7 6 5 4 3 2 1

REGISTERED TRADEMARK—MARCA REGISTRADA

PRINTED IN THE UNITED STATES OF AMERICA

PUBLISHER'S NOTE
This is a work of fiction. Names, characters, places, and incidents either
are the product of the author's imagination or are used fictitiously, and any
resemblance to actual persons, living or dead, events, or locales is entirely
coincidental.

Dedicated to my darling wife, Katherine.
Thank you for always believing in me.

Special thanks to my sister, Helen Bungert.
If not for your coaching and encouragement,
I might never have gotten started.

And special thanks to Buddha.
You taught me early in life that things
are not always what they seem to be.

I'd like to acknowledge the following people
for their assistance, encouragement, infor-
mation, and coaching throughout the writing
of this book: Juval Aviv, Debby, Dudley
F.B. Hodgson, I.L., Robert Jaeger, James
Keefe, Lilian Gilden, Hy Bender, Adam
Troy-Castro, Maniac, Avril Hordyk, Judy
Starger, Elena Andrews, Tom Deja, R.P.,
Donna Ellis, Jennie Grey, M.L., Sharon
Gumerove, B.M., Lisa Nowak, Michael
Higgins, Shawna McCarthy, and A.R.

Chapter 1

I arrived at eight forty-five A.M. An envelope had been placed on my desk, probably the night before. I imagined Higgins, the desk sergeant, swearing as he signed for the delivery, then asking one of his men to drop it on my desk. "Fucking feds think we're this guy's personal secretary," he had probably said, even though it had been more than six months since any hand-delivered correspondence was sent to me. I placed my jacket on the back of my chair and read the neatly typed label: MARTIN J. WALSH, FEDERAL BUREAU OF INVESTIGATION—CONFIDENTIAL.

I sat down and picked it up, my elbows resting on the desk as I read the label over and over again. *Could I finally be getting a new assignment?* I wondered. For three years I had been working as a liaison agent with the Los Angeles police department. A joint task force had been set up in response to a wave of bank robberies, muggings, and assaults believed to be the work of a leftist group called The People's Movement. I had co-ordinated efforts between the Bureau and the LAPD. Within two years the group had been so well infiltrated that nearly a quarter of their membership were either undercover police or FBI.

Aside from a few arrests for the Bureau and some requests for information by the LAPD, the past year had been uneventful. I still had a desk at the police station, but my phone seldom rang. I was all but forgotten, except for the direct deposit of my biweekly pay. I often wondered what would happen if I stopped showing up. Would anyone at headquarters ever notice?

Inside the envelope was a memo from the district chief ordering me to report to Senior Agent Richard Atwood. *Atwood? That's the Organized Crime Unit.* My wish could be coming true. Finally, some investigative work that would allow me to utilize the criminology techniques so painfully acquired in numerous courses and seminars.

I put my hands behind my head, tilted my chair back, and thought, *Whatever it is they want me for, it's got to be better than this assignment.* But the little voice inside my head reminded me: *Be careful what you wish for, you just might get it.*

After an hour of fighting Los Angeles traffic, I arrived at the Federal Building. I parked my silver Dodge Spirit ES in the subbasement lot. For the last six years, Amy and I had driven secondhand wrecks. This was our very first new car. I wiped a smudge from the side-view mirror as I locked the door. I fumbled for my identification card to summon the elevator to the basement. Nervous anticipation almost immobilized me. All the years of training and experience suddenly seemed dwarfed by self-doubt.

As I rode up the elevator, part of me wanted to run straight back to my do-nothing, go-nowhere job at the police station. Part of me also needed to know what lay ahead.

When I approached the reception desk on the eighth floor, I was greeted by a pleasant-looking woman in her early forties.

"Mr. Atwood is expecting you, Mr. Walsh. You can go in," she said warmly. "It's the second office on the right."

"Thank you," I said.

The window in Atwood's office door had a hairline crack, which made a pattern resembling that of the profile of a person's face. I found myself staring at it, my hand on the doorknob, when the sound of Atwood's voice brought me back into focus.

"Come on in, Martin!" he said robustly. His voice was hoarse from years of smoking cigars.

"Good morning, Mr. Atwood. You . . . wanted to see me, sir?" I said. *Calm down, for Christ's sake. You've been out of the academy for over six years. Stop acting so tense.*

He motioned for me to sit in the chair across from his desk, and he lit his cigar.

Atwood's office was a shrine to his career. Awards, citations, press clippings, and photos covered the walls. He also had the most incredible collection of police department patches I had ever seen. Many agents collect and trade them like baseball cards. He must have had a thousand of them.

"Cigar, Martin?" Atwood stood, leaning over his desk. He held the cigar between his index finger and what was left of his left thumb. I remembered hearing that he had lost it while investigating the Petricci organization in New York. He'd been assigned to get in tight with Fortunato Petricci, the then Godfather, and gather evidence to convict him of racketeering. While working as Petricci's number-two man, Atwood found himself in the middle of a squabble between the Petricci and Bonavici crime families. He was jumped by a couple of Bonavici thugs and they sliced off his thumb with a tin-snipper. They must have figured that if they could show Petricci how easily they could get to his number-two man, he would curtail his expansion into the firearms market. The story around the Bureau was that even as they were threatening to cut it off, Atwood had told them to go fuck themselves.

"You might want to start, Martin." He laughed, and then started to cough violently.

"Would you like a drink of water, sir?" I said.

Atwood motioned no with his good hand and cleared his throat. He spit into the garbage pail and fell back into his desk chair.

"I'm gonna give these things up someday," he said, taking a puff on his Macanudo.

"Martin, you are, of course, familiar with The Henchmen?"

"Of course. I mean . . . yes, sir!"

I sure was familiar with The Henchmen. These guys were the most notorious motorcycle gang in the country. I had personally handled the liaison efforts between the LAPD and our offices in a case involving Henchmen just eight months ago. Three of those boys are now doing twenty to life for killing a guy who they said was breaking into their clubhouse. They murdered this poor bastard by hanging him from the ceiling by his feet and playing piñata with his skull. Two of the bikers actually had pieces of the guy's brains sticking to their clothes when they were arrested. When the LAPD requested information from the Bureau on the two suspects, we supplied them with details of six different cases in which the two bikers were wanted for questioning.

"There is sufficient evidence, Martin, that motorcycle gang members have heavy ties to organized crime. By the way, it's 'Richard.' Can that 'Mr. Atwood' and 'sir' shit, okay?"

"Sure, thanks."

"We have reason to believe The Henchmen are involved in extortion, murder for hire, arson, and a host of other nasty activities. Let's face it. It's never been a secret that these guys are criminals. Only now it seems they've become well organized and have expanded their operations to major cities around the country. A sort of Mafia on wheels. Take a look at these."

He tossed four black-and-white photos to the edge of his desk. I picked up snapshots of the bodies of two Mexicans who had been murdered three weeks ago.

"What a mess," I said. "I read the police report on this one. These guys actually had their testicles cut off. Their throats were cut, and the medical examiner found evidence that they were tortured for hours before they were finally killed."

"Exactly," said Atwood pointedly. "There's only two possible reasons for this kind of overkill. Either the killer or killers wanted to send a message, or they're complete psychopaths. Or both."

"And you think The Henchmen did this?"

"Damn right I do, Martin. Nobody goes farther, faster, and more viciously than The Henchmen. And a witness saw two bikes outside the victims' apartment building around the time of the murder. She said the riders were wearing colors. Her description of their jackets matched The Henchmen's insignia very closely."

"I don't remember reading that in the police report," I said.

"That's because it wasn't there. We conducted our own investigation."

"Isn't this a local matter?"

"Not since we've learned who the Mexicans were. They were identified as Pedro Morales and Juan Mendez. Both from Queens, New York. Both suspected of running drugs and guns around the country. They were known to have frequented The Henchmen's clubhouse in New Jersey."

"A little interstate commerce," I said.

"Precisely. We suspect The Henchmen operate cross-country, moving drugs and weapons and generally controlling activities in some areas—either in concert with or in the place of traditional organized crime."

Atwood looked me up and down, the way an inspector general surveys his troops. *He wants me to go out,* I thought to myself. *This son of a bitch wants me to go out! No way! I'm married and have a kid. Investigations are one thing. You interview potential witnesses, question suspects, study documents, make reports. But undercover? Deep cover? No thanks.*

"Mr. Atwood, if you're thinking of sending—"

"Martin!" he interrupted powerfully. "First of all, it's 'Richard,' remember? And I would like to give you the opportunity of a lifetime. A chance to make supervisor. You can write your own ticket. Any assignment. Anywhere."

Supervisor. Any assignment. I felt myself being drawn in, seduced by the promise of a promotion. A second ago I'd been ready to flatly refuse. Now I wanted to hear more. It can happen like that, in a moment. Sometimes things that are the furthest from your mind pop in and *Blam!* your whole life is never the same afterwards.

I thought back to the time in my life when I'd first decided I wanted to work in law enforcement. I was nine years old. On my way home from school I found a wallet with over eighty bucks in it. Eighty bucks! To a nine-year-old that was all the money in the world. There was no identification in the wallet, only a receipt from Jovino's Shoe Repair. I wanted so badly to run to the nearest toy store and buy Mr. Machine, the walking, talking robot, but part of me wouldn't go for it. I ran straight to the shoe shop and Mr. Jovino identified the owner through the repair ticket.

The owner turned out to be a retired Treasury Department agent by the name of Roger Wolfe. Wolfe had spent much of his career as an investigator for the Bureau of Alcohol, Tobacco and Firearms, often going undercover in Mississippi, Alabama, and Louisiana to bust up moonshine operations. He told me that I was made of the right stuff: integrity and brains. He gave me a ten-dollar reward and told me he could use some help around his house on the weekends if I was interested.

The pay was fifty cents an hour, and every Saturday from then until I went away to college I mowed Roger Wolfe's lawn, painted, scrubbed floors and, when I was really lucky, helped him clean and oil his gun collection. On those occasions Mr. Wolfe would tell me stories of how he and his special team broke up moonshine operations in Mississippi, and how they were considered the real "Untouchables" by the press. Becoming a government agent was all I thought about. To me there could be no better life than one spent enforcing the law. Integrity and brains.

Atwood stood up, walked over to the window, and looked out.

"We want these bastards, Martin," he said with his back to me. "And I think you'll be the man who gets them." Atwood turned abruptly and looked straight at me. *My move.* I could have said, "No, thank you" and walked away. Instead I blurted out:

"What do I have to do?"

Atwood opened his eyes wide, and the left side of his mouth twitched to form a satisfied smile.

"You have to disappear, Martin. Become part of their world."

"Why me . . . Richard?"

"Well, for one thing, your knowledge of motorcycles. Your age and physique also make you perfect for it." He began to glance through a file on his desk. "Says here you're a karate champion, and an ace motorcycle mechanic. I understand you paid your way through college by working at a motorcycle repair shop."

"Part-time, yes. I haven't been on a bike in almost ten years though," I said. I had never thought I'd get back into bikes like this. My heart was pounding and my palms were sweaty, as I listened to Atwood explain this assignment.

"Here's the deal, Martin. You go under for six, eight months, tops. You contact me and two or three other case agents only. You can call home, but no visits. We can't risk your being tailed. I'm sure you wouldn't want that, either."

I nodded.

"If any emergency comes up at home, we'll bring you out. If things get too hot, we'll bring you out. You'll get paid automatically through a special account. Not too different from how we do it now. All the other details of your assignment will be determined and fully disclosed during your training."

Atwood returned to his chair and folded his arms, waiting for my reaction, for questions. I couldn't focus on a single one to ask him.

"Okay, I'll do it," I found myself saying. "When do I start?"

Clearly Atwood sensed I was uneasy, and he warmly assured me that he would be there for me and my family.

"We're partners now. From now on your concerns are my concerns. Take the rest of the day off, then report to Dalton Leverick tomorrow morning at the Brentwood facility. Dalton is our resident expert on motorcycle gangs. He'll teach you everything you'll need to know, and then some."

Atwood stood up and opened the door. "By the way, stop shaving. We have to make a biker out of you."

All the way from Atwood's office to the parking garage I wondered whether I'd done the right thing. I was tempted to run back and tell him to forget it. I drove the car out of the garage into the bright afternoon sunlight. The reality of the commitment I had just made hit me hard. The drive home seemed unusually long, as I wondered how I was going to explain this to Amy.

Bumper-to-bumper traffic gave me time to rehearse—"Amy, I've just accepted a dangerous assignment"; "Amy, I'll see you and Alex in six months"; "Amy, I have an opportunity to do something really important"—but there was going to be no good way to say it.

My concentration was broken by the rumbling of two motorcycles passing the stalled traffic between lanes. "These lawless punks think they own the highways," I said out loud. My thoughts raced back and forth between the bikers and my family. I remembered an incident where one of the Henchmen had killed a woman and her four-year-old son. The papers said she had tried to run away from the biker and he'd shot them both. Suddenly I was angry. At that moment my personal crusade for law and order became more important than the prospect of a promotion. I hated these low-lifes and all they stood for. As the bikers rode away I pointed my finger like a gun, as a child would play cops and robbers, until they were completely out of sight. Hating them was an easy way to justify my decision to go after them.

I arrived home at two-thirty in the afternoon. I must have sat in the car for forty minutes before I decided to go inside and tell my wife that her husband was about to take off for six months. When I walked in, Amy was in the family room playing with Alex, our four-year-old son.

"Hello, Martin," she said affectionately. "You're home early. What's wrong . . . ?"

"Nothing," I said, trying to sound surprised at her question.

"After eight years of marriage, I can tell when something isn't right with you."

She had me pegged. "Alex, why don't you play in the yard for a few minutes while Mommy and I talk," I said. With a little coaxing from his mother, he complied.

"It's about an assignment. A good one. One that will lead to a promotion and security for our family."

Amy frowned. "I don't understand," she said. "Exactly what kind of an assignment? What will you have to do?"

"I'm being assigned to an undercover operation. It's not much of an operation actually, just an information-gathering assignment." I thought I could lessen the impact—play down what my actual duties would be. I couldn't tell her I would be rubbing elbows with the lowest form of scum the stinking streets have ever produced. "I have to gather evidence against a motorcycle gang. It's really no big deal. I just can't live at home for a while."

Amy's look turned sour.

"How long is 'a while'?"

"Six . . . eight months, tops."

"Bullshit. Bullshit! Bullshit! Bullshit!" she yelled. "I'm not going to stand for having you away from home for six months. *Six months?* Jesus Christ, Martin! What the hell do I tell Alex?" She turned away from me and looked out the window to where he was playing in the backyard. "Do I say, 'I'm sorry, son, but you can't see Daddy for the next two hundred nights because he's off chasing some bad guys around and can't come home'?" she asked sarcastically.

I put my hands on her shoulders, and for a moment we both watched Alex roam the yard in search of new and different stones for his collection. I gently turned Amy around and kissed her softly.

"I love you," I said. "I wouldn't do this if I didn't think it was the best thing for our future."

"This is unbelievable, Martin. If you go, I don't see you for half a year. If you turn it down, you'll resent me for denying you this opportunity to advance in the Bureau. Alex and I lose, either way." She pushed away from me, looking down and shaking her head. "Do what you have to do." She then joined Alex in the yard.

We didn't say much to each other for the rest of the evening. Long after Amy had fallen asleep I was still awake, staring at the ceiling and thinking just one thought: *What the hell am I getting myself into?*

Chapter 2

I blinked my eyes, and the digits on my alarm clock changed from 2:10 A.M. to 6:32 A.M. "Oh, shit!" I muttered out loud, as I popped out of bed. Amy woke up almost as abruptly.

"What time is it?" She sat up, resting on her elbows.

"I'm late. I have to hurry," I said.

"I guess there's no chance you'll change your mind."

I sat on the side of the bed and gently placed my hand on her soft cheek. She looked at me with pleading eyes. I wanted to stay. I really wanted to stay, but she knew as well as I did that there was no way that was going to happen. She knows that once something is in my mind as strong as this assignment was there's no stopping me.

"I love you more than I will ever be able to express," I said. "These next few months will pass quickly, and then we'll have the rest of our lives together."

She took my hand and kissed it. "I'll miss you, too. So will Alex."

Amy slipped on her blue silk bathrobe. God, I love her in that robe. She went to the kitchen to put on a pot of coffee while I got dressed. On my way down the hall I opened the door to Alex's room. He was holding his stuffed animal while he slept. He clutched it tighter as I kissed him on his forehead.

"See ya, champ. Take care of your mommy for me," I whispered softly, as I closed the door to his room.

After two quick cups of coffee, during which neither Amy nor I said much, we embraced for what seemed like a long time by the front door. As I walked down the path to the driveway, I could hear the click of the bolt as she locked the door.

The training facility was located in Brentwood, thirty miles east of my home in Oakville, a Los Angeles suburb. The facility used to be a summer camp for the underprivileged in the forties. In 1951 funding dried up, and the place was closed. In 1964 the Bureau purchased it from the state and converted it into its West Coast training site.

The facility was divided into four sections: the recently added north section for anti-terrorist training; the south section for basic training; the east section for heavy weapons; and the west section for special assignments, where I was to spend the next three weeks learning how to be a biker.

I arrived at the administration building at nine A.M. It was sunny that morning and I had forgotten my sunglasses. I held my hand above my eyes to block the sun's glare as I walked up the steps. Once inside I picked up my assignment sheet and registered with the duty clerk.

"You're due to report to Training Room 7 at nine-thirty, Mr. Walsh," he said, as he clocked in my sheet and handed it to me without ever looking up from his desk. "Here are the keys to your room. When you get outside turn left, walk straight about a hundred and fifty yards. It's the third building, room C."

"Thanks."

"You're welcome, sir," he said, looking up for a moment.

The sun was at my back as I walked toward the dormitories. It beat down on the back of my head with almost personal intent. I started to feel irritated. The strap on my garment bag was bothering my shoulder, so I carried it by hand the rest of the way. It was about eighty degrees now, and my irritation was growing with every step. When I arrived at the steps of the dorm I felt like I'd just run a marathon. The heat, combined with my nervousness about the assignment, had drained me. Getting little sleep the night before added to my lackluster condition.

The room was the standard one-bedroom issue: two sets of bunk beds, two chairs, a desk, and a coffee table. It looked like it hadn't been painted since 1960. Normally two or three agents room together during training. I figured they had me here alone due to the special nature of the assignment. Getting used to the idea that you're out there alone in deep cover started here.

Training Room 7 was set up with about a dozen chairs, a podium with a director's chair next to it, and a couple of blackboards. I was early, so I sat down and waited. At about nine-forty a man in his early forties came into the room and sat in the director's chair. He placed some files and books on the podium.

"Welcome, Martin," he said, "I'm sorry I'm late."

"That's fine."

"My name is Dalton Leverick. I'll be training you on the specifics of the outlaw motorcycle gang." Leverick's speaking style was crisp and articulate. Of average height, and athletically built, he had the look of a drill sergeant. His hair was short, almost a crew cut.

Tattoos on his forearms, long since faded, suggested a tour in the military.

"Good to meet you, Dalton. How do I get started?" I asked enthusiastically.

"We get started by studying our targets. You'll need to read this." He reached up to the podium and grabbed a thick loose-leaf binder.

"What is it?" I asked, as he opened the binder and rummaged through the pages.

"It's like a reference manual. It has the criminal history of every member of the Los Angeles chapter of The Henchmen. That's the mother chapter. We'll be concentrating our efforts there. There are also facts about the club's hierarchy, suspected mob connections, and locations of chapters throughout the United States."

"How many are there?" I asked.

"Near as we can figure, about twenty. St. Paul, Chicago, Des Moines, Phoenix." He flipped through more pages and tapped his finger on the book when he found the appropriate one. "Paterson, New Jersey, and New York City," he continued with the list. "There's a Philadelphia chapter, two near Pittsburgh, and one in Atlanta, Georgia. There are three in Florida. We're not exactly sure of the cities there, since they change so often. The group has had a lot of trouble with a rival gang called The Outcasts. That gang also has several chapters in Florida. The threat of warfare keeps The Henchmen moving down there. I think they just set a chapter up in Jacksonville."

"How about here in California?"

"Besides the mother chapter in L.A. there's a chapter in Elmwood, San Pagano, and a few more scattered around the southern part of the state."

"How many members in each chapter?"

"Anywhere from a low of six or eight in San Pagano

to thirty or so in Los Angeles. It's hard to keep track. A half-dozen of them get killed each year in bike accidents and street violence. There's never a shortage of new prospects, though, all wishing to one day become official members."

"Is the plan for me to become a prospect?" I thought that sounded like a logical way to infiltrate their organization.

"That would be preferable, but may not be possible."

"What do you mean? Why?" I asked.

"The Henchmen are very suspicious, and always watch for law enforcement attempts to bring them down. They usually have prospects, or strikers as they're sometimes called, commit crimes before they can be considered for membership. These crimes can range from petty larceny to murder."

"How, then?"

"I'm working on a plan of action. I should have all the details handled in a week or so. Once I determine its feasibility, I'll brief you.

"The Henchmen have many friends of the club who are trusted, as much as any outsider can be, to do business with them. They also have a lot of legitimate businesses. For example, this guy."

Leverick tossed a file over to me that contained photos and fact sheets on several of the Los Angeles members. On top was a guy named John Weeks, a.k.a. Fat Jack. As I flipped through the pile I saw that all the bikers had aliases or nicknames. Leverick explained that the bikers only call each other by these aliases. Some members don't even know each other's real names. Half of them don't even have proper mailing addresses. Fat Jack was one of the lot who did. In fact he owned his own home, was married with two kids, and ran a moderately successful vending-machine business.

"Where does a guy like this fit in?" I asked.

"We're not exactly sure. Not all Henchmen are full-timers. Some, like Fat Jack, have decent jobs and families. Weekenders, who attend major parties and events. However, if they're called by the chapter presidents they'll drop everything and do whatever is asked of them—including murder. The club and the colors always come first. We had a case two years ago where eight members of The Hombres, a small local club, jumped one Henchman at a gas station near Route 36. They held a gun to his head and told him they'd blow his brains out if he didn't take off his colors. The Henchman refused and they shot him dead. We suspect the chapter president declared open warfare, because within four months of the incident four Hombres were dead, three were in the hospital, and the club was disbanded. Fat Jack was arrested for one of those killings. The prosecutors couldn't make it stick because of a sudden case of witness amnesia."

"Intimidation?"

"What do you think?"

"Got it. So what's next?"

"For the next week you study. Memorize that manual. Review it until you know everything the Bureau knows about The Henchmen: their women, favorite music, favorite beer—everything. You'll be a biker before you leave here in three weeks. And keep that beard growing—you'll need to look the part."

For the next six days I slept, ate, and lived bikers. I was amazed at the complexity of the network The Henchmen had put together. I was also amazed at their biker lifestyle. These guys are way outside the mainstream. I mean *way* outside. They have their own set of laws, even their own wedding ceremonies. The Henchmen have no respect for society and society's laws. The bikers very existence mocks everything that is decent.

On Sunday night I called home. Amy was supportive, but she couldn't hide her pain and fear behind comforting words.

"Are you all right, Martin?" she asked.

"Sure, honey," I said. "It's going real smooth. The first week is mainly textbook work. A lot of reading and studying. How's Alex?"

"He misses you. I told him you were like a superhero—going off to fight the forces of evil. He liked that. You *are* his hero, you know, and mine too."

"I do, sweetheart. Thanks."

Amy and I talked for about an hour. She understood that for the next six months our conversations would be few and far between. The deeper I went under, the less opportunity I would have for outside contact.

Leverick and I met for breakfast Monday morning. We had developed a good relationship during the past week, and I was comfortable that he was part of the team. We discussed the next stage of the training.

"I understand that you're an accomplished martial artist, Martin," he said.

"I used to participate quite a bit. I haven't done much in the last couple of years, though."

"Well, we're going to get back in the ring for a couple of days."

"Back in the ring?"

"Not exactly the ring as you know it from your karate days. Report to the gymnasium at eleven o'clock and I'll show you what I mean."

I had known there would be some specialized physical training. After going over the manual and several case histories, it was clear that these guys were less

than conventional fighters. In one incident a Henchman allegedly bit a guy's nose off during a skirmish
at a rock concert. This type of fighter doesn't respond
well to conventional self-defense techniques. I started
to become a little apprehensive as I watched the omi-
nous hand of time shift toward the eleventh hour.

The gymnasium was set up like a padded living
room. Chairs, tables, and other pieces of furniture, all
thickly padded with foam rubber and cloth. Leverick
arrived exactly at eleven.

"Surprised to see it set up this way?" Leverick
asked.

"A little. Why the furniture?"

"I believe that you don't train a fighter for the street
or saloon the same way you train him for the ring.
I've seen too many so-called 'trained' fighters get their
asses kicked when the real thing came down, because
the environment they trained in was too controlled.
In a real situation you don't have the luxury of padded
floor mats and a two-hundred-fifty-square-foot boxing
ring. When an agent has to fight, it's usually in close
quarters. In an alley, an apartment, or barroom."

Leverick handed me a pair of Chinese fighting
gloves.

"Put these on," he said with a slight smirk, amused
at my apprehension. The gloves fit well. I punched at
my open palms alternately to get the feel of them.
Chinese fighting gloves are designed with the same
padding as professional boxing gloves, but the fingers
are free, unlike the "mitten fit" of the traditional
glove.

"Are you ready, Martin?" he asked.

"I guess so. For what, specifically?"

"Okay, Charlie, come on in!" Leverick yelled.

Through the doorway came a figure who looked like
a cross between Big Foot and The Wild Man of

Borneo. He stood about six-five. He had huge, solid arm muscles, and reddish-brown hair that was almost shoulder-length.

"Who's *that*?" I demanded.

"That's Charlie Red. He's a freelance bad-ass. We fly him in from New York from time to time when we need to train an agent in the realities of the street. Like I said, that bullshit we teach in basic won't fly out in the real world."

"I suppose you want me to fight him?"

"No, just keep him from killing you."

"Great. Just great, Dalton."

The hulking figure approached me slowly, no emotion on his face. Just a man who'd showed for work this morning to do his job. And his job was to throw me a beating. We circled each other in the middle of the mock living room. My opponent certainly looked as if he'd been in a few scrambles on the street. He made the first move—lunging at my neck with both arms extended. I immediately bent at the waist, slipped under his left arm, and thrust a solid right-hand punch to his left temple. Without losing his balance, he shot a right which grazed my jaw and sent me backwards, falling over an easy chair or whatever that mocked-up piece of shit was supposed to be. I sprang to my feet in time to meet the menace head-on as he leaped.

The force of his body knocked me back about ten feet across the room. As I staggered up to one knee, the thundering impact of his hammer-like fist on the back of my neck sent my face crashing to the floor. He then placed me in a headlock of iron that started to drain me of my strength, spirit, and will to live. Leverick got on his hands and knees, placed his face near mine, and shouted, "You'd better get resourceful, asshole! This ain't basic! Forget everything you ever learned and fight for your fucking life, man! You don't get a second chance!"

Red was breathing down my neck. I estimated the position of his head and whipped my left hand back over my shoulder with the thumb extended and my fist tightly closed. With a painful grunt, his grip on my neck loosened. As he reached for his injured eye, I twisted and snapped an explosive elbow strike to the bridge of his nose, sending him onto his back. He pushed himself up slightly with his hands and attempted to shake off the blow. I leaped to my feet and came crashing through his jaw with my right foot. I lay back panting, repeating with every exhausted exhale, "Shit, oh shit, oh shit."

"Very resourceful, Martin. Very resourceful," Leverick said, with pride in his voice.

Charlie Red regained consciousness, and left as silently and as ominously as he'd appeared. Leverick instructed me to take the rest of the day off and relax.

That second week entailed a lot of physical activity. The morning encounters with Charlie Red were less vicious, but every bit as draining as the first one. By Saturday I was feeling pumped up, ready to take on the world. Simply busting these thugs wasn't going to be enough. I wanted to get a piece of them on the way down. Leverick must have sensed this, because he took me aside that afternoon for a brief sitdown.

"How are you feeling, Martin?" he asked.

"Great, Dalton. I feel strong. I can't wait to get out there."

"Listen, I don't want you to get over-anxious. Your job is to record events, not engage unnecessarily in violence. I've been training agents for special assignments for over six years, and I can tell when someone starts to hate."

"Hate?"

"Yes. You've had to rely heavily on aggression to get you through the training this week. The aggression you've developed towards The Henchmen has served you well. Now it's time to let it go."

"I don't understand," I said. I was a little puzzled. After all, we're the good guys and they're the enemy. It's us or them.

"You have to be emotionless during this operation," Leverick said. "Any extreme is dangerous. Feelings of love or hate for a subject can jeopardize an operation. Or worse, an agent's life."

"What am I supposed to feel?"

"Be like a doctor, removing a cancerous tumor. He doesn't hate the tumor, and he's detached from the patient. He's single-minded and purposeful. His actions are calculated and result-oriented. Are you hearing me?"

"Yes. Loud and clear. Thanks."

Dalton was right. I was becoming too emotionally charged. He put things back in perspective for me that afternoon.

"This is going to be a little different from any investigation you've ever worked on before," Leverick continued.

"Meaning?"

"Meaning we have a game plan that can be altered at any time. If nothing concrete comes your way while you're investigating, we'll have to set up some transactions—weapons, drug buys, etcetera—in order to build a case. You'll need to record and communicate with Base I every time you witness a crime being committed."

"Base I?"

"You'll be given a special number to call. Your statements will be transcribed, and 302's prepared for your signature so warrants can be issued. At times I'll personally answer that number. Other times it will be manned by Atwood, whom you already know, and by special agents Fred Parkins and Molly Samuels."

"Molly Samuels? I remember seeing her name in one of the reports."

"Yes. Molly was part of a team we put together three years ago. She tried to work her way into The Henchmen by posing as a young girl looking for some biker action. We terminated the investigation when two Henchmen tried to rape her on a barroom pool table. Molly was able to get away, but by then we knew it was foolish to try to infiltrate the group that way. She knows a lot about outlaw bikers and will be extremely useful to this investigation."

"Who *else* is in on the assignment?" I asked, with more than a touch of disgust in my voice. "I can see the *Tribune* printing details before things even get under way. I'll get my balls shot off the first time I try to make contact with them."

"Don't worry, Martin. Besides you, me, Atwood, Parkins, and Samuels, nobody knows the whole story."

"The whole story?"

"There will be players along the way. Local cops or agents may be brought in for a specific role to facilitate your assignment, or, and I hope this doesn't happen, get you out of a jam."

"You mean if I get caught?"

"Not just that. You could find yourself involved in a conflict with another club. We don't want you injured while fighting for these guys, for chrissake. Or you could find yourself hanging around with one of the prospects, when he decides to carry out one of his instructions from the club."

"Instructions?"

"When a guy becomes a prospect," Leverick continued, "he has to perform certain tasks to prove himself loyal to the club. These can be anything from robbing a liquor store to shoplifting to murder. Prospects are carefully scrutinized to see if they can show class."

"Class?"

"Yeah, it's a bikers' interpretation of the term. It simply means 'worthy to wear the club's colors on your back,' 'being a stand-up righteous dude,' and all that crap. Then after an initiation ritual, the prospect becomes a full-fledged member. We'll bring people in to the extent necessary to get you through situations like these. Also, our plans to set up drug buys and other activities will be altered according to information you relay to us. If you get enough just hanging around these guys, we won't have to set up any major operations of our own. My guess is that you'll see plenty of action from day one."

During the third week of training I learned to customize a Harley-Davidson motorcycle, outlaw-style. An outlaw biker can dismantle every nut and bolt on a Harley and put it back together in a matter of hours. By the end of the week Leverick was timing me at just under five hours. The training was winding down and, despite Leverick's talk about emotion, I was winding up. This was going to be one of the biggest busts of the decade, and I was going to be the one responsible. Agents in the academy would hear how I'd brought down the most notorious outlaw motorcycle club in America. I fantasized about media interviews, talk shows, possibly a book. I was hooked. Hooked by whatever drives people to achieve the impossible.

On Sunday morning I met Dalton for my last session.

"Morning, Martin," he said.

"Hello, Dalton. I guess I graduate today." I was feeling a little cocky.

"*Au contraire*, my boy. This is where the schooling really begins. I just got the green light from Atwood last night. After today you'll be known as James Randall, alias 'Dr. Death.' "

"You make that one up yourself?"

"Not at all. Long before the name became a cliché, used to death in pro wrestling and in B-movies, Randall was a member of a bike gang from Vancouver called Satan's Saints. He was also head of their hit squad. The Saints live now only in outlaw legend, but they made quite a name for themselves a while back. In 1976 they took on, in an all-out war with the Canadian authorities, half an army division. Eighty soldiers were killed, and all but four of the sixty-four members of the Saints died as well. Two were later killed during an attempted bank robbery. One died in an automobile accident in Quebec, and the fourth, James Randall, died of a drug overdose in South America."

"South America?" I asked.

"He took up with some mercenaries. Apparently they must have paid him in cocaine."

"Won't any of The Henchmen know what he looks like?"

"We've had to dig real deep to get this information. Atwood called in some favors from a CIA contact. We couldn't even find a photo of Randall. Some of the old-timers will probably remember his name, but I would bet that all outlaw bikers know of the infamous Saints, and the battle that wiped them out. Randall was only twenty years old at the time. He'd be thirty-six today. Just two years older than you."

"So how does Dr. Death get in with them?"

"First thing we have to do is to get you tattooed."

"Tattooed? Don't you think that's a bit much?" I

was gung ho and all, but placing permanent scars on my body was a lot to ask.

"Relax, Martin, we aren't going to scar you," Leverick said reassuringly. "The lab guys recently got hold of a process by which we can create a removable tattoo. It was invented by the Japanese government when they were trying to infiltrate the Yakusa. The Japanese Mafia are well known for their colorful tattoos, and none of their agents was willing to have a permanent garden of colors painted on his back either. The paint can be removed by laser. It's painless and leaves no scars."

"Do I get a choice of pictures?" I asked, only half kidding. I thought the least they could do was let me pick out the tattoo myself.

"No." Leverick's answer was automatic. "I've already planned which ones you'll wear. And one in particular is vital to your cover."

He showed me a photo of a corpse. The dead guy had a bearded, almost Christ-like head, and on his chest there was a crown of snakes.

"Every member of the Saints," Leverick added, "had this tattooed on the left side of his chest shortly after initiation. We'll also put an eagle on your right forearm with 'Live Free or Die' written under it. On your left shoulder, a knife dripping with blood reading 'Death is certain, life isn't.' Both classic biker tattoos. We'll take care of that tomorrow morning at the research facility in Harrisdale."

"Then I go find the Henchmen, right?"

"Not exactly. One of the members is scheduled to be paroled in two weeks. We're going to send you into Boldero to get to know him. He's sure to recognize the Satan's Saints tattoo. We'll arrange to get you in tight with him. My guess is he'll invite you to come around and see him when you get out."

"Who knows I'm there?" I asked cautiously. The thought of being inside those prison walls with fifteen hundred rapists, thieves, and murderers, any one of whom would cut my throat in a moment, scared the hell out of me.

"Besides the Base I group, only the warden, Bill Pierce, and two of his senior guards. You remember the name 'Leo Ryan'?"

"Senator?"

"Congressman."

"Yeah, Congressman Ryan . . . Killed by the Reverend Jim Jones in Guyana."

"That's what he's known for. Terrible tragedy. But a couple of years before he developed his hard-on for Jim Jones he had himself placed in Folsom Prison for a week to expose the inhumane conditions there. Pierce was warden then, and Richard Atwood coordinated the whole thing for Ryan. Pierce had himself and the two supervisors transferred to Boldero eight months ago. You'll be in good hands."

Leverick began to gather up the papers and photos.

"One of the guards is going to stage an altercation with you in front of the biker so you can make an impression. This guard will have instructions to protect you the whole time you're inside. Are you ready?"

"I'm ready." For something like this, I had no idea what "ready" was supposed to look like.

Chapter 3

I found the handcuffs uncomfortable as I was led through the gates of Boldero Prison by two burly state marshals. The marshals, arranged for by Richard Atwood through the Department of Corrections, stared straight ahead as they led me through the first checkpoint. Seemingly just two obedient employees, transporting another transferred prisoner, ignorant as to my true identity and wary of potential violent behavior.

We stopped in front of the guard's post, and I could see my reflection in the window of his booth. The vigorous workouts with weights during my training had made my six-foot-two frame more physically imposing than I had thought it could be. That, combined with my long, unkempt brown hair and beard, gave me the appearance of a cross between a healthy (and perhaps a little less crazy) Charlie Manson and some pro wrestler.

"Prisoner 35288990 from Sacramento," the raspy-voiced marshal stated, as he handed the guard a clipboard with my transfer sheet on it.

"Just what we need, another troublemaker," the guard said with disgust as he initialed the sheet. He handed it back and motioned with his head. "Straight ahead through Checkpoint B."

"Thanks, chief. Let's go."

The marshals escorted me to the second checkpoint. We passed through a metal-detector, were cleared by another guard, and proceeded inside. The cuffs and shackles were removed and I was released to the custody of a third guard.

"Cell Block A . . . er . . . Randall," said the guard, as he glanced at the paperwork. As we walked through the corridor I noticed that the cells were all empty. Three tiers of human cages awaiting their inhabitants' return from the prison yard, mess hall, or showers.

"In here," the guard instructed. "Don't leave the cell. Yard time will be over in a few minutes. Everyone'll be back for lock 'n' count." As he turned and walked away he mumbled something like "Enjoy your stay." A little prison-guard humor, I supposed.

The cell contained only an upper and lower bunk, a seatless toilet with a single faucet sink attached to it, and a small stool and table. Never in my wildest dreams could I have imagined myself inside a prison cell, planning a charade which, if it failed, could cost me my life. My thoughts flew to Amy and Alex. I wondered what they were doing right that very moment. Maybe Alex was throwing one of his famous tantrums over not wanting to eat lunch. Amy would eventually triumph, with that special blend of love and reasoning she so expertly mixed together. *Man, do I miss them!* I shook the thought from my mind. *Got to stay alert. Can't get melancholy thinking about home.* I forced myself to concentrate on the business at hand and continued to scope out the cell.

The lower bunk had pictures of naked women taped to the wall. Half were of girls straddling motorcycles. It was obvious this was my target's bunk, so I decided not to invade his space. I removed my shirt, climbed onto the upper bunk, and waited, listening to the distant sounds of radios and the occasional shouting of profanities echoing through the halls.

I was startled by the sudden appearance of a tall, muscular prisoner who looked to be a well-preserved fifty. He stood at the entrance to the cell, silent and imposing, scoping out the new guy on the block. I stared straight into his eyes. I wondered if he'd behave like one of those monkeys in the zoo the teachers had always told us not to stare at because they would find it threatening. Of course all the kids in the eighth-grade class immediately began to stare away, causing the small creatures to flip out and scream and dance— to our endless delight.

Fortunately for me, after about thirty seconds the inmate, seemingly satisfied, started to walk away. It was then I noticed the other figure, who had previously been out of view. I was shocked to see what I first thought was a woman, her finger through his belt-loop, following along closely. The young prisoner was dressed in halter top, short pants that exposed part of his butt cheeks, and high heels, which he seemed to have little trouble walking in. His face was soft, and he wore eyeliner and lipstick. He shot me a coy look as he passed the cell.

I closed my eyes for a moment, thinking about the unfortunate individual I'd just seen. He'd probably been sent up on some bullshit possession charge and, not being rich enough, got sent to the big house for two years. He would have been lucky to just do his two years and get out. They probably turned that kid before he'd been here a week. Poor little bastard.

My thoughts of pity were abruptly interrupted by the growl of a six-foot-three, two-hundred-thirty-or-so-pound inmate inquiring about my identity.

"Who the fuck are you?"

I turned slightly on one shoulder and gave him a hard, cold look. I knew that to answer him quickly would be a sign of weakness.

"Who the fuck's askin'?" I replied. I was scared, but couldn't let him know it.

"Look, scumbag, I fu—" He stopped in mid-curse, his eyes widening as he saw the Satan's Saints tattoo on my chest. "Son of a bitch! You're a fuckin' Saint! No shit?"

"No shit," I said unkindly. I had to concentrate, keep the act going.

"I thought all you guys were dead. Killed, after you chilled about three thousand cops."

I hopped down from the bunk to greet my inquiring friend face-to-face.

"Obviously not all of us . . . and not quite three thousand cops." The lies came to my lips with an ease I found surprising. The fear was quickly turning to excitement. I would have no trouble winning this gullible oaf's confidence. "I'm Jimmy," I said as I extended my hand. No need for last names.

"My friends call me Dog."

"Okay, Dog, good to meet ya. Looks like we'll be sharing this house."

"Not for long, my man. I'll be getting out of this hole in two weeks. Then I'm gonna grab my old lady and ride for two days. Only gonna stop to eat, drink, and fuck. How long you got?"

"Already put in fifteen of a sixteen-month clip. They pulled me from Sacramento 'cause we were 'bout to get it on with the niggers there in a big way. They must have figured if they transferred out the gang leaders from both sides, the rumble wouldn't take place. The shit's gonna blow there no matter what they do." Again the lies flowed easily, and Fenway bought it all the way. He didn't comment, just nodded as if he'd heard it all before. After about thirty seconds of silence he added, "When you get out, man, look us up. I ride with The Henchmen."

He rolled up his sleeve and showed me The Henchmen insignia tattooed on his right forearm. "You can prospect for me if you want."

"Dr. Death doesn't fucking prospect for nobody," I asserted abruptly. Fenway smiled. My instincts had served me well. An outlaw like Randall would never lower himself to prospect status. Fenway's eyes widened. "Dr. Fucking Death! Holy shit! You come look up me and my friends. I'll hook you up."

"House check!" shouted an inmate from about three cells away.

"Here we go again," said Fenway.

"How often do they toss you here?" I asked.

"Depends. Sometimes once a week. More, if somebody gets shivved in the yard."

A guard walked into our cell and ordered, "Okay, you know the routine, turn around." Fenway was facing the back of the cell. I could see the guard from the corner of my eye as he searched under the mattress of the top bunk. The guard abruptly turned toward me. "Hey, Mack, wise up! You face the fucking wall during house check! Got it?" The guard smiled slightly, pulled a homemade knife from his pants pocket, and proceeded to slip it under Fenway's mattress.

This was it. I was supposed to say something and get in tight with the biker by exposing the guard's attempt to plant the blade. My mind was screaming *No, no, you stupid idiot, we don't need to do this! I'm in! I'm in tight already!* but there was nothing I could do. I felt I had to proceed with what had been planned lest they try something too obvious and screw me up completely.

I turned toward the guard and shouted, "Hey, hack, you pulled that shit from your pocket! No fucking way, man!"

Fenway turned around in time to see the guard holding the mattress up with one hand, the blade in the other.

"Shut the fuck up, asshole!" the guard ordered as he drove his club into my gut, just hard enough to look authentic. He turned toward Fenway.

"Don't move, motherfucker!" he ordered. I had doubled over, as if the blow to my stomach had been effective, but I could still see two more guards come rushing into the cell. My head exploded in pain. Darkness. Silence.

I woke up about four hours later in the prison infirmary. As I opened my eyes I recognized Dalton Leverick standing at the foot of the bed. He was dressed as a doctor—white coat, stethoscope, the whole bit.

"Oh shit, I died and went to hell," I said with some irritation in my voice.

"How are you, Martin?" Dalton asked with concern.

"Great. Just great. I had it made with the guy. He bought everything I had to say. He practically invited me to join the goddamn club. There was no reason to pull that house-check bullshit. What the hell went wrong, anyway?"

"When two of the other guards heard the commotion they thought you and Fenway were attacking the guard in your cell. It wasn't meant to be that way, Martin. I'm sorry."

"Those stupid pricks could have killed me."

"It could have been worse."

"How's that?"

"The biker could have smelled a rat and cut your throat while you slept."

"I'd rather take my chances with the bikers. No more setups with assholes who are going to get me hurt. I'm better off alone than with help like that. I don't know if this prison thing was such a great idea, Dalton. I'd like a little more say from now on in what affects my life during this assignment." I rubbed my head as if for emphasis.

"Sure, sure, Martin, don't get so excited. Nothing like this will ever happen again. Guaranteed." Leverick picked up a chart and pretended to write as one of the inmates passed us with a bucket and mop on his way to the toilets. After he was clear, Leverick returned the clipboard to the front of the bed. "I'll personally make sure of it," he added.

"So what's next, Dalton?" I asked, with a touch of eagerness in my voice. In spite of a splitting headache my adrenaline was pumping. I wanted to get right back in action.

"You spend a week here in this room. You'll need that time for your head to heal. The story among the general population is that a stand-up guy from up north got hurt during lock and count. Next week, about a week before Fenway gets paroled, a story will be circulated that you got transferred out. That isn't uncommon. Troublemakers from other penitentiaries are often bounced around until they finally end up in solitary confinement, or get killed. In a few weeks, you make contact with Fenway. Then the real game begins. Clear?"

"Yeah, real clear. Christ, Dalton, what the hell am I supposed to do here for a week?"

"Just keep your ears open. Remember, the prisoners have elaborate networks. Some of them run huge operations from inside the prison. Usually they give instructions through visitors, ordering murders or setting up major drug deals. Many of those situations may involve The Henchmen on the outside. You've got a name here now. During the next week any prisoners brought to the infirmary will know about James Randall, a.k.a. Dr. Death, the righteous brother who took on three guards his first day inside. If anyone takes you into their confidence, make it known that you plan to hook up with The Henchmen when you get out."

"I guess I'll see you when I get out."

Leverick came closer to me and pretended to examine my head wound.

"One more thing. There's a nurse here. His name is Freddy. He's one of ours. If there's any emergency or any message you need to get to me, go through him."

Two days passed without any contact with other prisoners. Freddy came by my bed a few times to see if I needed anything. There was never a mention of who he really was. He treated me like any other patient. His manner was professional and distant. On the third day they put a prisoner in the bed next to mine. He was of Mexican descent, probably second- or third-generation, thirtyish. His name was Rafael Mendez. His street name was Poppi.

"Hey, you Dr. Death, ain't you, man?"

"Yeah," I answered, without looking up from my copy of *Penthouse*.

"Your name's all 'round the joint, man. Say you killed three guards."

I practically laughed out loud. The way the story had gotten changed around reminded me of the telephone game I used to play in school.

"Just a little hassle, that's all."

"Yeah? Well, everybody wants to meet Dr. Death. This guy, Dog, has been talking a lot about you, bro. He sent you a message. Says, 'Thanks, brother, see you on the outside.' You going out soon, man?"

"About a month. They said they wouldn't slap on any more time if I kept my mouth shut about certain things. They'll probably bump me to segregation at Folsom, seeing how mixing with the population gets me in trouble. Know what I mean?" Mendez was nodding his head up and down the entire time I was talking.

"Yeah, man. I sure do. Maybe if you get in with The Henchmen we can do some business when you get out."

"You getting out too?" I asked.

"No, but I still do businesses. My people outside are very loyal. I have someone running things until I get out in about three."

"What are you here for?" I asked.

"They busted me on some bullshit weapons charge," Mendez answered. "I sold two guys a couple of niners. They turned out to be feds. They fucked up and couldn't make the sales rap stick, so they settled for possession. The fucking judge gave me the max of five to seven. Hard-ons."

Poppi was a cool piece of work. He smiled a lot while he spoke, but his ruthlessness was obvious. He seemed like the type of guy who would shoot you in the head, rape your wife and daughter, and celebrate by taking a few friends out for Chinese food using your credit card. He stood about five-eleven, a hundred-eighty pounds. Slim but powerfully proportioned, his jet-black hair and pencil-thin mustache gave him the appearance of a Spanish bullfighter.

"So, what's your interest in The Henchmen?"

"Niners, man. You can't do business in L.A. unless you do business with them. I got the product the people want, but I can't reach the buyers. They control the streets, and they got connections all over the country."

Mendez was referring to the nine-millimeter pistol. This semiautomatic weapon was fast becoming the weapon of choice for street-level drug dealers, hit men, or just about any other vermin who gave himself permission to take a human life just because he thought it necessary. The pistol has a twelve-shot clip and is easily concealed.

"Why are you talking to me about it? Why don't you talk to them?" I asked.

"Can't do it, bro. I didn't even get the message for you straight from Dog. We think The Henchmen killed two of our people last year. I can't even talk to one of the motherfuckers. If I do, I'll get my balls cut off. My own people would do it, but my attitude is fuck it. That's past, now it's time to make some bread. I figure with you as a middle man, I can turn over about fifteen hundred pieces in the first two months."

"You got that many pieces in hand?" I asked with genuine interest.

"No problem. I got them stored in a warehouse in East L.A. Here, take this number." He handed me a napkin with a phone number written on it. "Just tell them Poppi gave you the number. They'll be expecting your call."

"All right, Poppi, let's give it a shot." I put the napkin in my shirt pocket and went back to reading my magazine. Mendez lay in his bed, softly singing in Spanish. My thoughts drifted to my wife and son as I slowly fell off to sleep.

On Wednesday morning I was transported about thirty miles east to a local police department holding pen. From there two marshals picked me up, drove me to a café near Route 40, and turned me over to two agents waiting outside in a blue Olds 88.

"Hi, Martin, I'm Molly Samuels," said the thin, dark-haired woman. Molly was a lawyer from Berkeley. She had joined the Bureau in 1983 after graduating at the top of her class. She could have had her pick of law firms to work for, but instead chose to become an agent. I later learned that her father had been killed on-duty while serving as a police officer in Hollywood.

"Nice to meet you, Molly," I said, applying a little schoolboy charm.

"This is Fred Parkins." Parkins leaned against the car, arms folded. He smiled slightly and nodded his head. I returned the gesture. Parkins had a certain arrogance about him. He was tall and slender, with blond hair and blue eyes. He looked more like a beach bum than a special agent. His father owned one of the largest accounting firms in the state. Parkins was himself a CPA, with plans to take over the firm one day. The fact that he wasn't in for the duration made me very nervous.

"Great to have you on the team," Parkins said.

"It's great to be had," I said, expecting at least an ice-breaking chuckle from my colleague. None was forthcoming.

As we drove, I filled them in on my encounter with Fenway and my discussion with Mendez. Parkins was familiar with the Mexican's business and the location of the warehouse.

"We'll check it out," he said, as he lit a cigarette with the car lighter. "Mendez's people used to control quite a bit of the drug and weapons trade in Southern California until about five years ago. At that time The Henchmen got wise to the opportunities they were missing. Even the mob doesn't want to mess with these guys. They're too crazy for most of the old families' blood. Although this doesn't stop them from subcontracting mechanic work from time to time."

"Here, take a look at these." Samuels handed me an envelope containing some police photos.

"Who's this?" I asked, looking at a picture of a guy, dressed in a business suit, slumped in what looked like an office chair, his head bleeding from a bullet wound between his eyes.

"That is, or should I say 'was,' Ralph W. Dixon. He ran a chain of massage parlors and was in over his head to local loan sharks," said Samuels.

Parkins interceded. "We think The Henchmen made the hit. In particular, Luis Morgan, the club's sergeant-at-arms. Dixon must have anticipated the visit to his office. He had placed a microcassette recorder inside his desk drawer before the incident took place. Listen." Parkins inserted a tape in the car stereo. I listened intently to a man's last moments of life:

"Who the hell are you?" The voice obviously Dixon's.

"Time's up, asshole. Twenty-five thousand *now*," the other voice demanded.

"I don't have it." Dixon's voice trembling now. "Tell him five more days . . . three more. Yeah, just three more."

"No more." Then the *pop* sound of a low-caliber revolver. Then the sound of Dixon's last gasp for air.

"Is that all?" I asked.

"That's it," said Samuels.

"What makes you think Morgan made the hit?"

"Descriptions given by people in the building lobby and on the street outside," answered Parkins. "They all say a man about six-three, two hundred-fifty pounds, with long black hair and beard, left the building at eight-thirty. The coroner's report clocks the time of death between seven and nine.

"We suspect Morgan's the club's main hitter. He more than likely handles all the subcontracted hit work from the Mob. The local police are investigating the murder, and my guess is that they'll pick Morgan up eventually. Then, when the witnesses learn that he's a Henchman, there'll be a few sudden cases of amnesia."

"I hope one day I'll have the pleasure of meeting Mr. Morgan," I said, with a twinge of arrogance. I was feeling pretty sure of myself at that moment. I think now that it must have been something about Parkins. I wasn't able to put my finger on it then, but I just couldn't relax around the guy. I was overcompensating by trying to appear seasoned and confident. With the exception of getting clocked over the head the prison work had gone well, so I guess the feelings were partly genuine.

We arrived at Leverick's home in Sherman Oaks, a Los Angeles suburb about twenty miles from the center of town. Atwood and Leverick were waiting for us when we arrived shortly after four P.M.

"Hello, Martin! Great to see you, kid!" Atwood said enthusiastically, his face glowing like that of a father welcoming his son home from college.

"Good to see you, too."

"Of course you know Dalton Leverick."

"Of course." I reached out and shook Dalton's hand. "Dalton."

"Martin. Nice job inside."

"Piece of cake."

"How's your head?"

"Like iron." I tapped the side of my head with my knuckles.

"Okay, Lead Head," joked Atwood. "Let's get started. First of all, here's the phone number to Base I. Memorize it. One of us will always be there. Report everything, no matter how minor. We'll prepare the 302's from whatever information you relay to us. When the case is made and we're ready to move we'll pull you in, have you sign the forms, obtain the warrants, and make the arrests. We'll need names, dates, and the time any incident occurred."

"As I mentioned to you already," Leverick interjected, "it may be necessary from time to time to bring in other agents or local law enforcement. This won't be done without your prior knowledge, and only if it's critical to making the case. Okay?"

"Sure, that's fine." I had long since cooled down about the prison guard incident.

"Here are the keys to your apartment, Martin," Samuels said as she handed them to me. "Apartment 3F, 425 Wilkes Street. That's just four blocks from Mike's, a bar The Henchmen frequent. And it's only six blocks from The Henchmen's clubhouse on Fourth Avenue.

"Here's your driver's license, James T. Randall. It's all the ID you'll need, and it's probably twice as much as some of The Henchmen have. And this is the key to a garage leased in Randall's name. You'll find a Harley 74, chopped, stripped down, and ready for the road." Samuels smiled as she handed me the keys.

"Now what?" I asked.

"Now you just move into the neighborhood," said Leverick. "Drive around a little each day. Be seen around town, especially in front of Mike's bar. In about two weeks, seek out Fenway."

"The rest is improvisation, buddy," said Parkins.

This guy annoyed me every time he opened his mouth. I shrugged him off.

"Let's go. We'll take you within a few blocks of Wilkes Street," said Samuels, as she ushered me toward the door. I said good-bye to Leverick and Atwood, then left with my two escorts.

Chapter 4

Mike's had been a biker bar since 1947. At that time groups like The Main Street Fighters and The Young Angry Sons of Bitches (later to become the first chapter of The Henchmen) frequented the place. The original bikers were made up mostly of World War II veterans who'd had trouble adjusting to civilian life. By the late fifties dozens of motorcycle gangs had sprung up all over the country, with the largest concentration in Southern California. By the early seventies The Henchmen had pedaled their influence up and down the state, as well as to several states across the country.

The bar was particularly noisy this night, because Jerome "Dog" Fenway had just been released from Boldero Prison after serving more than two years of a seven-year conviction on assault and attempted murder charges. The entire East Los Angeles chapter, except for those still serving time, were assembled at Mike's for the celebration of Dog's return.

The head honchos of The Henchmen always sat in the same part of the bar. There was a booth in the back that had a clear view of the entrance, so the head Henchmen could monitor all the comings and goings while there. In their absence, the booth remained empty.

Kurt "Counsel" Benson, the club's president since '72, and his four officers invited Dog over to sit with them. It was understood by club members and the regular patrons of Mike's that no one was to cross the line to that back booth without an invitation.

"Brother." Counsel to Dog. "Welcome back, man."

"Yeah," said Henry "Hank the Shank" Becker, the club's vice-president.

"Welcome home, blood." He raised his beer mug slightly, then took a gulp. Hank had rotten teeth, long hair that looked almost like dreadlocks, and thin, bony fingers with long, dirty nails.

Luis "Iron Man" Morgan, sergeant-at-arms, threw a small patch onto the table. "For you, brother. It's an original." Dog picked up the patch with the double S's in the form of lightning bolts—the insignia of Hitler's infamous SS—and placed it in his vest pocket. "Thanks, bro," he said. Iron Man nodded.

"Tell us 'bout how ya got sent up," said Victor "Crazy" Crawford, the club's road captain and security officer.

"Yeah, I love that story." Vincent "Little Vinney" Brown, the secretary and treasurer. "Nobody fucks with the Dog."

Dog picked at his beard and looked up at the ceiling, as if trying to recollect an incident that had taken place twenty rather than two years earlier.

"I think it was July . . . maybe August. Yeah, it was August. My ole lady and me had a tent set up in the mountains and was 'bout to settle down for a nice afternoon nap when some stupid-ass, young punk faggot forest rangers tell me I gotta move the fucking tent to the public campground. Now it's only a piece of canvas on a rope, one end tied to my Hog, one to a tree. But that's not the point. Point is the punks showed no respect."

The four bikers listened intently, as if hearing the story for the first time.

"So I stab this one dude, right? The other asshole runs like a motherfucker. So I figured I'd better split, right? Figure there's gotta be enough time to get laid first, though. This dude's layin' on the ground, bleedin' and cryin' for his momma or whatever, I'm fuckin' away in my tent and bingo—half the fucking troopers in the state are on my ass before I even come.

"So when they bust me, right, this trooper asks me why I hung around. I told him, 'I didn't think you fuckers would be back so soon, and I wanted to get laid. Kicking the shit out of some asshole always gets me horny.' "

The bikers laughed and pounded the table. Counsel rose from his seat unsteadily. He lifted his pitcher of beer and bellowed:

"Yo, listen the fuck up!"

The bar immediately fell silent, the assembled bikers growing as attentive as a class of Catholic schoolboys when the Brother taps his ruler on the desk.

"Tanigh'," he continued, his words somewhat slurred, "we celabate Dog's return from the Big House. They don't make motherfuckers tougher than him."

Counsel gestured toward their reunited brother.

"Dog . . . I love you, man. May you ride free and die hard."

Counsel proceeded to chug the pitcher, as the entire bar chanted "Dog! Dog! Dog!" He officially ended his speech by smashing the pitcher against the table. The patrons roared, the sixty or so people in the bar that night sounding like six hundred. Ten minutes later, things had settled down to their usual chaos.

Counsel sat, arms folded, taking in the celebration, enjoying all that was his. The club's National President remembered the first time he'd come face-to-face with the legendary Henchmen.

He had been a first-year law student, working part-time as an auto mechanic. About thirty club members pulled into the station on the way back from an August run and asked to use the garage's facilities to work on their bikes. He knew of their reputation for brutalizing anyone who provoked them, so he granted their request. To his amazement, he found when they'd departed that every tool had been cleaned with gasoline and returned to its original place. The floors had been swept, and every drop of fuel and oil paid for.

It was only a matter of time before he became obsessed with this band of marauding cyclists. He relished the thought of being free and riding hard with this modern-day James Gang. Like Robin Hood's righteous band of fighting men, their retaliation was always total, their purpose pure and focused. No one dared to take on these warriors en masse. They were the nomads of city life, the heroes of kids brought up on comic books and pro wrestling. He knew in his heart that he was an outlaw biker—and knew The Henchmen was his future club.

It took Counsel a year of prospecting before he got his colors. Two years later he was elected unanimously to the post of president, after killing three members of The Outcasts, a rival club, in a knife fight at a San Francisco party.

Now he laughed to himself as he watched Dog guzzle beers and joke with the other bikers. Eight years earlier, Counsel had sponsored Dog for membership.

Iron Man nudged Counsel. "Hey, prez, you look like you're in another world. What's up?"

"Just diggin' my head, brother." Iron Man shrugged it off and returned his attention to the festivities. Counsel returned to his thoughts, the image of a slimmer, younger Dog prospecting for him.

The nervous striker walked past the idle patrol car for the third time. It was hot that afternoon, and Counsel was beginning to get irritated. He sat inside the van, waiting impatiently for the potential club member to fulfill his requirements. Glaring at the prospect, he pointed his finger at the patrol car and whispered intensely, "Do it, asshole!" The apprehensive candidate walked to the patrol car, opened the door, and urinated on the driver's seat. Counsel fell back laughing, as two uniforms exploded from the coffee shop.

Counsel pounded the dashboard as the two police officers bolted after their prey. Dog whisked down the avenue and around the corner, his organ still exposed.

"Assholes!" wheezed a now-out-of-breath Counsel, as the uniforms turned the corner out of sight. Less than three minutes later, the two red-faced officers turned up the street without their target—out of breath, and furious at having been humiliated by a filthy punk.

About thirty minutes had passed when Counsel came upon the exhausted prospect, sitting on the steps of a shut-down social club on 9th Street.

"Get in, dipshit," he said with a broad grin.

"Jesus, those cops were pissed!"

"Hell, yes! You're lucky they didn't *shoot* your ass!"

"What's next, Counsel?"

"The last item, shithead, and then—if you play your cards right during probation—membership, and your Henchmen colors."

"Let's have it."

"Go to Chin's deli, pick up a six-pack of Coors, two packs of Lucky's, rolling paper, potato chips, a crunch bar, and a copy of *Mad* magazine."

"That it?"

"Yeah . . . and don't pay for shit."

"Wait a second! That chink's a crazy motherfucker! He keeps a double-barrel and a .357 under the counter. He wasted two niggers last year during a rip-off!"

"Listen, fuck-nut, I don't care how you do it. Waste him first, if you want to. Just get the shit and don't fuckin' pay, or you'll be a wannabe for the rest of your miserable life."

"Fuck you, Counsel. Let's go to the chink's."

By now Dog had been prospecting for five months, and he wasn't going to let some quick-triggered Chinaman keep him from his dream.

Counsel pulled the van across the street from Chin's. It was about seven P.M., and the streets were starting to get dark. They walked toward the deli, Dog looking like a boxer approaching the ring on the night of a championship bout. Cold, determined, but obviously masking a belly full of butterflies. He looked over at Counsel. Counsel nodded, as if to assure him that he would put his life on the line for him if he was truly at risk.

As they entered the store, Chin was sitting behind his counter watching a rerun of *Mission Impossible* on a poorly working black-and-white TV. Children could be heard laughing above the faint sound of Oriental music in the back-room apartment of the store. Counsel sniffed the air, enjoying the sweet aroma of the cooking smell from the back room. He flipped through the pages of a news magazine while Dog continued with his mission.

Chin sensed Dog's uneasiness and stood by his chair, expectant. With everything on the list except for the cigarettes and rolling paper, Dog began his approach to the counter, his eyes locked with Chin's.

"Two packs of Lucky's and a pack of E-Z wider,"

Dog demanded, with uncertainty in his voice. Chin reached behind and to the right, pulling two packs of Lucky Strikes off the cigarette rack without taking his eyes from Dog's. He then pointed to the display case of rolling paper on the counter. Dog slowly removed a pack and handed it to Chin.

Chin began to speak.

"Will there be anything el—" Dog's fist found Chin's forehead. Blood began to pour from his head and he fell against the cigarette rack. Dog and Counsel leaped through the doorway and ran across the street as car tires shrieked, narrowly avoiding the darting figures.

"Let's get the fuck out of here, Counsel!" cried Dog as Chin appeared in the doorway, shotgun in hand, bleeding from the head and crazy for revenge. Counsel pushed the gas pedal to the floor and sped away, as the dazed Asian pumped four shots at the escaping vehicle.

Things were simpler then, thought Counsel. *Much simpler*. The bikers partied at Mike's until two A.M., then moved the celebration to the clubhouse for the rest of the night.

Chapter 5

It had been three hours since he'd picked her up along the interstate, forty miles outside of Phoenix. She hadn't spoken a word, then or now. The white lines of the road held her with a hypnotic effect. Ed Mulligan, an independent trucker since '68, could stand it no longer.

"Do you talk, kid?" he asked.

"Sure I talk. What do you want to talk about?"

"How about the usual bullcrap? Where are you from? Where are you going? Some simple conversation, for crissake. We still got six hours before we get to Brawley. It would go a lot quicker if you'd lighten up a little, sweetheart. You said your name was Christy, right?"

The girl sighed.

"Right. I'm from Phoenix. I just got out of the Saint Agnes Home for children. I have no idea where my parents are and they don't give a fuck about me anyway. I'm going to California to get a job and enjoy myself for a while. You know—sun, fun, all that good shit. Okay?"

The tone of her voice sent a clear message: Leave me alone. Mulligan decided not to push it. The pretty, mysterious teenager could remain in her private world.

Christine Glidden, seventeen years old, born in Phoenix. She was the younger of two girls. She still remembered that day when she was eight years old. The screams. Her sister lying dead in the driveway, crushed by the wheels of her mother's car. Her mother being restrained and taken to the mental hospital. It was more like a dream now than a real memory. The months of being tossed around between relatives while her mother recovered and her father struggled to make a living as a bus mechanic.

She pulled an old photo from the pocket of her denim jacket, then quickly returned it. She massaged her temples as she thought of the day her parents had left her at Saint Agnes'. It had been a cloudy morning, just two days short of her ninth birthday. "I'm sorry, darling," her weeping mother had said. "Seeing you every day, I can't get over what happened to Laura. It won't be long."

She spent the next eight years yearning for a family, never understanding why her mommy and daddy had left her. Never understanding why they never came back.

Mulligan pulled into a truck stop twenty miles outside of Brawley. It was a mecca for drivers taking southwestern routes into California. A gas station, diner, and tavern, it was the most popular trucker's spot in Southern California. The Henchmen-owned establishment also catered to the honest trucker's need for a little boost to help him drive through the night. And it catered to the dishonest trucker's need to dump a load of hot TV's or stereos.

"Wait here," Mulligan ordered the teenager.

"Hey, where you going, man?" she asked.

"I have to talk to a couple of people inside. You just sit tight. Here, light up." He handed her a joint and a book of matches.

"Shit, man, you should have told me earlier you had smoke. Thanks."

Mulligan smiled as he shut the door to the cab.

Once inside the bar he ordered a beer for table number six.

"Sure thing," said the bartender, as he wrote a note on a small tablet and placed the sheet of paper on the waitress's tray. "There's two ahead of you."

"This one's too hot to wait," said Mulligan.

"I'll see what I can do."

Victor "Crazy" Crawford and Henry "Savage" Rivers were sitting at the rear table with a trucker from Wisconsin. The trucker rose abruptly and left with his two hundred dollars of methamphetamine as the waitress handed the note to Savage.

"It better be worth it," said Savage. "Tell him to come over."

The waitress waved him over and Mulligan sat down with the expressionless bikers.

"What you got?" asked Crazy. The clean-shaven biker had piercing green eyes that looked deep into Mulligan's. It was like looking into the eyes of Lucifer.

"I got a sweet young thing sitting in my rig. She can't be no more'n seventeen or eighteen. I told her I could take her as far as Brawley. Interested?"

"How much?"

"Three hundred," said Mulligan.

"Fuck off. One-fifty," countered Savage.

"Make it two. Come on, she's a *pretty* young thing."

Savage looked at Crazy, who shrugged indifferently.

Mulligan returned to his rig to retrieve the pretty teenager.

"That was good weed, man," she said happily as Mulligan climbed into the cab.

"Listen." Mulligan lowered the radio. "How would you like to party with some cool guys from a motorcycle club? They'll take you all the way to Los Angeles if you want, or San Francisco, or wherever."

"Wow. Who are they?"

"The Henchmen."

"Oh man, fuck yeah. Those guys are the coolest. Thanks. Thanks a lot, man."

"Don't mention it, kid. I'm glad to help out."

Mulligan drove off with two hundred dollars in his pocket. Christine drove off on the back of Savage's bike. As they glided gracefully between lanes on the highway, her hair lashed wildly around her face. *A princess on a white knight's horse,* she thought. *Imagine, the most famous motorcycle club in the country taking me to Los Angeles.* She had never felt so free.

The apartment was exactly what I had expected. A crapped-up one-bedroom in a run-down part of town. Leverick had even been thoughtful enough to furnish the damn thing for me. A mattress, no box springs or covers, on the floor to sleep on. A chest of drawers that looked like it belonged in a museum and a cracked mirror completed the scene. An old easy chair with a couple of springs broken sat next to a table and lamp in the living room. An open sleeping bag served as an area rug, and a milk crate supported a black-and-white TV set. The kitchen and bathroom should have been condemned. Maybe a few tons of Brillo could have made a dent. There was beer in the refrigerator. Christ, he even had empty pizza boxes on the floor. In short, it was perfect.

My first ride on the Harley was a little unnerving. The bike I'd trained on hadn't had its handlebars quite so high. It would take a few days of cruising around the neighborhood before I could master the chopper.

I made frequent trips past Mike's bar and the clubhouse. By this time, I figured, they must know exactly where I lived and who I was. After two and a half weeks my hunch proved correct. It was a Saturday morning. I was just about to settle down to some Saturday morning TV when there was a loud bang at the door. When I opened the door I was tackled by an animal whom I'd briefly had the pleasure of meeting while in prison.

"Hey, brother, how the fuck are you?" he asked as he pinned me to the ground. He then gave me a big, wet kiss on the lips.

"I'm great, Dog. How the hell are you, man?" I asked, as I slipped out of the position with a move any high school wrestler could have managed. I then climbed on his back and attempted to get him in a headlock. He dumped me off his back with ease and we both laughed at our childish reunion. I didn't immediately notice the other biker who'd come in with Dog until he yelled at us from my easy chair.

"Shut the fuck up, you guys! Pee-wee Herman's coming on!" The three of us watched the humorous opening of the kid's show. I found out later that it was a favorite among bikers. Shortly before Dog got sent away, he and few of the other Henchmen had gotten bit parts in one of Pee-wee Herman's movies.

"I'd like you to meet Little Vinney, Doc," said Dog, as he yanked him out of the easy chair and took the choice TV seat.

"Would you jump in my grave that fast, Dog?" Vinney protested.

"If it was this comfortable and had TV I would."

"Moron," Vinney mumbled. He extended his hand to me. "How are you, Doc? I heard about Boldero. Fuckin' hacks are always tryin' to fuck with the inmates." Vinney and I continued our conversation as we walked to the kitchen to get a beer. Dog continued to watch *Pee-wee's Playhouse*. I found it amazing that people so capable of violence and terror could turn into five-year-olds at a moment's notice. Or maybe the opposite was true. Maybe these fun-loving kids-at-heart could turn themselves into psychopaths at will.

"The word is you were approached by someone from The Medinos while you were inside," said Vinney. Vinney was one of the most unassuming-looking of The Henchmen. At five-eight, and slim, he looked more like a gymnast than an outlaw biker.

"Yeah. I wasn't sure if the guy was full of shit," I said.

"He's not. The Medinos control a lot of hardware imports. The trouble is, they can't distribute without our permission. And we ain't gonna give it."

"Let's make sure we're talking about the same thing, Vinney."

"Niners, man. He did tell you he had niners for sale?"

"Yeah, man, niners. For sure." I'd had to get him to say it. If something went wrong and we had to shut down the operation early, the case for conspiracy to buy weapons wouldn't stick if the language wasn't specific. He could claim he'd been referring to motorcycle parts rather than firearms.

"Here's the deal, Doc," said Vinney. "Make the call. Set it up for the day after tomorrow. We'll meet you at Mike's tomorrow night to go over the details. Okay?"

"Sure, Vinney. One thing," I asked. "How did you know I was approached by the Mexican?"

"The Henchmen have long arms and big ears, man. *Big* fuckin' ears. Let's go, Dog."

I was excited as I waited for them to ride away. It was all coming together beautifully. Integrity and brains. That's what it takes to succeed in law enforcement. After a few more minutes of congratulating myself I rode my bike to a deserted spot under Highway 64. During the construction of the highway, a public

phone had been installed across the street from the
workers' favorite diner. The diner had long since
closed, but the phone company had never bothered to
disconnect the phone. It was the perfect spot.

My conversation with the Mexican went smoothly.
But I was uneasy. This group held a blood vendetta
against the Henchmen, yet they were anxious to do
business. *Who's more dangerous,* I wondered, *the bikers or the Medinos?*

Molly Samuels was on duty at Base I when I called
in the information on the weapons buy.

"Do you want backup on this one, Martin?" Samuels asked.

"No need, Molly. Thanks. The Mexicans are eager
to do the deal and The Henchmen eager to buy. The
price is already worked out, so it should be a simple
deal."

I was lying. Something wasn't right with the deal, I
could feel it. But I didn't want some over-anxious
agent making matters worse by moving in too soon
and blowing the whole case. I'd rather take my
chances alone. Besides, I was going to have the most
powerful motorcycle gang in the country with me.
Samuels took down all the information and wished me
luck. Before I left I called home to check in with
Amy.

My calls had become few and far between since
leaving the training facility. Contact with Amy interfered with my ability to stay in character. She and I
had agreed I wouldn't speak with her too often while
on the assignment. She could call Atwood's home in
case of any emergency. This was upsetting for both of
us, but it was better that way.

As I rode back to the apartment, my thoughts were
with Amy and Alex and not on my riding. I accidently
cut off a pickup truck at an intersection, forcing the

driver to the shoulder. I rode up alongside the truck
and peered in at its shaken passengers.

"You all right?" I asked.

"You fucking freak!" the driver bellowed, a balding
man in his early fifties. His wife sat next to him, silent
but visibly shaken. "You could have killed us. Where
the hell do you come off riding like that? Don't you
have any goddamn respect for law and order?"

"I guess you're all right," I said as I rode away, the
driver of the pickup still cursing and shaking his fist.
I laughed to myself about what I must have looked
like to him. I rather enjoyed it that my appearance
and my apparent disdain for the law had rattled him
so much. If he only knew . . .

I arrived at Mike's early the next evening. None of
The Henchmen had arrived, and only a few of what
seemed to be regulars were drinking at the bar.

"What can I get ya?" asked the bartender, a short,
muscular man in his late forties. His face was hard,
stone-like. His eyes were tired. I wondered what those
eyes had witnessed in this bar over the years.

"I'll have a beer." He nodded, placed a napkin on
the bar, then filled a glass from the tap.

"Hi there," came a female voice from behind me.
"You must be Dr. Death."

"Who's asking?"

"I'm Christy. Word is all around the street about
you. Used to be a Saint, right?"

"Still am," I said. "Word travels fast, don't it?"

"Sure does, Doc." She sat on the stool in front of
me, her legs spread open. A sorry, drug-addicted
whore. Her vest bore a PROPERTY OF THE HENCHMEN
patch over the left pocket. Her legs and arms bore
black-and-blue marks.

"For a twenty, I can make you feel right," she said,

as she placed her hand between my legs and gently massaged my crotch.

I pushed her hand away. "I got business. Maybe later." Those terribly sad eyes locked into mine. It was as if she sensed my compassion. Her eyes grew watery.

"Sure, Doc. Maybe a freebee for you. Somethin's different about you, man. I can't put my finger on it. Somethin'."

At that moment I felt incredibly sad. For her. For me. For my wife Amy.

The sudden roar of motorcycles liberated me from my predicament. Christy quickly retreated to the rear of the bar like a frightened mouse. I spun around on my stool and faced the doorway. The rest of the patrons never flinched. They kept drinking and bullshitting as if they hadn't heard the thunderous approach of the outlaws.

Iron Man Morgan was the first to come through the door. It was customary for the sergeant-at-arms to walk into a public establishment first when traveling with the club's president. Counsel was next, followed by Little Vinney, Dog, Hank the Skank Becker, and Henry "Savage" Rivers. I was introduced to the members I didn't know and invited to sit down at the rear booth.

There was a white-tape line on the floor surrounding The Henchmen's table. At the edge of the line was a sign on a short metal post that read: DO NOT CROSS THIS LINE UNLESS YOU ARE INVITED. Nobody ever crossed it. Not even a member's old lady could just walk in and run up to her man. Even if she had money to give him, earned from a night of giving blow jobs to horny johns, she would still have to wait outside the line until summoned across.

"Let's have it," demanded Counsel. I couldn't see

his eyes behind the sunglasses. The shades and his long light-brown hair and beard made him resemble a hip, slightly overweight Jesus Christ. Lord knows, the members treated him like a savior.

"The Mexicans are anxious to make a deal," I said. "We can have their entire stock of fifteen hundred pieces and an option on a thousand more. It's set for tomorrow morning at eight o'clock."

"Where?" asked Savage.

"At the warehouse on Pier 40, by the tracks. They'll be waiting in a red pickup," I said, looking into his cold, piercing eyes.

I learned later that Savage and Iron Man were members of The Wild Bunch. About eight Henchmen from the L.A. chapter wore this patch on the front of their vests. It was issued to the club's killers. My cover's reputation was supposed to rival theirs, but they scared the hell out of me.

"All right," said Counsel. "Iron Man, Savage, and Dog go with you. No colors. No bikes. Take the gray van."

The club had three vans, which were kept in rented garages around East Los Angeles. The other two, a 1980 brown Caravan and an '86 blue Ford, were available on a first-come, first-served basis to all members. All three trucks were registered in the name of Alison Green, Victor Crawford's girlfriend.

"Do you have a piece, Doc?" Counsel asked.

"No. Not yet."

"Meet at the clubhouse at seven-thirty. Savage will give you one. What's your pleasure?"

"Doesn't matter really. A twelve-shot niner like the ones we're getting tomorrow would be nice."

"You got it. Let's have a few beers." Counsel motioned to Christy, who came running over with two pitchers of beer.

Mike's was becoming crowded. Many of the people who frequented the bar were regulars. The Henchmen never bothered them. In fact, many of them felt safer in that bar than in their own homes.

One story I heard was about a woman, Jenny, who had been followed to the bar one night by two men looking to collect on her dead husband's gambling debts. These guys must not have known, or didn't care, that this was a Henchmen bar. Despite her protests, they sat down next to her at the bar and harassed her until Counsel and Fat Jack lifted them off their chairs, threw them a beating, and tossed them into the street. They were both hospitalized.

By midnight The Henchmen had discussed fourteen murders, countless cases of rape, sodomy, and theft, and two future assassinations. One potential victim was a tough, street-smart police sergeant in New York and the other a writer named Ross who lived near San Francisco. The club was pissed at Ross for having written some revealing articles about The Henchmen for *World Weekly* Magazine. I was worried that I wouldn't be able to keep all this information in my head until I got back to my apartment to write it down. I, of course, had to brag of my escapades. My active imagination, and my access to Bureau files on "Dr. Death" Randall's alleged activities, made my tales convincing. Integrity and brains.

I heard a bike pulling up outside the bar. Aside from a couple of raised eyebrows, no one paid much attention. It wasn't unusual for members to come by Mike's throughout the night. I later learned that The Henchmen never met at Mike's without a guard on the roof with a thirty-thirty rifle and infrared scope. An attack from a rival club was a constant threat, real or imagined.

All Henchmen turned toward the door.

"What the fuck is that?" said Iron Man.

Walking through the doorway was something I had seen before only in sadomasochistic magazines. A leatherman, complete from his leather police cap to the spurs and studs on his boots. He walked right up to the white line and the dismayed outlaws.

"I have fifty bucks for anyone who has something I can choke on," lisped the leatherman.

The bikers looked around, their eyes bulging in disbelief. Then, all at once, they began laughing and slapping each other on the back. When the laughing had subsided, Hank the Skank stood up from his chair.

"Let's see the fifty, bitch," Hank ordered. The leatherman complied. Hank then whipped out his cock, ordered the man under the table, and enjoyed what he later described as the best blow job of his life. This assignment was beginning to get weird.

Chapter 6

It was a wet, chilly morning. Savage was already waiting inside the van when I arrived at the clubhouse at seven-fifteen.

"Get in, Doc," he said as he rolled down the window. I hopped in and sat on the passenger's seat.

"Here's your niner."

"Twelve shots?"

"Yeah, here are some more clips." He handed me three twelve-shot cartridges.

"We're just buying some guns, Savage, not going to war, man."

"You never know, bro. I don't trust these fucking Frito-heads for shit. I'm ready for anything. You'd better be too."

Our conversation was interrupted by a tap at the window. It was Dog and Iron Man. Dog was drinking a beer, holding the rest of a six-pack with his free hand. He looked like he was ready to go fishing or camping. Savage pointed toward the rear with his thumb. They piled in through the rear doors.

"Morning, gents," said Dog.

"Dickhead," Savage mumbled under his breath.

Dog and Iron Man immediately began assembling a tripod and a thirty-millimeter submachine gun. The van had special mounts which accommodated the tripods of various machine guns, as well as an antitank missile launcher.

"Ready for anything, eh, Savage?" I remarked.

"Fuck, yeah."

Now I was beginning to wish I'd asked for backup when I had the chance. These guys were ready for war. I wasn't prepared to get shot just to make a weapons buy. One minute I couldn't believe my good fortune, and the next I was wondering what the hell I was doing there. Integrity and brains. Roger Wolfe used to say to me when I was a kid, "Integrity will guide you to make the right decision. Brains will help you survive."

We drove for about forty minutes, discussing our favorite ways to waste somebody. I boasted of my skill with the niner and baseball bat. I must have sounded convincing, because the other bikers all seemed eager to boast of their own killing abilities. The method didn't matter much to Savage. If he had to choose, he preferred to work with explosives. A skill that he'd mastered while in the Army. Savage occasionally instructed chapter members on how to rig a remote-controlled bomb, using only dynamite and parts found in any common radio-parts store.

Iron Man loved the niner, the .38, and the ball peen hammer, which he always carried at his side, the way a carpenter carries his tape measure. One blow in the head from the likes of this psychopath could kill a man instantly. Dog, on the other hand, preferred to kill people with bad jokes.

"Hey, yo, listen. Why do bitches have two holes so close together?" Then, without waiting for our reply: "So when they get too fucked up you can carry them home like a six-pack."

The dock was vacant when we arrived. We were about ten minutes early, so Savage and I walked from the van to within eighty feet of the warehouse. He

carried the suitcase with the cash. We positioned ourselves directly in line with the back doors of the van.
In case something went sour, Dog and Iron Man would
have a clear shot.

The Mexicans were punctual. Three of them piled
out of the cab of a red pickup and approached us. A
paunchy, dark-skinned man in his early forties walked
in front. The other two, in their early twenties, if that,
lagged behind.

"Buenos dias, hombres," said the Mexican.

I nodded, saying nothing. Savage stood motionless.

"May I see the money, *señor*?"

"May I see the guns, *muchacho*?" Savage responded.

"Of course, *señor*. They are in the back of the
truck."

"Wait here," Savage said, handing me the suitcase.

"Your friend is not very trusting, *señor*."

"Neither am I," I said. I trusted this guy less with
each passing second. His eyes sparkled with greed.
His toothy smile was forced. I looked over toward the
pickup, and Savage had already opened one of the
crates. He gave me the thumbs-up. I knelt on one
knee and opened the suitcase so the Mexican could
see the cash. As I slowly handed the case up to
him, I noticed a small, round metal object behind the
dumpster near the warehouse. It looked very much
like the nose of an Uzi. The Mexican noticed the direction of my glance. He looked at the dumpster.
Then at me. Toward the dumpster again. I rose to my
feet. He reached behind and grabbed a gun from his
belt.

"Matalos!" he shouted, as he took aim at my head.
I dove toward his legs and brought him down. An
explosive strike to his nose with the heel of my palm
put him out. The doors of the van opened. Dog and
Iron Man sprayed the two other men with machine

gun fire. They were still reaching for their guns as their bodies were riddled with bullets.

The two men crouching behind the dumpster came out firing. Savage fell. I hit the ground and took out one of them with a shot to the head. Dog and Iron Man got the other one.

I picked myself up and, holding my gun outstretched from my body, moved slowly in a circle. Iron Man jumped from the van and picked up Savage. He was bleeding from the chest and leg.

"It's not bad," Savage said through gritted teeth. "How'd we do?"

"We got all the fuckers," Iron Man assured him. He then turned to me. "Doc, take the pickup and meet us at the clubhouse." Dog helped him lift Savage into the van. I grabbed the suitcase. We left five stiffs behind. I wondered if it had been a set-up from the beginning. Or had I simply discovered two extra men, brought along for security? I would never be quite sure.

Iron Man met me twenty minutes after I arrived at the clubhouse.

"Let's get these crates inside, then ditch this wetback piece of shit."

"How's Savage?" I asked.

"He'll be okay. Dog is getting him patched up now."

We carried five crates into one of the most fortified buildings I'd ever been in. It had more surveillance systems and weapons than most police buildings. After we'd unloaded the crates from the truck, Iron Man ordered one of the prospects to ditch the pickup.

"How about a tour, Doc?" Iron Man offered.

"Why not?" I accepted casually, hiding my excitement. Touring the clubhouse was not only critical to the case, I was personally looking forward to it.

The clubhouse was a three-story building attached to a double garage. On the first floor the walls had been knocked down, creating a triple-size garage area. Two vans and as many as forty bikes could be stored there at any time. The entire building was surrounded by an iron fence. Motion-detectors and closed-circuit cameras covered the entire perimeter. When the detectors were activated, an alarm sounded inside the club. If no one reset the alarms within one minute, the signals were diverted to the homes of Counsel, Iron Man, and Hank the Skank. The same was true if any of the burglar alarms on any door or window were activated. Every door was steel-reinforced, and every window had steel shutters with openings for gun ports.

The rest of the first floor was mainly a rec room. It had chairs, some couches, mattresses, a few tables, and a small kitchen. The kitchen had three refrigerators, two of which were stocked exclusively with American-brand beer.

Next Iron Man took me to the second floor.

"On this floor there's four crash rooms, Doc," he said. "Any brother can sleep here if he pays twenty bucks for each night. This is the security room." He pointed to the door at the end of the hallway. "Next to that is Counsel's office."

I remembered from the training manual that each Henchmen chapter had its own security officer. Months before a bike run takes place the security officer plans routes, contacts local law enforcement of the towns they will be passing through, and places scouts, with rifles, along the way. It's up to the security officer to ensure the safety of all riders.

"The Outcasts are our number-one security problem. Those motherfuckers would love to fuckin' ambush two hundred Henchmen on our way to the mountains."

Iron Man didn't mention that the security officer also keeps files on all club members and their families, old ladies, mamas; police and feds; and just about anyone else that might at one time or another be an asset or an enemy to the club. So important is he to the club that the security officer often doesn't wear his colors in public.

The third floor was the weapons and drug stash. In addition to the occasional guard outside the front of the building, the third floor was guarded twenty-four hours a day. Upon entering the third floor, you were immediately greeted by an automatic weapon-toting individual.

"Hey, Snake. This is Dr. Death, the last living member of the Satan's Saints."

"Doc." The stone-faced biker nodded. "You gotta have a patch before you can come up here on your own, Doc. Brothers have to sign in before taking anything. Street names will do it. We know who everybody is."

Any member could take drugs and weapons from the room they called "The Stash." Drugs had to be replaced by cash or by more drugs within twenty-four hours.

The club had an impressive arsenal. Over a hundred handguns, knives, clubs, and other small weapons were spread out on tables in the stash room. There were also several hundred plastic bags of methamphetamine, in tiny vials, ready for distribution. The Henchmen didn't bother much anymore with small-time, street-level dealing. Except, of course, if something useful could come of it.

"Everybody gets high, Doc," said Iron Man. "One of our brothers supplied a police lieutenant's daughter. The bitch gave us all sorts of info she got from papers and shit her father brought home. We had this gig going till she was busted for possession and sent to a rehab program."

"Tough luck," I said.

"Fuck it. That's why we try not to supply users anymore. We only sell weight, 'cept at some of the truck stops."

Iron Man brought me to the TCB (Taking Care of Business) room. No one was allowed access unless accompanied by the club president, sergeant-at-arms, security officer, or vice-president. This room was alarmed, and you had to know a four-digit code to gain entrance. I tried to see the four numbers as he pressed them, without seeming interested. I could only make out 5—9—2. The fourth was either a 3 or a 6.

This room was reserved for the heavy artillery. Thirty Uzi submachine guns, a 3.5-inch rocket-launcher, and fifteen AK47 Russian-made assault rifles. (I found this a bit ironic. The Henchmen had a reputation for being staunch anti-Communists. Apparently their hatred for the Reds wasn't deep enough to prevent them from purchasing this celebrated combat weapon.) There were also several crates of grenades and about one hundred pounds of dynamite, complete with wiring and timing devices for homemade bombs—all neatly stacked on one side of the room. The other side contained racks of M16's, probably over fifty in all, sawed-off shotguns, eighty .45-caliber handguns, thirty .357 Magnum handguns, and four bazookas.

"Some fucking collection, eh, Doc?"

Iron Man stood with his arms akimbo, lips stiffened, nodding his head in approval.

"Fuck, yeah," I said. "I was impressed with the shit you had in the stash room. But you could hold off a fucking army with the shit you got here."

He activated the alarm again as we left.

When we returned to the first floor, three club

members were sitting around a table. Among them was Monk, an ex-soldier and weapons expert. Monk often did guard duty on the roof of Mike's when regular meetings took place. I asked Iron Man why they didn't just meet at the clubhouse each week. He told me it was a tradition for the club's hierarchy to meet at Mike's—that was where it had all started. He also said that real club business was discussed in Counsel's office. The meetings at Mike's were nothing more than routine, except for the occasional deal brought in by outsiders. That's what I had been until this morning. The five corpses we'd left by the dock had changed my status—literally overnight.

"Monk, c'mere, man," said Iron Man. "This is Dr. Death."

Monk passed the joint the trio was sharing and approached us.

"Hey, Doc, heard you had some action this morning," he said.

"A little."

"A little, my ass. You took care of fucking business today, Jack." He gulped down the rest of his beer. "Listen, man, we need more beer for tonight's party. You want to take a ride, brother?"

"Party?"

"Yeah, we planned it as soon as we heard about you guys."

"Always down to party, Doc," Iron Man added. "Specially after a big score."

"What do you say, Doc?" asked Monk again.

"Let's go."

We took the blue Ford van.

"Smoke?" Monk asked as he offered me a cigarette, keeping his left hand on the steering wheel.

"Thanks."

"You looking to join the club, Doc?"

"No one's asked me so far, Monk."

"Somebody will, Doc. You can be sure of that." He cracked a half-smile, the other side of his mouth sporting the cigarette. "Ain't no way Iron Man would show you around like he did today if he wasn't sure you'd be in."

My reputation as a member of the Satan's Saints must have had a bigger impact on these guys than I had imagined. Still, it seemed too simple. Nobody becomes a Henchman that easy.

"I might consider it," I said, knowing full well that this response would surprise him. After all, The Henchmen are considered to be the outlaw's outlaw. The elite of the biker scene. You're either a Henchmen, a wannabe, a mortal enemy, or an outsider. I smiled and gave him a look that said *What do* you *think, stupid*? He nodded in silent acknowledgment. Monk wasn't much of a talker. In fact, it was his habitual long periods of silence that had earned him his name.

He had joined the club ten years ago when The Henchmen had absorbed his old club, The Warlords. The Warlords had over forty members then. Only twelve had the mettle to become Henchmen. The others just drifted away from the outlaw scene. Monk liked to think, to philosophize. He believed in reincarnation, and was certain that all The Henchmen had been Greek or Roman warriors in a past life.

Monk parked the van in front of Mike's. "Let's go," he said gleefully, "the fresh brew is waiting." As we walked into the bar my thoughts drifted. *How, during an all-night party, am I going to check in with Base 1? They must be shitting by now. Five corpses left by the docks, and no call from the man inside.* Deep *inside, and getting deeper by the minute.*

"Hey, Monk!" shouted Sam from behind the bar. "What's happening?"

"Give me a couple of kegs, Sam."

"Party tonight, boys?"

"Yeah. You know us, Sam. Life's a party, right, Doc?"

"You know it," I said, as I gave Monk the high-five. Sam brought up two kegs from the basement. He must have been pushing sixty, but he handled those kegs effortlessly. He was rock-hard, although the tattoos on his huge arms were fading with age. That and his white hair were the only things old about Sam.

Monk told me that even some of The Henchmen wouldn't have wanted to take Sam on. He'd been a middle-weight contender back in 1957, fighting out of Los Angeles. The story goes that Sam beat the shit out of two members of The Outcasts when he was in Arizona one summer. Apparently the two bikers got in an argument with Sam while they were drinking in a local tavern. Sam put both of them in the hospital that night. From the looks of him, I didn't doubt the story.

"You hungry?" asked Monk, as he placed the kegs in the back of the van. "How about grabbing a slice of pizza before going back?"

"I need to call my parole officer first," I said. "I'm two days late in checking in, and he's a real prick about shit like that." I had to take the chance. There was no telling when I would get a chance to call again. Henchmen parties often lasted three days or more. If Monk didn't buy that parole officer line, it was all over for the operation.

I started walking toward the pay phone near the entrance to Mike's. Tension was building in my gut. "I'll go with you," he said. I couldn't read him. Why did he want to come with me? Had I blown it? Or was I just being paranoid?

No sooner had I picked up the receiver than Monk grabbed my shoulder and spun me around. He reached inside his jacket. *Should I move on him*? was my immediate thought. He pulled out a quarter. "It's on me, man. I know how those fuckin' ballbusters can be."

"Thanks, Monk," I said, letting out the air I had stored in my lungs. This wasn't going to be easy. With Monk standing right there I couldn't talk freely. I punched in the numbers rapidly, too fast for him to memorize all the digits.

"Base One." *Thank God,* I thought. It was Leverick. Of all the people involved in the case, I felt the most comfortable with him. After all, he'd trained me for this assignment. He knew me better than anyone else.

"This is Randall," I said.

"What? Martin, is that you? Are you all right?"

"Yeah, yeah, sorry, man. I forgot," I said, knowing a parole officer's first question would be why I hadn't called. I looked at Monk and rolled my eyes in disgust. Monk snickered.

"You're not alone, are you?" said Leverick

"Right, I looked for work. Nobody's hiring, man, what can I tell ya?" Again I looked toward Monk, this time motioning with my hand near my crotch to further mock my fake PO. Monk started laughing.

"Okay, Martin. I guess you're all right. We received word of what happened with the Mexicans. Did they try to rip you off?"

"Yes. I'll call on time from now on." I placed the receiver near my buttocks.

Monk was weak with laughter.

"All right, Martin. Try to call within the next two

days and give me an update. I'll let the rest of the crew know you're well."

I hung up the phone and joined Monk in a belly laugh. We walked across the street to a pizza joint with our arms on each other's shoulders, laughing all the way at the Establishment that tried so unsuccessfully to control us. I thought again about Roger Wolfe. He must have been nearing seventy when he'd told me about one of his undercover assignments. At fifteen, I thought that was the greatest life a guy could have. He told about a time when he was working an illegal still in a small town outside of Jackson, Mississippi. "Sometimes you do some backslapping and drinking with your targets and you almost have a good time," he said. "But you can't ever forget why you're there. You're the greatest actor in the world, playing the most important role of his life. A role where if you forget your lines, you can get killed."

Once inside, Monk and I ordered four slices of pizza and two Cokes. Tony Marinaro, one of the last of the old store owners left in the downtown area, brought the food to our table. Marinaro was the type determined not to let crime, filth, and the general deterioration of the neighborhood drive him out.

"Enjoy, boys," he said with a thick Italian accent. "If you need anything else you ask, okay, boys?"

"Sure, Tony. Thanks," replied Monk.

"You've been coming here a long time?" I asked Monk.

"Shit, yeah. I think I was about eight years old when I first came into Tony's. Every Saturday I ran here when he opened at noon and ordered two slices and a Coke. The whole thing came to about forty cents. A lot has changed since then, Doc." Monk pointed out the window.

"See that karate school across the street?"

I nodded.

"That used to be a bakery. And that Gospel church next door used to be a movie theater. It's funny, you know. No matter where our chapters have their clubhouses, they always seem to be on the edge or in the middle of the worst fuckin' neighborhoods. I don't know if the raunch is attracted to us or if we're attracted to it."

"It seems to me that the real estate is cheap," I said jokingly. I knew full well why all the Henchmen chapters were in the middle of the worst neighborhoods. The drug trade. As one of their main sources of income, the manufacture and distribution of methamphetamine and its many derivatives thrived in the lower-class neighborhoods. Also, no middle- or upper-class street would tolerate a Henchmen clubhouse on it. The desperate existence of the poor areas of town makes possible things most of us see only in the movies and on television.

Monk and I were the only customers in Tony's, until six black men crossed the street from the karate school. They were all in their early twenties. Wise guys, who obviously studied the arts to be better able to intimidate people. Three of them wore stockings on their heads that resembled flesh-toned hair nets. They entered the pizzeria in an unruly manner. Pushing each other, throwing kicks and punches through the air. Monk acted as if he didn't notice the group. He kept eating his pizza and shaking his head up and down, like he was listening to music that only he could hear.

"Let's have a pie, old man," the tallest of the punks ordered.

"Yeah, wiff anchovies," added one of his buddies. "And make it snappy, happy."

"Ten minutes, boys. You relax, okay?" said Tony.

"No, *you* fucking relax, Jack," said another punk, this one now sitting at the table next to ours. Tony acted as if he hadn't heard the last remark. Two of them were now kicking their workout bags around the store like footballs. I looked to Monk in order to gauge his reaction to the intrusion. He kept eating as if the punks didn't exist. Tony came out from behind the counter and started to sweep the floor. One of the men grabbed the broom from Tony and motioned it toward his head.

"Boys, now stop this!" pleaded Tony.

"Eat shit, cracker," said the punk, as he swiped Tony on the side of the head with the broom.

"Get out! Get out now, or I'll call the police!" said the flustered old man.

"You ain't gonna call shit, peckerwood," said the man sitting at the table next to us, while the tallest of the group positioned himself between Tony and the entrance to the counter. Monk looked up for the first time since the men had entered the store.

"Split! *Now!* You fuckin' cocksuckers!" shouted Monk.

The tall one pushed Tony aside and walked up to Monk, stuck his finger in Monk's chest, and said, "Shut the fuck up, white boy. How da fuck you two dickface mothafuckas gonna make us split?" For a second everything became silent. The rowdies stopped playfighting and making noise. Every one—myself, Tony, and the rest of the punks—had their eyes on Monk and the man pressing his finger against the Henchman's chest.

Then came the distinctive crack of a snapped finger bone as Monk grabbed it and bent it back with vicious speed. A look of shock appeared on the tall one's face. As he stared at his mutilated hand in disbelief, Monk hammered an elbow strike which must have broken his jaw. The punk immediately dropped to the floor. Monk jumped on the table and leaped at the two men now approaching us. He knocked them off their feet. One of the others caught me with a straight kick to the stomach. As I doubled over I grabbed the top of the table, spun around, and caught my assailant across the side of his face with the table base. His face distorted terribly. Blood, saliva, and teeth spurted from his mouth as he fell to the floor. Before I could get my bearings, I found myself being choked from behind with the broom handle. I grabbed at the handle to lessen the pressure on my Adam's apple, just as one of the stockinged heads came leaping toward me with a flying kick aimed at my face. He was met with my foot in his groin as he leaped through the air. The three of us fell to the floor. I grabbed the broom and drove the end of the handle into the solar plexus of my attacker, leaving him and the ill-fated leaper squirming in pain on the floor.

Monk was giving the last two a final pummeling against the counter while Tony frantically telephoned the police. "We're done, Monk! Let's get the fuck out of here!" I implored.

"Not yet," Monk insisted. He walked over to the unconscious finger-pointer. The one who was the obvious ringleader of the group. Monk opened his fly and began to urinate on the head of the motionless body. This was a battle ritual for many bikers—like a cannibal warrior eating the flesh of his fallen foe.

Monk zipped his fly and started for the door.

"Come on, Doc. We have a party to go to."

Chapter 7

Bail was set at ten thousand dollars. This was the first time Kevin "Irish" McBright had been arrested since he had left The Henchmen eight months earlier. A state trooper had pulled him over for making an illegal right turn, and the car was searched after the trooper became suspicious. The charge—possession of two grams of cocaine.

During the twelve years Irish had ridden with the club, he had been pulled over and ticketed more than a hundred times. He had been arrested three of those times for possession of narcotics. Only then he'd had the club's bondsman and legal-defense fund. This time it was his wife, Sandy, who arranged bail.

Irish had no particular reason for turning in his colors to Counsel. He had just had enough. Years of hard riding, drinking, and fighting had taken their toll. He had to forfeit his motorcycle and blacken his Henchmen tattoos in order to leave. He was told the club would keep a watchful eye on him. He understood.

Sandy waited outside the courthouse while Richard Clement, the court-appointed lawyer, presented the bond and arranged for his release. Irish was brought into a small conference room and surrendered to his attorney.

"I'm Dick Clement," said the tall, slightly overweight lawyer.

"Are you gonna get me off on this piss-ant charge?" said Irish.

"Look, Mr. McBright, with your record they could give you seven years. Three priors for possession. Fifteen arrests in the last ten years for disorderly conduct. Assault. Attempted mur—"

"All right, all right. I know the tune," interrupted Irish. "I just think this is bullshit. Most guys walk without a problem for a diddlyshit amount of coke like that. It's not like I was selling the stuff or nothing."

"I might be able to get you a deal," said Clement. "I talked with a"—he flipped through the pages of his yellow writing pad—"Detective Roberts, this morning."

Irish's eyes widened. He sat up straight in his chair.

"I'm listening," he said.

"They want you to turn state's evidence against a member of the club who they believe strangled a prostitute two years ago. They believe you witnessed the murder. All charges will be dismissed if you're willing to cooperate."

Irish had witnessed the murder. He and Savage had been making the rounds together one Friday night, collecting from club-controlled prostitutes who were working the downtown streets and massage parlors. Savage thought the girl was lying about a trick that didn't show. When she was unable to produce the twenty dollars, he grabbed her throat and choked the life from her frail body. Irish had never questioned Savage's actions. A brother is always right.

The biker stood up. He placed his face close to Clement's and said, "Tell them to fuck off."

"Listen, I think you're making a mistake."

"I said, tell them to fuck off!" Irish was now shouting. "I may have hung up my colors, but I'm a Henchman for life! A Henchman doesn't rat on his brothers!

I'll do fifty fucking years before I turn punk! You got that straight?"

"Sure." Clement shook his head. "I got it straight. You're wife is waiting outside. Your hearing is in two weeks."

The party was already under way when Monk and I arrived with the beer. Motorcycles were lined up three-deep outside the clubhouse. There was an almost constant rumble of Harley engines. Some bikers would leave the party, kick-start their hogs, throttle the engine, then go back inside. Like a junkie needing a fix, a biker sometimes needs to feel the power of his machine between his legs.

Monk and I each carried a keg on our shoulders. Two large pans of ice were set up. We placed the kegs in the pans and affixed the spouts. The bikers converged on the beer, mugs in hand. Dog didn't bother to use one. He just put his mouth under the spout and began to guzzle.

"What the fuck took you guys so long?" Dog wanted to know, beer still dripping from his mouth.

"I had to take a leak," answered Monk. Dog shrugged his shoulders and returned to the beer line. Grateful Dead music was blaring, and some of the old ladies and mamas were dancing topless. The clubhouse was hazy with the smoke from joints and cigarettes. Now and again one of the bikers would join the girls, fondle one for a moment, then go back to drinking and smoking with his brothers. Counsel approached and handed me a small silver replica of The Henchmen insignia.

"Stick this on your vest. Leave it there until the party's over," he instructed. "A lot of the bros haven't met you yet. This will let them know you're a guest."

"Thanks." I pinned the insignia above my left pocket.

"Don't get pissed if someone looks you over," added Counsel. "Just make sure they can see the pin. Everyone will know you before the end of the night. You know, last summer a stupid fuck from *The Los Angeles Times* crashed one of our gigs. I guess he thought he'd get some fucking scoop or some shit like that. We tore him a new asshole that night." Counsel looked away for a moment. "Hey, there's Benny." He shouted, "Yo, Benny, come over here, man!"

Benny was about six-three and must have weighed close to three-fifty. He had long, unkempt brown hair, a full beard, and wore a Harley-Davidson headband. As he came closer, I recognized the young woman with him. *Oh, no!* I thought. The words almost slipped out of my mouth. *This woman works for the goddamn police department. My desk was only ten feet away from hers, for crissakes.* My heart rate increased, and I began to tremble slightly. If my cover was blown, these guys would cut my throat on the spot. *Okay, be calm, stay cool. She can't recognize me with my long hair and full beard.* I took a deep breath.

"Hey, Benny, meet Dr. Death of the Satan's Saints."

"What's happening, Benny?" I said. I nodded slightly toward his girlfriend. She just gave a disinterested half-smile. I didn't mean to stare, but my relief was intense. Counsel must have thought I was eyeing Benny's girl, because he later reminded me of the club rule: No club member or associate should mess around with a brother's old lady. A member's old lady wears a patch that says PROPERTY OF BENNY, or Iron Man, or whomever.

It was beginning to make sense. Benny's girlfriend was a PAA (Police Assistant Administrator). She had access to the whole goddamn computer network. I used to overhear frustrated officers returning empty-handed after trying to serve an arrest warrant on a Henchman. Obviously she had warned him. He had quietly disappeared until the warrant was old and had been shoved aside by more pressing business. These bastards had us more infiltrated than we ever had them. Until now . . .

By midnight I had met most of the Los Angeles chapter, except for Big Jimmy Hobbs and Fred "Lucky" Fletcher, who were both in jail. I sat down in an armchair, lit a cigarette, and tried to replay the day's events in my mind. One of the mamas, a heavy-set girl named Pamela, sat on the arm of my chair and handed me a joint. "How you doing?" she asked.

"I'm doing okay, babe, how about you?"

"Oh, I'm just fine, Doc. You want anything tonight, you just come see Mama Pam."

The thought of intimate contact with her made me ill. I wondered how many cocks she had sucked and how many assholes she had licked today. Besides making themselves available to any club member upon demand, women like Pam would also prostitute for the club. They turned over all of what they earned. The Henchmen gave them drugs and a small allowance for other essentials.

Pam wore her long black hair straight, so that it partially covered her left eye. The scars she attempted to hide had been made by Little Vinney's cigarette. Her crime: She'd bought herself a pair of shoes with some trick money.

"I'll let you know," I said, as I handed her back the joint. I laid my head back and closed my eyes. Despite the blaring music, I started to doze off.

As I drifted away my thoughts turned to Amy and Alex. I imagined my son sleeping in his little bed. I saw Amy reading a book, or maybe watching television. I missed her. There I was in the clubhouse of a major motorcycle gang, when I should have been home with my wife. I shook myself awake. Falling asleep was a dangerous thing to do at a biker party. I remembered from my training with Leverick that bikers don't take too kindly to people who fall asleep too early. Tattooing faces or setting crotches on fire were common penalties.

Lucky for me the attention at the moment was on Savage. He was being congratulated for today's victory. His right arm was in a sling, and he had a blood-stained dressing across his chest. I offered my seat.

"Thanks, Doc," he said in a low, weak voice.

"How you doing, Savage?"

"I'll be laid up for a while. Probably six weeks. Hey, somebody give me a fuckin' beer!" Pam came running over.

"Nice patch-up. Who did it?" I asked Iron Man. It hadn't been done in a hospital, that was for sure. All gunshot wounds had to be reported to the police. Savage would have been in jail, or at least held for questioning, if he had been taken to a hospital.

"A dude named Arthur Paterson. He's got a practice in his home. His daughter is one of our sheep." He was referring to Vicky Paterson. Iron Man had told her father that if he didn't patch up club members he would receive his daughter's head in a hat box. Paterson believed him. He would lose his license and face jail time if he was caught, but he had little choice. His name would be left out of my reports.

Around two A.M. Iron Man, Counsel, and Crazy went upstairs. Twenty minutes later, Crazy came down and invited me to join them.

He escorted me to the security room. It contained four file cabinets, with information on members and their families as well as on police officers, drug enforcement officials, local mobsters, ex-members, and anyone else the club took an interest in. I wondered if there was a file on me somewhere in there.

In the middle of the room was a conference table with four chairs. Iron Man and Counsel were seated. Crazy walked over to his desk. Except for his cutoff denim jacket and leather pants, he looked liked a corporate executive. He sat behind his desk, taking notes on a yellow writing pad. I sat at the table with Counsel and Iron Man.

"Take a look at this file, Doc," said Counsel, a cigarette dangling from his mouth. "His name is Kevin McBright. He used to ride with us. Now he's a liability, if you know what I mean."

"What's his situation?" I asked

"He just got busted and he's about to go punk on us," answered Iron Man.

"We can't afford ex-members with loose lips," Counsel said, staring straight at me. It would have been more appropriate for him to say that they couldn't afford ex-members, period.

"The most trustworthy person alive is a dead man," added Iron Man with a slight chuckle.

"You want me to take care of it?" I asked. My instincts told me to play it out.

"Yes," said Savage forcefully. "And soon, too."

"Within the next five days," added Counsel

"What does this do for me?" *Besides keep me alive,* I thought to myself. Iron Man and Crazy both looked over at Counsel.

"You get these," said Counsel. He laid a brand-new set of Henchmen colors on the table. "Just get the job done, and you're in."

"Then I guess I'm gonna be in." I slapped Iron Man a high-five and picked up McBright's file. *Now what*

*the hell am I going to do? Take what I have and call
in the operation? Kill the guy?* I needed to talk with
Leverick or Atwood as soon as possible.

"Let's get back downstairs and fuckin' *party!*" exploded Iron Man, pounding the table with his fist. We
returned to the party. At five the next morning, I
returned to my apartment and went to sleep. The lon-
gest day of my life had finally come to an end.

Chapter 8

In four more hours, Angelo's Cocktail Lounge would open for its after-hours guests. Angelo Vinetti always arrived at ten o'clock to take his place at the rear table, close to the stage. He would conduct business with local associates while he ate, occasionally paying attention to the strippers warming up onstage.

Michael "Zorro" Zoritella, the vice-president of The Henchmen's Philadelphia chapter, waited on the corner of Market and Second. He would not go in to see Vinetti alone. His instructions had come directly from the chapter president: Wait until he arrives, and then go in together. The Henchmen were always cautious when they dealt with the Mob. Zorro looked at his watch. Ten-twenty. He pulled a pack of Marlboros from his shirt pocket. "Shit," he said as he patted his pockets for matches. He let the unlit cigarette hang from the corner of his mouth as he continued to wait. Samuel "Whitey" Hilton rolled up in his blue BMW. Zorro got into the car and immediately pushed in the cigarette-lighter.

"Relax, man," said Whitey. "We're only picking up cash."

"I don't like dealing with this prick. He'd fuck us if he had the chance." Zorro took a drag of the cigarette and let the smoke out through gritted teeth.

"He knows better than that, bro," said Whitey. "They hire us because we can get the job done when they can't. They never would have found Williams on their own.''

Edwin Williams was one of the wealthiest drug dealers in Philadelphia. He worked for Vinetti and the Toritelli family. The Toritellis controlled forty percent of the drug traffic in Philadelphia. The Henchmen controlled forty, with the remaining twenty percent divided between the Colombians, Jamaicans, and independents.

Williams had committed one of the most serious offenses possible within that criminal organization. He had killed a law enforcement official without permission. When a judge who'd handled a case involving one of Williams' most profitable street-level dealers had refused to take a bribe, he'd had him shot outside his home in Malvern. Williams went underground, and the Toritellis hired The Henchmen to find and kill him. When someone disappeared into the labyrinthine city, there were no better stalkers than The Henchmen. They knew every alley, every dope dealer, and every flop house from Front Street to City Line Avenue.

It took them only eight days to locate Williams in an apartment on Cleveland Street. When the body was discovered, it was too badly burned to be properly identified without dental records. Two hookers had also been shot and burned. One survived a few hours in the hospital.

The police released a statement two days later stating that the male had been shot six times in the head before he was set on fire. The two hookers had each been shot once.

Zorro walked into the bar ahead of Whitey. Neither Henchman was wearing his colors. Whitey was dressed in a blue three-piece suit. Earlier in the evening he'd been handling some legitimate club business and had needed to look the part. He looked distinguished, with his gray, well-coiffed hair and his trim mustache. Zorro wore a Philadelphia Eagles sweatshirt and a pair of jeans.

Vinetti barely looked up from his plate as the odd couple walked through the door and sat down at his table. He motioned with his head, and one of his people came over to the table with two stacks of cash. Each stack contained fifty one-hundred-dollar bills. Whitey picked up one of the stacks and flipped through it. He placed it back on the table and looked straight at Vinetti.

"It looks light, Angelo," he said.

"Ten thousand. Count it."

"We get twenty. We always get twenty. Your man Famantia said you understood that." Whitey's voice was cool and steady. Zorro began thumping his burly fingers on the table.

"I pay ten. I always pay ten," Vinetti said. He laughed and looked around the room. His men joined in the laughter, right on cue. They stopped when Vinetti did.

"What the fuck is this shit?" fumed Zorro. "I told you we couldn't trust these scumbags!"

"Watch your mouth, punk!" Vinetti ripped the napkin from his collar and threw it on the table. "You fucking creeps are in over your head if you think you're going to get tough with me! I'll have your fucking balls for dinner!"

"No, I'll have *your* balls, motherfucker!" Zorro snapped, as he stood and reached behind him for his .38. A rapid succession of clicks stopped him cold. Two of Vinetti's lieutenants had their guns cocked and pressed against either side of Zorro's head. The bartender pointed a twelve-gauge shotgun, and a stripper aimed a .25-caliber semiautomatic that she had pulled from her boot. Vinetti leaned back in his chair, his pot belly supporting a poorly made necktie, and shrugged his shoulders.

"What can I tell you? They love me." He grinned.

Whitey calmly took the two stacks of money. He placed them in his jacket pocket and slowly rose to his feet. Vinetti's people kept their guns on Zorro, who had now lowered his hands to his sides.

"You owe The Henchmen ten thousand dollars," said Whitey. He turned around and proceeded to leave the lounge. Zorro followed cautiously, almost walking backwards, never taking his eyes off Vinetti's people.

Once outside, Whitey unlocked the passenger side of the car, as Zorro exploded.

"Shit! God fuckin' damn it! Shit, Whitey! We fuckin' backed down in there, man! What the fuck is going on? Shit!"

"Get in, man. I got it handled."

Zorro got in, slamming the door shut. Whitey picked up the car phone and motioned it toward Zorro like a shaking finger. "Nobody pulls that shit on us." He dialed the number one on his speed-dialer. Counsel picked up on the second ring.

"Yeah," Counsel answered.

"It's Whitey."

"What's up, Whitey? How are things in the City of Brotherly Love?"

"Oh, not bad. I'm just left feeling a little hungry after my meeting tonight."

A long pause.

"I see. What do you want to do about it?" asked Counsel.

"I'd like to take my friend to dinner. He deserves a good meal."

Another pause. Shorter this time.

"What's on the menu?"

"Oh, something hot. And very spicy."

"Who's your friend?"

"I'll spell it for you. H—Y—F—R—A—A—Y."

Another long pause. Whitey could picture Counsel deciphering the code which, during the last meeting of chapter presidents, they had both agreed to use when discussing sensitive matters over the phone. He knew Counsel would have his doubts. Killing Vinetti could be bad for business. Not that Counsel would be afraid to take on the Mob. But an all-out war would gain nothing. He would have to allocate too many resources to the Philadelphia area, thus hurting business in New York and other East Coast territories. Yet he knew Counsel wouldn't let his Philadelphia chapter down.

"When were you planning to go eat?" Counsel asked.

"Right now," replied Whitey. "This motherfucking minute."

Whitey immediately thought of The Henchmen's bylaw number seven, which states that no Henchman shall fail to retaliate fully when wronged. Counsel had little choice.

"Enjoy your dinner," he said before he hung up the phone.

Whitey smiled and placed the car phone back in its compartment. He removed a pair of gloves from the cradle and instructed Zorro to wait in the car. He then released the trunk lock. Inside the trunk was a set of golf clubs. He removed the red leather bag and reached inside, pulling out a disposable bazooka, standard army issue. He threw the weapon over his shoulder and took up his position behind a brown station wagon across from Angelo's. Inside he could see Vinetti, still sitting at the table with his two men. Vinetti was talking while he picked his teeth and gestured animatedly. Whitey squeezed the trigger slowly.

"Right in your face, scumbag," he said, releasing the rocket with a powerful *swoosh*. A second later Angelo's exploded, sending glass and debris in all directions. Whitey fell to the concrete, trying to avoid the flying glass, wood, and metal. A fiery form came running through the smoke into the street. Whitey couldn't tell if it was Vinetti or one of his people. It fell about three feet from the station wagon. Whitey watched the figure burn.

"Whitey! Whitey! Goddammit, man! Let's get the fuck out of here!" pleaded Zorro. Whitey dropped the smoking weapon to the ground and ran to the car. He hopped in, and the blue BMW sped down to Front Street and off toward the clubhouse in South Philadelphia.

The Bobby Jones concert was running an hour over-time. One of the most successful country-and-western singers, he sold out every city he played in. The crowd was roaring for a third encore. Barbara and Alice, two teenage fans, had become separated from their friends.

"Hey, Barb. Lez go up fron' and get a bedder look at Bobby," said Alice, her speech slurred from one too many beers.

"I don't know, Ally. Those motorcycle guys are keeping everyone away from the stage."

"Come on. Doan be a wimp. Lizzen, we're on our own. I'm sposed to be sleeping over your house. Your sposed to be sleeping over mine. We agreed we were gonna make this the bez night ever, right?"

"Oh all right, Ally," said Barbara hesitantly, "but I know I'm gonna regret this."

The two teenagers began to make their way down

to the stage. The outdoor, general-admission arena seated eleven thousand, and had standing room at stage level for five hundred. Six Henchmen bikes were parked near the stage with a sign draped across them: DON'T EVEN THINK OF TOUCHING THESE BIKES. The crowd was well aware of The Henchmen's reputation and kept a respectful distance from their motorcycles by standing behind the barriers.

Hiring The Henchmen to guard the stage was something Bobby Jones did whenever he played a city near a Henchmen chapter. Using bikers as bodyguards used to be fashionable among the rock bands of the seventies. For a dozen cases of beer and free admission to the concert, any band could hire The Henchmen or any other outlaw club. After the incident at Saratoga in 1979, however, only a few old-time friends of the outlaw clubs would hire the bikers. In Saratoga The Henchmen's New York City chapter had been hired by The Losers, a hard-rock band, to keep people off the stage. One of The Henchmen got into an argument over a girl. The boyfriend pulled a gun and shot one of the bikers in the leg. What they finally scraped off the floor when the ambulance arrived was a boyfriend beaten badly enough to have killed ten people. Every bone in his body had been broken. They beat his head so severely with a ballpeen hammer that his brain was exposed. No one was arrested. There were no official witnesses.

"Hurry, Barb! Thiz could be the laz song," said Alice, as she tugged on Barbara's arm. Alice, seventeen, was a bleached blonde who wore too much makeup. At five-foot-two and one hundred-fifteen pounds she was shapely and provocative. She was accustomed to using her looks to her advantage. At school, at home with her stepfather, and with her many boyfriends, Alice could always get what she wanted. Barbara, slightly taller at five-foot-five, had brown hair and brown eyes. She was more cautious than Alice, but was easily seduced by the excitement of a new challenge or experience.

The girls started their descent toward the stage. Gerald "Beef" Macruder, the sergeant-at-arms of the San Pagano chapter, was standing between the bikes and the stage. He swayed to the music, while keeping a threatening eye on the crowd. A baseball bat was slung over his shoulder like a foot soldier's rifle. Two of the Henchmen were sitting on their bikes. Mario "Slip" Zatela, the chapter's vice-president, talked with some of the crowd. He shared some booze and some smoke with the people closest to the barriers.

Sanford "Sandy" Collins, the chapter president, spoke to one of the stagehands. Sandy's brother, Lucky Joe, was the newest member. Lucky Joe had gotten his nickname because he'd been shot three times and survived. The remaining two members of the chapter were not at the concert. The San Pagano chapter had only the eight members required by charter. If one of the six members who were still on the street was killed or jailed, the club would have two weeks to find a worthy prospect or they would lose their charter.

Alice pushed her way to the front of the crowd. She stood next to one of The Henchmen sitting on his bike. "Nice bike," she said.

"I know it is," answered Frederick "Fred" Adams. "How ya doin', pretty girl?"

"Great, man. Bobby Jones is dynamite. Juz look at him up there. Heezza best." Alice started jumping and shouting as Bobby Jones began what would be the final song of the night: "Highway Woman." It was a trademark of the Bobby Jones Band to end each concert with this double-platinum hit. Barbara made her way over to Alice. "Shit, Alice. I almost got fuck-ing stomped trying to get up here," she said.

"Hey, how would you ladies like to meet Bobby Jones after the concert?" asked Fred.

"Get out, man! No shit?" said Alice.

"No shit. Let me just talk to my prez." Fred dis-mounted his bike and walked to the end of the stage to confer with Sandy. Sandy looked over at the girls, who were watching them carefully for the prez's ap-proval. Sandy smiled, gave Fred a kiss on the lips, and nodded his head yes. The two girls were ecstatic. They were going to meet Bobby Jones. The legendary Henchmen were going to introduce them.

"It's all set," said Fred eagerly. "There's a party at his hotel suite right after the concert. You can ride with us."

The concert ended at one A.M. Two roadies opened the side gates near the stage and the six Henchmen began to thunder out of the arena in pairs. Sandy and Slip rode first, followed by Fred and Bruce "Red" Tonnelly. Beef and Lucky Joe were in the rear. Alice rode with Fred. He placed her in front of him. She thought that unusual, but when she questioned him he assured her that he just wanted her to be safe. Bar-bara rode in front on Lucky Joe's bike. The bikes roared south onto Highway 395, the opposite direction from Bobby Jones' hotel.

The bikers took the girls to San Pagano, an old industrial town, thirty-five minutes from the concert arena. Barbara was the first to realize what was going on. She started to squirm in her seat.

"Let us go!" she screamed, turning to look at Lucky Joe. He grabbed her by the neck. "Shut the fuck up, or I'll drag your ass all over the street until your face is torn off," he said. A sinister delight shone in his eyes. Barbara started to cry. Lucky Joe laughed as they turned up Halston Street.

The San Pagano chapter was located in the middle of the industrial section of town. In the forties this had been a mini-boomtown, with factories and small businesses. Early in 1964 the shops started closing and people started to migrate to more prosperous areas. San Pagano is now a low-income community. Most of the factories are shut down. Few businesses remain. The ideal location for a Henchmen clubhouse.

The clubhouse was an old ranch-style home that had once belonged to one of the factory owners. The boarded-up factory still stood only thirty feet from the house. The Henchmen had bought it in '86. The bank had repossessed when the owners couldn't make the monthly payments. On the other side of the clubhouse stood a shabby bungalow that the factory owner had used to sleep guests. A family of eight now occupied the tiny three-room house. Living next to The Henchmen was something they had gotten used to. They were willing to put up with the noise and the occasional shotgun blast fired into the air. In fact, most of the neighbors welcomed living on a block where drug dealers and burglars dared not go.

Barbara was still crying and shaking. Alice, although aware of what was going on, had stayed calm. She figured she could charm her way out of this the way she always did. Lucky Joe had to carry Barbara into the house kicking and screaming. Alice, still being cool and no longer feeling the effects of the alcohol, was led in by Fred. He held her arm in a painful grip. She winced from the pain and fought back tears. Lucky Joe threw Barbara to the floor. Alice broke free from Fred's grip and ran over to Barbara. She tried to comfort her as the six bikers surrounded them.

"Hey, you guys," said Alice. "Don't you think this

has gone far enough? You've had your fun. You scared the shit out of us, now you can let us go."

"We haven't had our fun yet," said Red. All the other Henchmen started to laugh. Red picked up Alice and pushed her toward Fred. Fred caught her and pushed her at Sandy. They continued this for about three minutes, until Alice was dizzy from being bounced around like a beachball. Barbara climbed to her feet and tried to intercede on Alice's behalf. "Leave her alone!" she cried, throwing herself between Lucky Joe and Sandy. The two girls stood there surrounded by the six bikers. Barbara trembled, wetting her pants. Alice ground her teeth together. How dare these men treat them this way? Who were these animals with no compassion? Why did they delight so at inflicting suffering? Sandy stepped forward. The girls looked at him with a mixture of fear and disdain. With his long, straight black hair, square jaw, and high cheekbones, Sandy looked like a savage Indian of Western folklore. His huge, bodybuilder arms made him even more threatening. "Who wants to have the first dance?" he asked. Red turned up the stereo.

Both girls ran for the door. Fred grabbed Barbara and held her by the neck. Sandy caught Alice before she'd gotten more than ten steps away. He ripped open her blouse, exposing her breasts. She struggled and screamed as he tore the garment off her body. Fred held Barbara in front of him, with his right hand firmly under her jaw. He held her around her waist with his left hand, occasionally moving his hand down between her legs or up toward her breasts. He kept her turned toward Alice. "Watch carefully, cunt, you're next," he said.

Sandy pulled Alice's head back by her hair and put his mouth on her breast, biting her nipple. She struggled and hit him on his left ear. "Ow, you fucking little bitch!" he yammered. He smacked her with his open hand, almost knocking her unconscious. He clicked open his switchblade and held it to her throat. "You do that shit again and I'll cut your fucking tits off," he said, as he moved the blade slowly down her neck and to her nipple. She could feel the cold steel touching her as she lay there with her eyes tightly shut, trembling with fear, saying to herself over and over again that this must be a dream. Sandy motioned his head toward Joe. Lucky Joe grabbed Alice's arms and held her up. Sandy pulled off her pants and underpants. Slip and Beef each grabbed one of her legs. They suspended her in the air, spread-eagled. The chapter president then began to lap and slurp her genitals. Like a hungry dog he buried his head between her legs. When she was wet enough with his saliva, he dropped his pants and penetrated her. He came inside her quickly. They dropped her to the floor and Beef, Lucky Joe, and Slip violated her in every way imaginable.

Sandy sat smoking a cigarette and drinking a beer. Fred had Barbara doubled over a small table, naked. He sodomized her repeatedly while burning her butt cheeks with his cigarette. He had a dog's choker chain around her neck. He would tighten it each time she started to yell. The abuse of the girls continued for six hours. Having had their fill, the bikers dropped the brutalized teens on a street corner three miles from the clubhouse. The police found them half-naked, bloodied, and delirious.

Chapter 9

I was sitting in the most comfortable beach chair I'd ever been in. Seagulls soared through the air, diving occasionally to pick up a dropped piece of popcorn or a hot dog bun. Amy was helping Alex build a sturdy sand castle. "Daddy, come play with me, come play, come pla—" And then I was sitting in bed, my head spinning, my heart pounding. "Shit," I said out loud as I glanced at the clock. "Three-fucking-thirty in the afternoon." The previous day's events quickly asserted their reality. The Mexicans, the fight at the pizza parlor, McBright . . . Kevin McBright. *What am I going to do now?* I wondered. *Make arrests based on the weapons buy and drug stash?*

It was good, but not good enough. I had an opportunity to do something no other law enforcement officer had ever done: become a full patch-wearing member of The Henchmen. I needed to speak with Atwood or Leverick right away. Still wearing my clothing from the previous day, I called in to Base I from a phone booth down the street from my apartment. Fred Parkins was on duty. I gave him a brief update and asked him to arrange a sitdown immediately with all the case agents. I told him I'd call for confirmation in thirty minutes. The Base I operation had been set up so that everyone could be assembled for an emergency meeting within hours. Each member had to leave a number where he or she could be reached twenty-four hours a day. Atwood and Leverick carried beepers with a range that covered the entire country. Even if they were out of state, they could participate in a conference call.

The second call I made was to Amy. "Martin, are you all right?" Her voice was cracking. I could tell she was fighting back tears.

"I'm fine, Amy. I'm on the verge of something real big here. It might even take less time than originally planned. I could be home in two months."

I really had no idea whether or not I could be home that soon. I just couldn't think of anything else to say to make her feel better.

"How's Alex?"

"He misses you too, Martin. He's napping right now. You want me to wake him up?"

"No, let him sleep. Tell him his daddy loves him. Tell him it won't be long before I come home for good."

We talked for about twenty minutes. All things considered, she was holding up pretty well. I told her I'd call in a few days, but that she shouldn't worry if I went long periods without contacting her. The nature of the assignment was such that I might not be able to get to a phone without there being one of The Henchmen nearby. She said she understood. She also said she was frightened for me. I was too.

I had no recollection of riding my Harley home from the clubhouse. But there it was, parked next to the curb. I had a little trouble kicking her over, but after several adjustments to the carburetor she finally roared to life. As I was about to pull out, a red Mercedes stopped short next to me. I didn't recognize the driver, but a moment later the passenger door opened and out popped Christy, the club whore, whom I'd met at Mike's the day before. No sooner had she shut the car door than the driver sped away. I killed the engine and Christy strolled over and gave me a kiss on the cheek.

"Hi, Doc."

"Who was that?" I asked, motioning my chin toward the vanishing car.

"Nobody. A good tipper, but nobody. I had him drop me when I saw you. How ya doin'? Heard I missed a real good party last night."

I said nothing. I was due at Atwood's soon, and I had to find a way to get rid of her. She started to walk around me, looking over the bike. "Nice hog, Doc."

"Look, uh . . ." Always the actor, I pretended to forget her name.

"Christy!"

"Christy. I got to get going."

"Me too, Doc. Just wanted to say hi. Can you give me a ride to the West Shore Motel? I got a couple of dates."

What the hell. It's only five minutes out of the way. I motioned for her to climb on, still doing my strong, silent type routine. She mounted up behind me and I kicked the engine over on the first try. Somehow that meant something. I didn't want to embarrass myself in front of her while trying to get the engine started. I laughed to myself as I thought of something Roger Wolfe had said to me before I went away to the FBI Academy at Quantico. "Marty, there's nothing, with the possible exception of money, that has more influence over a man's behavior than a woman. I don't care if it's your mother, your wife, or a stranger on the street. Once a female enters the picture you had better be extra careful, because when it comes to women you'll find you instinctively want to protect them and impress them." He was right. As minor as my behavior at that moment might have seemed, I knew I was showing off for her. I would have to be more careful and not let my behavior be so easily influenced.

I rode into the parking lot of the motel, and again Christy offered her services before we parted company.

"Anytime, Doc. Thanks for the ride."

I sat there a moment, the engine idling loudly, and watched her walk toward the building. I could think of a hundred other things this sorry young girl should be doing right now besides whoring herself for The Henchmen. So many of these women wind up dead from drug overdoses or violence. I wanted to protect this pathetic creature, to save her from this life. I hoped it wasn't already too late for her.

It took me about thirty minutes to ride to Atwood's. Everyone was there, just like six weeks ago when I'd left the prison. Samuels had brought a bunch of 302's.

"Here you are, Martin," she said, as she handed me a stack of forms. "There's a separate 302 for each potential case. There's one here for the weapons buy and the subsequent shooting."

"They'd probably walk on that one. Self-defense," inserted Atwood.

"There's one for the weapons and drugs stashed at the clubhouse," Molly continued. "I've also included forms for the conversations you had at Mike's regarding the alleged activities of the eight members. Initial them all here and here." She pointed to the top left and lower right-hand corners of the form. "Handwrite any changes or additions, and initial them too." It took me about fifteen minutes to review the 302's. It all seemed in order. Indictments and warrants could be issued at any time.

"All right, let's get started," said Atwood, his cigar

in his mouth. "Marty, I didn't get the details from Fred. He said you needed an immediate meeting. Well, here we are."

"Here it is," I said through a deep breath. "They've asked me to kill someone." Atwood took the cigar out of his mouth. He nodded his head slightly, as if in approval of this new development. Samuels and Parkins sat silent, looking to Atwood to say something. Leverick was the first to comment. "Who, Martin? Who do they want you to kill?"

"An ex-member. Guy named McBright. Kevin. His street name is 'Irish.' The guy's looking at some serious time for a drug thing, and they think he's going to roll."

"Maybe you should just do it," said Parkins facetiously. Atwood rolled his eyes in disgust. I ignored the comment.

"Well, I guess that just about finishes the operation," said Molly Samuels. Her voice was strained with disappointment. She had counted on this one. Breaking the back of The Henchmen would have been a boost to everyone's career, but to Molly that part seemed unimportant. She was more concerned with taking the bad guys off the street than with any personal gain.

"What does it mean if we pull out now?" I looked around, posing the question to every member of the team.

"We could disrupt the mother chapter by arresting its major players," answered Leverick. "With the offer for you to take out McBright, we could get Benson on a conspiracy to commit murder charge. The weapons buy puts Morgan, Rivers, and Fenway away for at least seven, and we could shut down the clubhouse with the bust on the drugs and military hardware. That's *if* we can make everything stick."

"Shit," I said. "We were getting in good. Now it's blown."

Everyone looked at Atwood. He hadn't commented since hearing about The Henchmen's intention to chill McBright. He puffed on his cigar, smiling slightly as he scanned the table and making eye contact with each of us.

"Maybe we should let you shoot McBright." His comment lacked the facetious tone of Parkins'.

"What?" I asked.

"You're kiddin', right?" asked Leverick.

"No, I'm not. I mean, let's just say it was possible for us to make The Henchmen believe Dr. Death had carried out the hit."

"Impossible," said Parkins. "They'd want proof. You think they're a bunch of assholes?"

"Talk to me," I said to Atwood. I knew he was serious. "I'm in the club as a full patch-wearing member if we can do this."

"It's never been done, forget it," said Parkins.

"Shut up, Fred!" snapped Atwood. "You don't know what's been done and what hasn't been done. You think you know every goddamn thing that's gone on every year, year after year, since the Bureau was started?"

"So in other words, we fake it," I said.

"Yes, we stage the whole thing. It's been done before. Not many times, but it's been done." Atwood leaned back in his chair, hands behind his head, cigar in his mouth.

Leverick nodded his head in approval. "As crazy as this sounds, Marty, I think it could work."

"What about Martin's cover?" asked Samuels.

"Yeah, what about my cover?"

"It would be a bit complex," said Leverick. "Everyone would know just what they'd have to, and none of the players know you're FBI. Not McBright, not the coroner . . . nobody."

I turned to Leverick. "Can we really pull this off, Dalton?"

"Yes. I think we can. You set it up with The Henchmen that you have to study McBright's habits. When he comes and goes, shit like that. We'll get to McBright and have him vested before you hit him."

"Then what?"

"Then he gets announced DOA. The papers get their story. You get your proof for The Henchmen that the hit was made."

"Here's the deal," said Atwood. His loud, raspy voice was reminiscent of an old *Untouchables* episode. "Leverick, you make arrangements for a meeting at the Mayor's office. Include the District Attorney and the Police Commissioner. Samuels, you and Parkins are in charge of the medical team, death certificate, release forms for the body. Use your best people for this. Nobody knows about Martin. As far as all the other players are concerned, it's a witness relocation situation. I'll let the D.A., the Mayor, and Commissioner know we have a man under, and that this is pertinent to our case. Marty, you call me in two days for an update. Everyone set to go?"

Everyone nodded affirmatively. "What about McBright?" I asked.

"I'll handle him," said Leverick. "I'll offer to get all the charges dropped for the drug bust. Marty, you have to engineer a couple of drive-bys past McBright's house. Use one of the club's vehicles so he'll recognize it. If possible, take someone along who he may recognize as well. We'll get plenty of surveillance photos, if necessary, to show McBright. I'll convince him it's real."

"What about a wire, maybe a recorded conversation

with one of the club's officers? That would help convince him," suggested Fred Parkins.

"No way," I said. "These guys are always checking each other for wires. If you don't come around for a couple of days they give you a big bear hug. Partially because they miss you, and partially because they want to make sure you didn't turn punk while you were gone and cut a deal with police or the DEA."

"Don't worry," said Leverick. "I'll have enough. You just make those drive-bys, Martin."

"I'll make 'em," I said. "Oh, shit . . . one other thing. They have one of their people working as a Police Administrator downtown. I recognized her at the party. She's probably been feeding them information for years. It's no wonder that every time the police go to serve a warrant the club member is nowhere to be found."

"Parkins, you handle that one," Atwood ordered. "Make sure she's not arrested yet. I don't want anything endangering this case, or Martin. Especially Martin." Atwood shot me a wink.

"You got it," answered Parkins. "I'll recommend they give her a transfer right away to a job with less access to police files. We can at least slow down their flow of information."

Atwood stood up. "Okay then, who wants pizza?"

I arrived at Mike's at about ten P.M. Dog and Iron Man were at the bar having a beer and bullshitting with the bartender. A member I hadn't met yet was playing pool in the back room with one of the locals. There were three women with them. One of them appeared to be his girlfriend. In between shots he would stop to tongue-kiss her and run a hand over her butt. There was no one sitting at The Henchmen's regular table. Since I wasn't a member yet, I couldn't sit there without an invitation. I ordered a beer and leaned against the wall to watch the pool game.

Counsel, Dog, and a member I hadn't met yet arrived at eleven. "Come on over, Doc," said Dog.

"Hey, Dog. How's it goin', man?" I sat down next to Counsel. Dog went to the pool room to bring the other member over. Iron Man was still at the bar.

"This is Smitty."

"Smitty," I said, as I shook his hand.

"Doc, Smitty used to be real close to Irish before he left the club," said Counsel. "He'll take you past his house so you can get started."

"I'd like to take a couple of days to watch his movements, who he lives with, you know."

"He lives with his old lady, that's all. Just Sandy and him in a three-room bungalow," said Smitty. Smitty looked like an old-timer. His colors were dirty and worn. He was thin, with huge veins on his tattooed arms. He had a Fu Manchu-style mustache and bushy eyebrows. All he needed was a hook, and he would have made a perfect pirate.

"Does he work?" I asked Smitty.

"Yeah, most times. He paints boats down at the marina."

"Good, we can take a cruise past his place tomorrow and check it out. Can we use one of the vans?"

"Sure," said Counsel. "Take the blue Ford. You can get the keys from Snake at the clubhouse tomorrow morning."

The rest of the night we spent drinking beer and shooting pool. I was lucky that Smitty had been willing to come along on the McBright thing from the beginning. I didn't even have to ask. I found out that night that Smitty had been with the club since the late sixties. He bragged about beating the shit out of two cops in Laconia, New Hampshire, back in 1979. Laconia is the biggest bike run on the East Coast. It takes place every June, and over twenty thousand bikers attend. Smitty said the cops tried to give him a ticket for running a red light. He was willing to take the ticket, but when the cops asked him to peel his colors they went too far. It took six more cops to bring Smitty under control. He did eighteen months in jail for that. He referred to his stretch in prison as "the time I went on vacation."

Chapter 10

The RV needed a tune-up badly. It had been backfiring ever since Sam and Louise Ginsberg had left Albuquerque. "When are you going to get this junk pile fixed?" whined Louise, in between bites of her tuna melt.

"Come on, Lou, stop breaking my balls. After this run we'll have enough money to fix up this baby and party for a couple of months. Any more orange soda in the cooler?"

"I'll check," Louise sighed. She huffed and puffed as she maneuvered her five-foot-two, two-hundred-forty-eight-pound frame to the cabin. "Only root beer and cola!" she shouted.

"Give me a root beer." Louise warmed up her tuna melt in the microwave before struggling back to her seat. She handed Sam the can of root beer.

Louise and Sam had been married for over twenty years. Sam had worked as an accountant for a mob family in Vegas, and Louise had been a coat-check girl in one of the casinos. They were married the night they met. The Varrantino family controlled the hotel that Louise worked in. Sam worked for the Boracchis, a rival family, so Louise had to quit her job at The Pyramid. In 1973, when the FBI broke the back of the Boracchis, Sam did three years. He refused to testify against the family, in spite of an offer of amnesty and witness relocation for him and his wife.

While in prison he met an associate of The Henchmen. He set Sam up with the club after his release. He began as a distributor of drugs and weapons in the Los Angeles area. After a while he began making regular runs to major Eastern cities, with caches of marijuana and methamphetamine. Louise stayed home at first, but eventually became a partner. For the last six years they'd been making runs six to ten times a year between California, Chicago, and New York.

"This soda's piss-warm," complained Sam. "Remind me to get some ice when we get to Pedro's."

LAST GAS FOR 80 MILES—6 MILES AHEAD. The sign was so weather-beaten it blended in with the harsh, golden-brown background of the desert. Louise was sleeping, her head thrown back, snoring, her sandwich still in her hand. Sam turned up the volume on the tape deck to drown out her annoying snorts. His throat was sore from the desert heat, and his sweat-soaked T-shirt hugged the fat on his body like an extra layer of skin. With his stubby, hairy fingers he tried to adjust the air-conditioning controls. "Shit, it's hot as an oven out there, and this fucking thing won't pump out no more cool." He looked at the thermometer. The inside temperature was eighty-one degrees. He took another gulp of soda.

He steered carefully past Pedro's gas pump and stopped the camper next to the garage. There were two bikes parked under a sign that read PEDRO'S—GAS, FOOD AND DRINK. A young blond-haired woman, a little on the plump side, was soaping down the forks, handlebars, and wheel spokes. A mangy dog walked lazily toward the camper and lay down in the shade the bulky vehicle was now providing. "Wake up, Lou." Sam nudged her. "It's already after three. I want to be back on the road before five o'clock. Why don't you get the cabin ready?"

Louise just nodded. She smacked her lips a few times, swallowed, then frowned. "Any soda left in that can? My mouth tastes like a camel's ass."

"Just a sip." Sam handed her the warm, flat beverage.

As she awkwardly climbed out of the vehicle, her sandwich fell to the ground right in front of the panting dog. It gulped it down in one bite. "Fucking dog." Louise opened the padlock on the side door of the camper. The floor had been built up eight inches, to provide a false bottom that could conceal drugs for transport to the East. Louise stepped inside and began opening the clips that held the back wall onto the camper. When she was finished she moved to the outside of the camper and started to remove the screws that held the facade covering the opening to the storage compartment.

"*Buenos tardes,* Señor Ginsberg," said Pedro, a small-framed Mexican in his late forties. "Tacos today, *muy especiales.*"

"Maybe later, Pedro, I'm a little rushed right now. Maybe I'll just grab one of these." Sam helped himself to a KitKat bar from the counter. As he peeled off the foil wrapper, he looked around Pedro's store. *It never changes,* he thought. The store was littered with car and motorcycle parts. With the exception of members of The Henchmen who might work on their bikes when they had business at Pedro's, the parts and garage were seldom used. Occasionally a motorist would happen by and need a fill-up, or a new fan belt and some water or coolant for the radiator. The old desert road wasn't traveled much anymore. In fact, it didn't even appear on any of the new maps.

Behind the counter were two soda coolers and some scantily stocked shelves, containing potato chips, cookies, soup cans, and other non-perishables. Pedro slept on a cot in the back room. This dilapidated service station was his home.

The back room contained a stove where he did all of his cooking—Mexican dishes mainly. Guaranteed to burn your taste buds and give you heartburn for two days. The stove had an exhaust that extended through the roof. Another pipe, barely noticeable, came up from the floor and joined the stove exhaust. The smell of fried beef and Mexican spices made the taste of the candy bar less enjoyable for Sam. As much as Sam loved to eat, he could never get used to Mexican food. "Okay, Pedro, let's go down."

"Ciertamente, señor." Pedro removed a poster from the wall next to his bed, a poster of Marlon Brando in the movie *The Wild Ones*. It revealed a numeric dial pad with a blinking red light. He punched in the numbers 9—9—2—2. There was a distinctive click, and a small section of the floor rose slightly. Pedro reached down and pulled the door open. Sam walked sideways down the stairs, his three-hundred-pound girth making it impossible for him to walk straight down. He huffed and puffed with every clumsy step. Pedro lowered the door and returned to his stove and his fried beef. The trapdoor automatically locked behind Sam.

Sam was now inside The Henchmen's drug-manufacturing lab. Unlike the dingy, disorganized shop above it, this underground room was the epitome of cleanliness and organization. It was almost square, measuring fourteen by thirteen feet. Four sets of fluorescent lights hung from the eight-foot ceiling. Sikati Kim, a U.S.-born Korean, sat at a large aluminum table, mixing the proper ratio of phenylacetone and N-methyl formamide. He would then cook the mixture for six hours to make the granular white methamphetamine.

Kim had been a freelance chemist in Los Angeles

until three years ago, when The Henchmen had informed him that he would be their exclusive manufacturer. To ensure his cooperation they'd moved him to this secret lab, where he manufactured millions of dollars' worth of the drug each year. Although he was seemingly free to come and go as he pleased, he remained a prisoner of The Henchmen's ever-growing need for the drug.

Two members of the Los Angeles chapter were also in the lab—Arnold "Park" Parker and Little Vinney. They were bringing a supply of crank back into Los Angeles. They were also there to supply Sam and Louise for their run east and to record this month's transactions. As treasurer, Little Vinney kept the books for the club's drug operation. The club had sent him to an extensive course in business accounting and computer programming early in 1980 to bring the operation into the modern age. The computer base contained an extensive list of customers and drop-off points throughout the U.S. and Canada. If a name wasn't on that list, he or she didn't buy from The Henchmen. A name could be added to the list only if supplied by a chapter president. Chapter presidents communicated directly with the computer via a modem and telephone lines. Little Vinney was transmitting order confirmations to Houston, New York, Philadelphia, and New Jersey, complete with delivery date and pickup point. The confirmation order for New Jersey read MERCHANDISE ENROUTE— ETA N.J. TPK 14–99. The Paterson, New Jersey chapter would consult their code list and determine the exact location of the delivery point. Each city had over five delivery points that alternated at the discretion of the member in charge of distribution. This ensured the safety of the deliveries.

Park greeted Sam by the stairs. "Hey, Sammy. Pretty

soon you won't be able to fit down those stairs." He patted Sam's huge stomach.

"Yeah, yeah. I'm gonna go on a diet . . . as soon as I lose some weight." Sam laughed, patting his belly.

"Some KitKat?"

"No thanks, Sam. Where's Louise?"

"She's getting the camper ready. We're a little behind schedule, and I want to get out of here as soon as possible."

"No prob, everything's ready to go." Park pointed to four rows of plastic bags. Each bag contained two pounds of methamphetamine. There were one hundred bags in all. "Your first stop is Chicago for twenty bags, then Philadelphia for forty, New Jersey for eight, and New York for the rest."

For the next forty minutes Park and Sam went over road maps, planning routes and timetables. Park would contact the other chapters and let them know the route Sam was taking into their area, and they would have the option of dispatching an escort when the camper was close to the drop-off site. This would be done for the security of the shipment, since many of the points of delivery were on the edges of dangerous neighborhoods.

"Okay, let's get started," said Sam.

"Here, Sam, here's your bread." Park handed Sam an envelope containing five thousand dollars in one-hundred-dollar bills, his standard fee for a four-city run.

Park and Little Vinney carried the bags outside and began loading them under the floor of the camper. Louise was inside Pedro's kitchen, giving him advice on how to make his tacos tastier. After the drugs had been loaded, Sam returned the paneled facades to the back of the camper and padlocked the side door.

"Come on, Lou, let's go." Sam beeped the horn.

Louise appeared in the doorway with two of Pedro's tacos in her hand.

"I'm coming, goddammit, I'm coming." Some of the taco filling oozed out of the sides and fell to the ground as she scurried toward the camper, taking bites along the way.

"How can you eat that shit Pedro makes?"

"If I can suck your dick, I can eat this," answered Louise.

The couple laughed as they cruised back onto Route 71.

"Get me a soda, will ya, honey?"

Chapter 11

He woke at the same time every Saturday, six-fifteen A.M., happy as a child on Christmas morning. This was the day that Eddie "Popeye" Burns took his solo rides from Los Angeles to Santa Barbara. He'd ride for four hours, only stopping at a gas station to use the bathroom or have something to drink. That was the way it had been every Saturday for the last ten years. Unless he was in jail, or part of a major Henchmen run.

"Popeye? That you, honey?" mumbled his wife, Dierdre, as she placed a pillow over her head to block out the morning sunlight. Popeye said nothing. She went back to sleep. He pulled his road-beaten Levi's over his thin, well-toned legs and clasped his "Hooded Executioner" insignia belt buckle. Over his jeans went his leather chaps with Western fringes. Next his steel-toed, seventeen-inch-high leather boots, complete with cigarette pocket and knife-holder. It was already seventy-five degrees out, so a T-shirt would do it. Lastly, it was time to put on a biker's most prized possession, his colors. The leather vest always sat on the back of a chair, patch facing the bed. He carefully removed it and placed his arms through the holes. First right, then left. Then a slow twist of his body toward the mirror to view his coveted uniform.

Popeye was as proud of his patch today as he had been the day he got it fifteen years ago. He was now thirty-eight, but his body was as lean as that of a man of twenty. His huge forearms had earned him his nickname, and many opponents in barroom brawls and hamburger-stand scuffles had been sent into oblivion by his thunderous blows. He motioned a strike with his right elbow toward the mirror. He was pumped and ready to roll. He looked in on his eight-year-old daughter, Angel, then left the house.

Popeye always kept his bike covered in thick plastic, even though it was kept in the garage. A 1955 Harley-Davidson, with a 1957 panhead engine. Candy-red paint covered the frame and gas tank. It had a springer fork, and narrowed sixteen-inch ape handlebars. Ninety percent of the exposed metal was chrome-plated and shone like new. Popeye grabbed a rag off the workbench and cleaned a smudge off the side of the headlight. He carefully escorted his bike to the street, mounted it, primed the ignition, and kicked it over on the first try. "That's forty-two in a row," he said proudly. Popeye held The Henchmen record for the most starts on the first kick: sixty-one.

He throttled the engine a couple of times, then thundered down the street, grinning, the wind against his face. Only when he rode his bike was he truly at peace. The endless conversations in his head about the way things could be, should be, and might be suddenly came to a halt. The aliveness that in most respects he had cut himself off from since he was a child could be experienced again.

His pleasure trip was interrupted as he turned onto Route 44, a winding, seldom-traveled road. A dark gray van pulled to within inches of his rear wheel. Popeye accelerated to avoid a collision. "Fucking assholes!" yelled Popeye, as he gave the intruders the middle finger. The van accelerated once again, this time striking him. Popeye was forced over the embankment and into a ditch. He was thrown from the bike, smashing his head and back against the ground. The van stopped. Popeye bounced up, dazed and angered. He looked over at his broken-up hog, the engine still running, then up at the van.

"Cocksucker! I'll fuckin' kill this asshole!" Popeye started to make his way up the hill as the door on the passenger side of the van opened. Brian "Shooter" Riggs, the sergeant-at-arms for the Seattle chapter of The Outcasts, emerged with a shotgun in his hands. He met Popeye's face with the double-barreled weapon. Popeye stood still, staring down the twin holes. Joe "Skinny Joe" Walters appeared next to Shooter.

"All right, fuck-nuts, peel that fucking patch *now*!" demanded Skinny Joe.

Shooter said nothing. The wind was blowing his thin, scraggly hair in front of his dark sunglasses. He bit nervously on his lower lip as he cocked the hammers into position. "You heard the man, dipshit, lose the jacket!" he ordered.

Popeye looked disdainfully at Skinny Joe. He stepped forward, his nose almost touching the gun metal.

"Take it off, asshole!" growled Shooter.

The barrel of the shotgun was starting to shake. Popeye took a step back.

"Fuck you, pussy. Pull the trigger, but you ain't getting this," said Popeye, tugging slightly on the collar of his vest. Shooter gave a painful smile and squeezed both barrels, ripping into Popeye's skull. The force of the blast sent Popeye down the hill, where he came to rest on his now stalled Harley. His body lay draped over the bike, his Henchmen patch in full view. The two Outcasts approached the body cautiously. Shooter lowered the weapon and stared at his victim. Skinny Joe began to remove Popeye's colors. "Nice leather vest. I'd like to—"

"Take your fucking hands off that vest!" Shooter demanded, as he kicked Skinny Joe in the rib cage. Skinny Joe crumpled over, a look of shock on his face.

"What the fuck is wrong with you, man? We *came* to pull his fucking patch! Let's pull it, and get the fuck out of here!"

"You dumb, skinny shit! I should blow *your* fucking head off too! You don't know nothing, man! He had balls enough not to give it up. More balls than you'll ever have. Get in the fuckin' van! This dude gets buried with his patch." The warriors left without their scalp. Popeye lay lifeless on his metal horse. It began to rain.

The front doorbell rang a half-hour before Kevin McBright had to wake up for work. "Shit. Motherfucker," he said as he glanced at the clock. "It's only five-thirty. Another fucking half-hour before I have to get up. This fucking shit-for-brains is gonna get his ass kicked." He threw on some dungarees, grabbed the baseball bat he kept by the bed, headed for the door and threw it wide open.

"You dumb motherfuc—"

"Kevin McBright? Dalton Leverick. FBI." Leverick flashed his badge.

"Look, man, my trial ain't started yet. I don't gotta to talk to no motherfucker with a badge about nothing. So get the fuck out of my face, before I shove that badge up your ass!"

"I need to speak with you, Kevin. It concerns your and your wife's safety," Leverick said in a low, serious voice.

"Listen, man," said McBright, pointing the bat like a huge index finger. "First of all, my name is 'Irish.' Only my mother calls me 'Kevin.' Second, I can handle any trouble that comes my way, so fuck off."

"Ten minutes . . . Irish." Leverick held both hands out in front of him. "Ten minutes, then I'll fuck off if you want me to."

McBright stepped aside, allowing room for Leverick to pass. "This better not be more fed bullshit."

Leverick and McBright walked over to an old, dusty sofa. Leverick sat down on the edge of the couch. McBright sat on the coffee table directly facing him. He rested his hand on the end of the baseball bat, tapping his chin against his knuckles, sometimes lifting the bat and tapping the floor.

"Your old club has put a contract out on you. They think you're going to roll over on them because it will get you off the drug bust."

"Bullshit! Bullshit, man!" McBright stood up. The bat fell to the floor. Leverick remained calm, watching McBright carefully, knowing the man could reach down for the baseball bat at any moment. Leverick moved his hand slightly toward the inside of his jacket, hoping McBright wouldn't get nutty on him. If he had to shoot him, he could blow the whole operation. He could see it all: paperwork, inquiries. Leverick continued to reason with him.

"I can prove it, Irish. Right now," said Leverick in a smooth, steady tone.

"How the hell you gonna prove that bullshit?"

By this time Sandy was awake and pressing her ear against the bedroom door. Experience had taught her not to interfere in her husband's business. She touched the scar on her upper lip, and thought back to the night in Mike's bar when Irish had smacked her for offering her opinion. Although she had been defending her husband's position in that argument with Counsel, McBright told her that Henchmen women never question and never interfere in a man's affairs.

Eight stitches and six years later, she still remembered that lesson.

"Come with me," said Leverick. He pulled a small pair of binoculars from his coat pocket. "Let's go around back and you can see for yourself." He led McBright out the back door and around by the front porch. From there he could get a clear view of the Henchmen van parked almost two blocks up the street. "Look through these." Leverick handed him the binoculars. "Look at that blue van about a block and a half down the street on the left-hand side. Recognize anyone?"

"Shit!" exclaimed a surprised McBright. "It's fuckin' Smitty! Smitty, you fuckin' pirate! I don't know the other dude. You?"

"I know of him. He used to ride with the Satan's Saints in Canada. They call him Dr. Death. He's the trigger man on your hit."

"We'll see about that shit," said McBright, his face now red with anger. He dropped the binoculars to the ground and headed toward the rear of the bungalow. Leverick stumbled to pick them up and followed McBright. McBright went to the bedroom and started loading his rifle. Sandy sat on the edge of the bed, naked. She made a feeble attempt to pull the sheets over her body when Leverick entered the room.

"Irish, wait, man, this is stupid!" pleaded Leverick, his voice soft but intense.

"I'll blow *both* those mothers away right now! Move aside!" His eyes were wide, his breathing short and quick. Leverick remained in the bedroom doorway.

"Wait . . . there's a better way. A way that will guarantee your safety and keep you out of the joint." Leverick shot a glance at Sandy. She remained seated on the edge of the bed, her firm breasts exposed.

"I'm listening," said McBright hesitantly. His breathing started to return to something a bit more normal.

"I have it all set up if you're willing to go through with it."

"Have *what* set up?"

"Your death . . . and subsequent relocation."

"What?"

"Witness protection."

"Get the fuck out of here!" McBright bolted the rifle and started toward the doorway. Leverick stood firm, his hand inside his jacket.

"Look, you don't understand." Leverick placed his left hand on McBright's chest. He continued to keep his right hand close to his service revolver. "We just make it look that way. They think they made the hit. You and Sandy move to a new city with new names and a new job, and we bust the motherfuckers who want your ass dead."

McBright began to relax. He stepped back and sat next his wife on the edge of the bed. He started shaking his head. "I don't know. I just don't know. Maybe they ain't looking to do me. Maybe I should go talk to them."

Leverick walked over and looked straight into McBright's eyes.

"A minute ago you wanted to blow them away." Leverick's voice became harsh, almost abusive. "You know goddamn well why they're there." Leverick pulled a small note pad from the inside pocket of his jacket. He flipped through the pages vigorously.

"Steven Wilkin. You probably knew him as 'Bolt.' " McBright nodded.

"Fat Dougen, remember him?" Leverick flipped the pad closed and returned it to his breast pocket. "They burned him, his wife, and their two kids while they slept in their trailer. The Henchmen don't have too many ex-members, do they?"

There was an awkward moment of silence before McBright let out a sigh, then spoke.

"How you gonna do this?"

"When the time comes, you wear a bulletproof vest. You leave the rest to me."

McBright looked over at Sandy. She nodded.

"Okay," said McBright, looking down at the ground, defeated. "When do we do it?"

"Our sources tell us the hit is scheduled for day after tomorrow. They're going to hit you before you go to work. About the same time I came here today. I'll bring the vest over tomorrow night and stay in the house as backup. If the house is being watched at the time, I'll come around back sometime during the night."

"Wow, I'm feeling safer already," McBright said sarcastically. Sandy laughed.

"Go to work today. And tomorrow. We'll keep an eye on the house. Sandy will be safe, Irish, don't worry."

"It's all right, baby, I'll be all right. Let's do it the way he says," said Sandy. She somehow sensed that she wouldn't be beaten this time for offering her opinion. McBright looked at her and smiled with a warmth she had never before experienced.

"You'd better hurry," said Leverick. "You're gonna be late for work."

Leverick left as he had arrived, via the front door.

We had been sitting since five A.M. Smitty's chainsmoking was getting on my nerves.

"Look," said Smitty. "That dude's coming out now."

"He looks like a fed if I ever fucking saw one.

These motherfuckers are so hungry for information they'll lean on a dude for life. Squeezing him for every last bit of shit they can get," I said. Leverick and I had discussed whether or not he should go to McBright's while I was scoping out his place in the company of one of The Henchmen. We decided it would add credibility to the story about McBright rolling over, so we went with it.

"That fucking rat. Let's do him now, man. Let's fucking do him now," insisted Smitty, lighting another cigarette from the butt of the last one.

"Patience, my man Smitty. Patience. The day after tomorrow his rat mouth will be permanently shut." Smitty took a deep drag on his cigarette, as if he were taking in my words along with the smoke.

"Yeah, yeah." Smitty turned to me, hand in the shape of a pistol. "Pop him one for me, Doc."

"Sure, Smitty, sure thing," I said. I was finding out that, next to pissing on someone's colors, the worst thing you could do to The Henchmen was turn rat. A rat could not avoid retribution. The Henchmen's arm is long, and their memory longer. And this poor fuck wasn't even going to turn in the first place. He was just a victim of the gang's paranoia. And of our manipulation of his life.

Chapter 12

"*After the beep, leave your name, your chapter, and a telephone number where you can be reached for the next four hours. . . .*"

"This is Lieutenant Kyle, LAPD. We found this number in the wallet of one of your members. There's been a shooting. You can reach me at 644-7—"

"What shooting? Who?" said Counsel, hastily picking up the receiver.

"Edward Burns," said Kyle coldly. "We've already called his wife. She's at the morgue now, identifying the body."

"Then why call me? All of a sudden the police department calls every number in a guy's wallet?"

"No, Mr. Benson?"

"Jesus Christ, what makes you so sure my name is Benson?"

"This telephone number is registered in your name. It's unpublished, and you've had it since 1977. You give it to all L.A. chapter members and all presidents and vice-presidents of other national chapters."

"All right, all right, I get the point. The man has friends at the phone company and knows a little something about the club. Big fuckin' deal. Who killed Popeye?"

"Don't know. He was shot by the turnoff from 44. I was hoping you might have some idea."

"I don't. You be sure and let me know if you find out anything, officer," said Counsel bitterly.

"Sure, sure. So you and your gang of merry men can take the law into your own hands and cut his balls off. That's not the way it works in our society, Mr. Benson."

"We don't live in your society, Mr. Kyle. We have our own laws, our own rules."

Counsel was certain that this was an Outcasts hit. He had warned members not to fly colors solo. He had also warned all the California chapters that members of the Seattle chapter of The Outcasts were rumored to be visiting associates near the Mexican border. Extra caution was advisable.

"Look, I know this is probably falling on deaf ears, but I implore you to let us handle this."

"We take care of our own. We don't ask anything of the police. A brother is dead. Some fuckin' low-life slime took him away from us. If you get him, fine. If I get him, fine. That's all I have to say."

Counsel hung up the phone. He depressed the speed-dial button for Hank the Skank. Counsel's vice-president wore a pager so he could be reached twenty-four hours a day. Within minutes Hank had returned the call. Counsel instructed him to go to Popeye's wife and make all the funeral arrangements. All members within one hundred miles would attend, wearing full colors. The next call was to Crazy. As the security officer, Crazy would handle surveillance and secure routes to the cemetery for all attending chapters.

The immediate business handled, Counsel sat in his easy chair, looking through old snapshots of the club's run to Sturgis, South Dakota, in August, 1986. Each August some fifty thousand bikers descend on this small town on the edge of the historic Black Hills. The Henchmen are treated like royalty whenever they attend a major run like Sturgis. Counsel laughed to himself as he looked at Popeye chugging beers with a couple of college kids. The Henchmen never paid for a drop of beer the whole time they were there. Everyone wanted to be seen partying with a Henchman, and Popeye ate it up. He would get fifteen bucks a photo from anyone wanting a picture. He came home that year with over three hundred dollars.

"So long, brother," said Counsel. "You lived free and you rode hard. I hope heaven is a highway and you're on it, man."

Counsel was filled with feelings of regret and anger as he finished his second six-pack. He crushed the empty can and threw it without aiming toward the wastebasket. It lay on the floor with the other eleven.

Counsel had been asleep for about four hours when he was awakened by the distinctive ring of his cellular phone. Very few members and club associates had the number. Since cellular phones are more difficult to trace than regular phones, Counsel could talk openly only on this line.

"Yeah," said Counsel groggily. His throat was scratchy and his mouth dry

"Counsel, this is Pat." It was Patrick Helmsford, police captain at the 7th Street Station in East L.A. Helmsford had been on the Henchmen payroll for the last seven years. He would feed information on roadblocks, drug busts, warrants, movements of rival bike clubs, and anything else his status in the department made him privy to. For fifteen hundred dollars a month, Helmsford used his influence to take pressure off the Henchmen's businesses. The massage parlors and strip joints needed the police to keep a blind eye to a list of violations a mile long. In July of 1987, he had warned The Henchmen of a major sweep that was about to take place on the strip. Every other massage parlor and strip joint was closed for a week because of violations. Only the Henchmen establishments had their houses in order on the night of the raids.

"What is it?" Counsel. Impatient.

"Look, I heard about your boy, I'm sorry."

"Send me a sympathy card. What do you got for me?"

"It's the San Pagano chapter. They've really fucked up this time. A couple of high school girls were found on a street corner Saturday morning. They were in shock from what the examiner describes as 'a night of rape and torture.' Witnesses at the Bobby Jones concert said they saw them leave with bikers."

"So what?" interrupted Counsel. "Don't other bike clubs attend concerts?"

"Not this one, Counsel. Your guys were paid body-guards that night, hired to work the crowds near the stage. They definitely left with Henchmen. What's worse, one of the girls is the niece of the lieutenant-fucking-governor of California. We've got orders right from the chief to pressure you guys any way we can. That includes raids on your clubhouses, harassing your strip joints, bars, and parlors. Even your goddamn body shops and restaurants are going to get the once-over."

"Those fucking assholes. So what the fuck can we do?"

"They gotta come in, man. The girls are too scared to talk, or arrests would have been made already."

"Forget it. They're Henchmen," said Counsel defiantly. "They would die before they fuckin' came in."

"Well then, you better get ready for the biggest harassment campaign since 1975, because it's gonna come down hard if I don't have some Henchmen meat to throw to the wolves."

"I'll see what I can do," said a disgusted Counsel. "You just get the info on the raids and shit if it starts to happen soon."

"As always. But it may be bigger than both of us this time."

Counsel placed the phone back in its holder and walked slowly to the bathroom. He splashed cold water on his face and looked at himself in the mirror. His head ached as he thought to himself: I'm *the one who has to make it all work out. Those fuckin' idiots.*

He'd always known that sooner or later the San Pagano chapter would go too far. It was only two months ago that Red Tonnelly had beaten two people nearly to death for honking at him at a red light. And Slip Zatela almost had the whole chapter busted three weeks before that, when he raped the waitress at an all-night donut shop in Reno. Only fear of the club's retaliation and intimidation of the witnesses had saved them from being arrested. They had to go. They were too wild and bad for business. Counsel returned to his chair, drank another beer, and went back to asleep.

Christy put the twenty in her purse and laid it on the end table. She removed her shirt and climbed onto the bed. Her customer, a pudgy man in his early forties, sat up in bed with his boxer underwear and black, calf-high socks still on. "You're gonna have to relax if you wanna have a good time with little Christy now, baby."

"Well, I . . . er . . . I don't relax very easy," said the nervous john. The blinking VACANCY light of the motel sign cast an eerie shadow on the wall. He stood up and walked to the window. "Do you mind if I close these blinds? The blinking lights are distracting," he said.

"Sure thing, sweetie," said the now naked Christy,

her arms stretched above her head. She crossed her knee over her left thigh, giving the john a view of her shapely buttocks. He fumbled with the drawstring and managed to get the blinds about three-quarters of the way down. Christy moved to a kneeling position as he turned toward the bed. She gently placed her hand between his legs and began stroking his penis until it protruded from the awkward-looking underwear. She then gently pulled his shorts to his knees and took his organ deep into her mouth. The john moaned as she moved her head back and forth with increasing intensity. Then she moved her mouth away and continued to stroke hard with her hand.

"I can keep this up all the way, if you'd like," she said as she looked up at him, her eyelids half-closed, licking her lips slightly.

"Yes, oh Jesus, yes, don't stop," said the trembling customer. Christy reached to the side of the bed, where she had carefully placed an opened condom. She slipped it in her mouth before continuing the fellatio. She moved her head back and forth while she gently squeezed his testicles. "Oh God, oh God, oh yeah. Here it is. . . . Here it is." He held his breath and his body convulsed. Christy removed the filled condom and discarded it in the bin next to the bed. The john never noticed. He collapsed on the bed, his boxer shorts wrapped around his sock-covered ankles.

"You were great. You were the greatest," he said, out of breath.

"Sure I am, honey, it's what I do. Now get dressed and get going. I got a full night ahead of me."

Christy watched from the window as her john crossed the street. The flashing lights from the motel sign began to produce a hypnotic effect. She began to reflect, to soul-search. She remembered the night she'd come to Los Angeles on the back of Savage's motorcycle. He had made her feel special. He took her out for Chinese food and brought her around to all the biker spots. People turned their heads to get a look at the Henchman and his date. She felt special having this strong, manly specimen pay so much attention to her. Attention she had previously known only as a small child. She also remembered Savage taking her to this motel. To this very same room. He had made love to her for what seemed like hours. Anyone she had ever slept with before was just a boy compared to this strong biker.

She moved to the bed and lay down, continuing to replay scenes from the past in her mind. She remembered another Henchman coming up to the room in the middle of the night and Savage saying, "Now it's time to take care of my friends," and how he had beat her almost unconscious when she refused. She began to cry. The memory of that night was still vivid. One after another they had piled into the room. There must have been six. Or was it eight? She couldn't remember for sure. They all had her. Some of them twice. Savage told her it was part of her "training" and that she was now working for them. The only way out was by her death.

Her heart started to beat faster as she relived the fear she'd felt that night, and she replayed Savage's words in her mind: "If you ever try to run away or go to the cops, we'll eventually find your ass. And when we do, we won't stop beating and fucking until you're stone-cold dead." The only solace she could find was in a crack pipe. The Henchmen generously supplied all their addict girls with drugs. In fact it was a requirement, part of the "training" process. Through fear and drug addiction these slavemasters controlled their stables.

The sadness and emptiness slowly turned to unbearable pain. Christy opened her purse and removed the only picture she had of her family. She walked toward the window, still crying, looking at the pictures of those she remembered once loving. Her father, mother, and sister. A picture taken before Christy was born. Her heart beat faster. The flashing lights seemed to match the tempo of the beats. The knock at the door meant the next john had arrived. She would perform once again and hand over her earnings to her captors. They would throw her some drugs, the way a farmer feeds his pigs. "No! No more!" she cried. "Mommy, Daddy . . . I love you!" were her last words as she leaped to the only option for freedom available: her death.

Chapter 13

Jerry Robinson ran halfway home from school. He wanted to be home by three-thirty to watch his favorite cartoon shows. Jerry was a good student. All A's and B's on his last report card. He always resisted the pressure from his friends at school to do drugs and drink alcohol. The local pushers were even harassing him to deal crack for them. Using minors to deal crack was becoming a popular vehicle for inner-city pushers. Kids weren't immediately suspect, and they wouldn't have to do hard time when caught. Jerry spotted Billy Ray Collin's limousine as he turned up Broadway.

"Oh, shoot!" cried Jerry. "It's Billy Ray!" Jerry started to run faster. Only two more blocks and he would be home. Home, the sanctuary where he had lived with his mother and father since his birth twelve years ago. Home, on the very same street where The Henchmen had had their clubhouse for the last ten.

The Paterson police say that 33rd between Broadway and Fourth Avenue is probably one of the safest streets in New Jersey. During the last ten years only six burglaries and four muggings have been reported. All of these incidents had taken place while The Henchmen were away on bike runs.

Billy Ray was fairly new to Paterson. He had made over a quarter million dollars selling crack in Astoria, New York, until a local mobster turned up the heat and forced him to seek his fortune elsewhere. Eight months ago he and his gang had set up shop in Pater-son. He used mostly neighborhood kids to sell his drugs, but occasionally recruited people from Newark and West New York. Most of the neighborhood feared him. It was rumored that Billy Ray and one of his goons had butchered a deli owner for refusing to sell crack for them from his store. His body was found in a dumpster behind the store. They'd cut him into sev-eral pieces with a chainsaw. The chainsaw was recov-ered at the scene. No fingerprints.

Billy Ray spotted Jerry running down the street and ordered his driver, JJ Smith, to head him off at the next corner. The huge car stopped just short of hitting him. Jerry froze for a moment. As soon as Billy Ray stepped out of the car, Jerry darted again toward home.

"Get in, you stupid little motherfucker!" ordered Billy Ray. Jerry kept running. Billy Ray slipped back into the car and ordered JJ Smith to continue the pursuit. They caught up with Jerry outside his home. Billy Ray jumped out of the limousine and grabbed Jerry by the back of his shirt, almost choking him. Jerry began to cough. "You're all right. Don't be such a little pussy," said Ray.

"I didn't do nuffin. What you boderin' me fo?" asked Jerry.

JJ Smith turned off the engine, walked to the left side of the car, and stood, arms folded, while Billy Ray continued to badger Jerry.

"Look here, you stupid niggah, you ain't got no choice in the matter! You gonna deal for me at school or you gonna get yo ass busted!" threatened Billy Ray.

"You doan scare me, Billy Ray!" said a tearful Jerry. "Da Henchmen are my friends! They kick yo butt good!"

Billy Ray laughed out loud. "You think those white motherfuckers give a shit about a little niggah like you? Boy, if this was Alabama or Mississippi, they'd call themselves the KKK instead of The Henchmen! You *are* a dumb-ass kid, ain't ya?"

Billy Ray had good reason to believe The Henchmen hated blacks. His brother-in-law, Barry Roosevelt, had done time in Folsom Prison. He used to tell Billy Ray stories at Sunday afternoon barbecues. Stories about jailed Henchmen and other bikers who would quickly align themselves with white supremacy groups like the Brothers of Arian and the American Nazi Party. In fact, a Canadian motorcycle club called The Devil's Chosen had been denied access to a Henchmen-sponsored run because they had a black member. Billy Ray was confident that The Henchmen would never interfere with his recruiting process for young dealers.

"I won't do it, Billy Ray! You're a bad man, and I hate you!" Jerry started swinging his arms wildly, trying desperately to punch Billy Ray. JJ Smith, still leaning against the car, laughed at Jerry's futile effort. Jerry's mother, returning from work, spotted the men confronting her son and began to run up the street.

"You let go of my boy!" she screamed, dropping her bag of groceries as she ran. She was intercepted by JJ Smith, who threw one arm around her waist as she struggled and screamed at Billy Ray. Windows started to open, and neighbors began to poke their curious heads out to see what the commotion was all about. The yelling came to an abrupt halt with the thunderous roar of four Henchmen motorcycles turning up the street. Jerry kicked Billy Ray in the shin and bolted across the street to The Henchmen's clubhouse as the four bikers pulled up. "I'm gonna laugh when they smack that little niggah in his face and send him home crying," said Billy Ray.

Billy Ray watched anxiously as Daniel "Dirty Dan" Goldman stood listening to Jerry's whimpering explanation. Billy Ray's anxiety turned quickly to genuine concern as the hulking six-foot-four, two-hundred-ninety-pound biker gently patted Jerry on the head and shot a menacing glance across the street. Dirty Dan clicked his fingers in the direction of his cohorts and pointed toward Billy Ray and JJ. The four bikers began to walk slowly across the street.

"Shit, JJ, let's get the fuck outta here, man! Those fuckers are coming over here!" said Billy Ray, as he leaped into the back of the limo. JJ immediately let go of Jerry's mom, who ran to greet her son halfway across the road. Before they could get the limo rolling, two Henchmen, Bobby "Bones" Blackwell and Dirty Dan, climbed into the backseat with Billy Ray. Henry "Grease" Bartley, a jolly-looking sort with a huge belly and hands as big as a gorilla's, stood by the driver's window. Only The Henchmen insignia and the bottom rocker of his colors, which read NEW JERSEY in bold black letters on a white background, were visible through the glass. The Henchmen used to have city names as the bottom rocker of their colors, until Counsel gave instructions to all national chapters to strip the city names and use only the state. Counsel figured that in states with multiple chapters it would be harder for the police to narrow down their suspects when Henchmen colors were spotted.

The fourth Henchman, Edward "Stoned Eddie" LeCamp, followed JJ into the front seat and sat beside him, one arm over his shoulder. "Hiya, pal! Nice day, eh?" said the Canadian-born biker. Stoned Eddie had been a member of the Montreal Sinners before moving to the U.S. He'd been a member of The Hench-

men since 1982. Henchmen lore had it that Stoned
Eddie had killed three Outcasts by beating them to
death with a motorcycle kick-stand during a rumble
in Binghamton, New York. This feat earned him his
Henchmen colors, as well as the vice-presidency of the
Paterson, New Jersey chapter two months later.
Stoned Eddie placed the cold steel of a six-inch hunt-
ing knife to JJ's throat.

"You just sit tight, eh, and maybe I won't cut your
neck. Okay, brother?"

JJ said nothing. Just a few short gasps for air, and
a wide-eyed look that begged for mercy.

Bones pulled a .25-caliber pistol from his boot and
held it to Billy Ray's temple. Billy Ray gasped, held
his breath for a moment, then let it out in short, stut-
tering bursts. "What the fuck you want with me, man?
I ain't done shit to you," said Ray, his voice high-
pitched. Dirty Dan held up a five-inch combat bayonet
in front of Ray's face. "See this, you stupid nigger?
This is the steel that's gonna cut off your balls." He
slowly moved the blade down Billy Ray's body and
stuck the point lightly against his crotch. The smell of
human excrement filled the air as Ray's sphincter mus-
cle loosened.

"Oh shit, man," said Bones. "This motherfucker
shit his pants." Dirty Dan didn't laugh. He leaned
over and spoke softly to Billy Ray. "This is *my* block,
shithead. Don't fuck with anybody. Clear?" Ray nodded, out of breath, embarrassed, and beaten. "Now
get the fuck off my street."

The limousine drove off as the four Henchmen returned to their bikes. Dirty Dan turned and met Mrs.
Robinson's grateful eyes. He nodded. She took her
son by the hand. "Let's go, boy. You have homework
to do before you can watch TV."

*   *   *

Joseph Famantia bit his nails as he waited outside Don Toritelli's office. His right-hand man, Mario Calvecci, waited with him, sharing his nervousness. They both knew Toritelli's temper well, and they were the bearers of bad tidings. "Give me another smoke, Mario. I hope he's ready to see us soon. I want to get this over with."

"You and me both," said Calvecci. "What do you think he's gonna do?"

"Don't know. He's gonna want to get even real bad. Real bad." Famantia brushed some cigarette ashes off his tie. "You know, Mario, a cunt in Barbados bought me this tie. You like it?"

"Sure thing, boss. I always like a yellow tie with a blue jacket."

"Think so?"

"Yeah."

Both men turned toward the mahogany doors as Toritelli's *consigliere,* Jack MacDonald, emerged from the office. "Don Toritelli will see you now, gentlemen," said the young lawyer. Calvecci stood by the door as Famantia moved forward. Famantia stopped three feet from Toritelli's desk.

"Don Toritelli, I'm sorry to have disturbed you this evening."

"Tell me, Joey, what is so important that it cannot wait?" said Toritelli, his Italian accent thick and his voice deep. For a man of sixty-seven he stood tall and strong. His gray hair was well groomed. His dark, sunken eyes hid many of his wrinkles, and although some said he never smiled, he still possessed all of his teeth.

"It's Angelo, Don. He's . . . he's dead."

"Dead? Who? How?"

"They hit the lounge. Tonight. Some kind of explosion. We're not sure who, but we think . . ." Famantia hesitated. He had set up the deal. He knew Angelo wouldn't give The Henchmen their twenty G's, but he never thought they'd do anything about it. Never thought for a minute they'd have the nerve to hit a Toritelli-owned establishment. "We think it's the motorcycle club. The Henchmen."

"Why?" inquired Toritelli, his face starting to redden.

"One of the cocktail waitresses survived. She told Mario that two of The Henchmen argued with Angelo minutes before. She said she thought Angelo was going to shoot them right there in the lounge."

Toritelli's eyes widened and he began panting. *"Dead!"* he bellowed, as he pounded the top of his oak desk.

"Dead! Dead! Dead! Dead!" he shouted, as he hammered the desk again and again. "I want all those fucking slimy, hippie bastards dead! I want that fucking clubhouse of theirs burned to the ground! Take a hundred men if you have to! I don't want a single Henchman left alive in this goddamn city!" He shook his fist at the air, then bit his forefinger as he growled away his anger. He fell back into his chair. Exhausted, he motioned for Famantia and Calvecci to leave.

"What do we do first?" asked Calvecci, as the two men left the office building at 18th and Broad.

"We put the word out. Only guys who are in line to get made. Everybody gets their bones after we hit them." Famantia knew that many of the old blood might not be up for a hit on The Henchmen. He also knew that the younger guys would be willing to accept the job. For a guy to "get made" was the Mob equivalent of a Henchman getting his colors. Ever since FBI agents like Joseph Pistone had infiltrated the Mafia in the late seventies, mob families across the United States had tightened up on procedures for accepting new members. Now you had to "earn your bones" by making a hit. Famantia figured that young men, hungry to become members of the Toritelli family, would jump at this chance to bring down The Henchmen.

"Talk to Ricky Moose. He's got the best line on available guys."

"When do we hit them, Joey?" asked Calvecci.

"Not sure. We need to find out when they have their club meetings. I'll have one of our people inside the police department check it out. I'm sure they have files on these guys. Let's meet at Eddie's tomorrow afternoon. Three o'clock."

"Sure thing, Joey. Three o'clock."

Calvecci walked down 18th Street to catch the subway at Market. Famantia hailed a cab.

He tapped the flashlight against his hand to give it some more juice. "Damn, I should have put new fucking batteries in this," grumbled Peter "Pete" Jacobs, as he made his way through the dark tunnel underneath Front Street in North Philly. He was looking for the junction box that tied in the buildings between Westmoreland and Lippincott to the Philadelphia Power Company electrical network. "Come on, baby, just a few more minutes," Jacobs pleaded with his fading light.

As he came up to the rusted, metal cover, the light died again. One more whack against his hand gave him enough light to read the tags near the terminals: 1118 FRONT STREET. "That's it," said a pleased Jacobs. He then removed the rubber-handled wrench from his tool bag and proceeded to loosen two of the hot wires that provided the building with electrical service. Once the bolts had been loosened, Jacobs removed the wires from the terminals and tapped the circuit opened and closed six times. He repeated this procedure a half-dozen times within ten minutes. "This ought to give them a little flicker," he said. He then returned the wires to their secured position and tightened the bolts. The flashlight held out until he had made his way through the tunnel and back onto the street.

Chapter 14

Smitty was already waiting outside my apartment when I woke up. From my window I could see him bopping his head up and down to the music from the van's stereo. Today was the day. The day I was to hit McBright and earn my Henchmen colors. I had telephoned Base I the night before to tell them the hit was on. Molly assured me that everything was set. Dalton had set it up with McBright. He would walk through his door at six-thirty A.M. and I would shoot him in the chest point-blank with a .22-caliber pistol. Three shots to the heart. His vest would save his life. I wondered if Dalton had told him that the shots might still knock him on his ass and leave a black-and-blue mark the size of a basketball. I tucked the pistol in my belt and went out to meet Smitty.

"Morning, Doc. Nice day to off somebody, ain't it?" said Smitty. His eyes were bloodshot from too much speed and not enough sleep.

"Sure is, Smitty," I said, as I tapped the pistol in my belt.

"Oh, about the hardware, man. Counsel says he wants you to use this. It makes more of a statement." He reached behind him and pulled out a sawed-off, double-barreled shotgun. *Oh, shit. At point-blank range, the blast from the shotgun may rip McBright's face off. Even with the bulletproof vest he may not survive the hit at that range. What the hell am I going to do now?*

"Hey, not for nothin'," I said. "I kinda like the .22. I feel comfortable with it. Ya know, it's sort of like a baseball player and his favorite bat." I tried to make light of it.

"Look, man, I hear ya. It's Counsel—he's real up-tight lately. One of our brothers was killed yesterday. Popeye. Know 'im?"

"No. What happened?"

"Not sure. We think he was hit by The Outcasts. Counsel's checking into it. He's going nuts over it. Just use the fucking double-barrel, man. No big deal, right?"

"No big deal." I clicked open the barrel and looked at the two shells in the chamber. I had to make it seem like no big thing. "Nice," I said, as I closed the chamber and held the weapon in my hands, looking it over. The barrel was sawed off to within two inches of the fore-end. This was done for two reasons. First, it made a powerful weapon easy to conceal. Second, for a close-range hit, the shorter the barrel, the wider the spread of buckshot.

I was tempted to lay the barrel across Smitty's temple and arrest him right there. We could still bring down a lot of Henchmen with what we had so far. But at the very same moment I said to myself, *No. I'm in this too deep. I'm gonna play it out. I'll figure out something.*

The ride to McBright's took twenty minutes. Smitty and I spoke about bikes, pussy, and guns. His knowledge of weapons was impressive. At times I had to recall my training classes at the academy, and the countless hours talking with Roger Wolfe about his gun collection, just to keep up with him.

When we arrived at McBright's, Smitty pulled over

opposite the house, just slightly past his doorway. "This is it, Doc. Six-twenty."

"Time to rock and roll," I said as I leaped out of the van, the shotgun concealed under my jacket. I quickly crossed the street and crouched beside the wooden porch to McBright's house. I looked at my watch. Six twenty-three. He would start to open the door any minute now. I would leap to the doorway and blast both barrels into his chest. I tried to think fast. How was I going to make Smitty think I'd shot him, without really killing him with the spreading buckshot?

Maybe I could kick him in the chest, knocking him back into the house, out of sight. I could then empty the gun into the ceiling or floor, giving Smitty the sound effects without the visual. We would have to let McBright in on the fact that it was a phony hit. *No good,* I thought. Then it hit me.

I clicked open the barrel and removed the right shell. My back was to Smitty, so my activities were out of sight. I removed the crimp from the shell with my teeth and emptied half the buckshot onto the ground. I quickly recapped the shell and placed it back into the barrel. I had barely gotten the barrel closed when I heard the door latch open.

I leaped onto the porch and pulled the trigger of the right barrel. McBright fell back into the doorway. I could hear McBright's wife screaming. There was no sign of Leverick. With my back still to Smitty I pulled the left trigger, this time aiming toward the wall. McBright was barely conscious. He wouldn't remember the second shot. I would leave it to Dalton to explain away the shot on the wall. That's if McBright even thought to ask about it. I turned and ran across to the van. The streets were still empty, except for a passing motorist who had to brake to avoid me as I ran across the street.

"What the fuck happened?" asked Smitty as we drove off.

"I let him have a single barrel first. I aimed slower with number two. It made sure of him. Real sure. Dig?"

"Yeah. I got it, Doc. Nice job. Let's get some breakfast."

Dalton Leverick darted from the bedroom, Sandy McBright at his heels.

"Oh my God!" she cried. Leverick knelt next to McBright and placed two fingers on the side of his neck. He lifted his eyelid and looked at his pupils. "Dilated," he said. "He's in shock."

"You fucking bastard!" shouted Sandy. She knelt next to Leverick, gently touching her old man's forehead. "You fucked him up! You said the vest would protect him! What happened?"

"He'll be fine, Sandy." Leverick placed a hand on Sandy's shoulder. "Try to stay calm. The blast from the shotgun caused this temporary shock. I've seen it before. He'll be okay." Leverick unhooked a small transmitter from his belt and pulled open the antenna.

"Bad Boy, Bad Boy, this is the Baker, come in, over."

"This is Bad Boy. Go ahead, Baker, over."

"We're ready to make the delivery, over."

"Be there in two, out."

Leverick returned the device to his belt. Several long seconds passed before McBright started to come to.

"What the fuck?" said a groggy McBright. "My chest feels like I got hit with a sledgehammer."

"That was a shot from a twelve-gauge. We're real

lucky. The gun must have recoiled hard. The second shot ended up in your wall." Leverick stood up and pulled off his jacket as he heard the siren of the approaching ambulance.

"Sandy," said Leverick. "I want you to wait five minutes and then call the police at the number I gave you. Everything's arranged. We'll take Irish to the hospital. We've had a government physician temporarily assigned to St. Katherine's Medical Center. He'll sign the death certificate. We'll switch toe tags with a John Doe who'll be sent to the morgue with his new name, Kevin McBright."

Molly Samuels and Fred Parkins walked through the door rolling a stretcher, both wearing EMS uniforms. Parkins tossed Leverick a jacket and cap. He put them on and assisted McBright onto the stretcher.

"Sandy," he said. "Meet us at the medical center after the police finish questioning you. You remember what we went over last night? You know what to tell them?"

Sandy nodded.

"Then what?" asked McBright. Parkins buckled the straps around McBright's chest and legs. Samuels then held open the front door as Parkins and Leverick began to roll the stretcher out.

"Then we take both of you to a safe house, until we can work out your new identity and figure out where we're going to place you," said Leverick.

"Do we get a choice?" asked McBright.

"Quiet, Irish," said Leverick, patting him on the head. "You're supposed to be dead, remember?

Fenway pulled ahead of Snake and pointed to the side of the road. Snake nodded, and both bikers pulled their machines over and turned off the engines.

"What's up, Dog?" asked Snake.

"That bar we passed, about a mile back."

"Yeah?"

"There was a van in front of it. I think I recognized it. Looks like an Outcast's. The one they brought to Sturgis last year."

"Let's check it out," said Snake.

The bikers returned to the vicinity of the tavern and discreetly placed their bikes about fifty yards away from the entrance. They walked to the window and peered in.

"Look," said Dog. "It's that prick Riggs and that skinny fuck."

"You think they did Popeye?"

"Don't know man, but shit, what the fuck are they doing down this way anyhow? I mean . . . we got a vendetta, right? We gotta move on 'em, right?"

Not all Henchmen took the club vendetta as seriously as Dog. Those who did would not let a member of the Outcasts get away alive, no matter what the circumstances.

"What's our next move?" asked Snake.

Dog looked around. A young boy was walking up the road, swinging a stick back and forth.

"That kid, he's the ticket. Give me ten bucks." Snake complied, and Dog approached the boy as he neared the two bikers.

"You want to make ten bucks, kid?"

"How?" said the boy, looking inquisitively at Dog. Dog removed his amber-tinted sunglasses and made eye contact with the boy.

"Just go into that bar and yell as loud as you can, 'Outcasts are a scumbag club and suck Japanese dick.' " Dog knew this would rile them. One thing all outlaw bikers share is a common disdain for the Japanese. Bikers have been known to set foreign cars on fire at major motorcycle events. Anyone coming to one of these events as a spectator must use caution if he owns a Toyota or a Honda. The two bikers waited as the boy went inside the bar.

Within seconds the boy came running out, past Snake and Dog and then around the back of the building. The two Outcasts burst through the door, in search of the offender. Riggs and Skinny Joe stood for a moment, motionless, as they realized they were now face-to-face with The Henchmen.

"So long, scumbag," said Snake, as he squeezed the trigger on his .44 Magnum. Riggs fell dead to the ground with a bullet in the middle of his forehead. Skinny Joe instantly raised his hands above his head.

"Wasn't me! Shooter did him! Fuckin' Shooter! Not me, man!" cried Skinny Joe.

Dog removed his knife from his boot and threw it straight into Skinny Joe's throat. Blood spouted from his neck as his arms shot straight out to the sides, his whole body convulsing. Then he dropped, his body lying across Riggs'. Dog walked over and reached down for his knife. The blade made a squishing sound as he removed it. He wiped the blood on his pants and placed the knife back in his boot.

Some of the patrons of the tavern started to exit to view the commotion. Snake and Dog ran to their bikes and took off in a cloud of dust. They had turned their vests inside out, so no one would recognize their colors. No one except the boy had seen their faces. Ten dollars richer, he would be nowhere in sight when the county sheriff arrived.

As they sped down the road, Snake would occasionally remove one hand from the bars and extend both feet to the side, mocking the manner in which Skinny Joe had convulsed before he dropped. Both men would laugh, as their taste for death sent adrenaline rioting through their bodies. Both were wired, fearless, mean-spirited. No regrets about the murder of Riggs and Walters. Just excitement.

The two bikers slowed down as they approached a vehicle on the side of the road. An elderly woman, about seventy, sat on the driver's side of a tan 1967 Rambler, as her husband tinkered with the engine. She couldn't see him through the raised hood, but would turn the key to no avail when he shouted instructions to her. She spotted the two Henchmen in her rearview mirror. *Oh no,* she thought to herself, *my worst fear is about to come true! Here we are, two elderly people, helpless, alone.*

Her husband, unaware of the bikers' presence, continued to trifle with the engine. The woman's heart rate soared as she watched them approach the car. She tried to speak, to warn her husband, but she could not. She was paralyzed with fear. The two bikers passed her on either side of the car, converging on her husband. Seconds later, Dog opened the door and reached toward her.

"Excuse me, ma'am," he said as he turned the key. The car started instantly. "I told your husband to have that carburetor cleaned as soon as possible."

She sat in the car in disbelief as the Henchmen rode away.

"Move over, dear," said her husband. He took his place behind the wheel as she maneuvered herself to the passenger side. "What nice young men."

Chapter 15

"How many?"

"I'm thinking, I'm thinking!"

"Goddammit, Mario, how long are you going to take?" said Famantia.

"All right, all right! Give me two, Eddie." Eddie Farcone complied.

"Now maybe we can get on with it!" said Famantia, slightly agitated.

"What do you say?" asked Calvecci.

"Twenty," said Farcone.

"I'll see it," said Famantia eagerly, "and raise you ten."

"I'm out." Calvecci folded his cards and crossed his arms.

"Let's have it," said Farcone.

"Pair of ladies and a pair of twos."

"Shit. You lucky fuck. That's six in a row."

"What can I say, Eddie? My momma raised me right."

Eddie Farcone pushed himself away from the table. "Let's take a break. Another round?" The two men nodded their acceptance and Falcone grabbed the bottle of Johnnie Walker from the shelf. He poured Famantia's first. "You know, Joey, we had a little electrical problem here."

"Yeah?"

"Yeah. Last night we lost power a couple of times.

Everything went black. We had a game going back here, and out front was packed. The girls brought in over five grand. Johnny said he was going to keep the place open even if he had to use fucking candles on the girls' tits."

"So what happened?"

"Nothin'. Some guy came from Philly Electric this morning. He said the wire to the meter was loose. I guess Johnny called them."

Famantia pulled a small notebook from his jacket pocket. "Okay, let's talk about the Henchmen hit. Did you talk to Ricky Moose, Mario?"

"Yeah. Moose can have forty guys. Needs twenty-four hour's notice."

"Good . . . good. I found out that The Henchmen meet day after tomorrow. By about nine o'clock, the entire Philadelphia chapter should be there. I got ten guys all set to go. Eddie?"

"Five. Maybe more."

"That should do it. Hell, there's only about twenty of them."

"What about getting into the clubhouse?" Farcone returned to his seat at the table.

"It shouldn't be too hard. My man at the police department tells me there's some Puerto Rican schmuck doing time who owns the house to the left. On the right-hand side there's just some old lady living alone. I'll have two of my guys go into her house early. We'll lock her in a closet or some shit. The houses are attached, so we just gotta worry about the front, back, and rooftops."

"Ricky Moose says he's got an explosives man if we need him," added Calvecci.

"We might. We can blow a fucking hole right through the wall from one of the other houses if all else fails." Famantia smiled as he made the statement. His flabby chin expanded as he sunk his neck into his chest. He looked menacing enough, but inside he was filled with apprehension. *We'd better not miss,* he thought. *I'm on the line this time. If I fail, I know what the consequences will be.*

"Come on, ante up," said Eddie.

"I'm in. How about you, boss? Boss! Jesus, you're a million miles away. You in?"

Famantia threw a chip in the pot.

We were gathered tightly around the television. Iron Man was leaning so far over me I was practically supporting him on my back. Counsel fiddled with the fine tuning. "Come on, Counsel!" pleaded Little Vinney. "I can't see fucking *through* you!"

"Fuck you, man. Suck my dick," said Counsel jokingly as he moved away from the set.

The four of us waited patiently in Counsel's office for the six o'clock news to begin. News of McBright's death had to appear on television or in an article in one of the major papers. I shared their anticipation. I kept wondering to myself, *Did it go off smoothly? Did they get McBright's death certificate done? Did McBright really get killed?* Although I had let some of the shot out of that shell, I had hit him pretty hard. Counsel stood up, hesitated, then moved to his desk, as the newswoman began the details of the shooting— and death—of Kevin McBright. Atwood had done it. That slick son of a bitch. The team had actually pulled it off.

The segment ended. Without missing a beat, Counsel handed me a new leather vest, complete with Henchmen colors. He kissed me on the lips and hugged me.

"Way to go, Doc! You're a Henchman now, brother! Ride free and die hard!"

"Thanks, man," I said.

I accepted similar congratulations from Iron Man and Vinney. We were interrupted by the ringing of Counsel's phone. The TV news continued as he took the call.

When he'd hung up, Counsel looked concerned. For a moment, he stood silent. His huge, tattooed arms were folded tightly, his brow creased.

"What is it?" asked Iron Man.

"It's Philadelphia. That was Whitey on the phone. They're planning to hit the clubhouse tomorrow night."

"Who?" I said.

"We had a little misunderstanding with some business associates of ours—the Toritellis. One of our guys in Philadelphia—Pete, what a fuckin' genius!— he planted a listening device in the back room of a Toritelli bar. He heard them planning the whole fuckin' thing."

"What do we do? Go out there?" asked Vinney.

"No. Whitey says he's got it handled. He talked to the Paterson chapter. They're only two hours from Philadelphia. There'll be twenty of them there tomorrow afternoon. With almost twenty brothers in his own chapter, he'll have more than enough power to defend the clubhouse. One thing . . ." Counsel looked at me. "Dirty Dan needs someone to make a pickup for him."

Counsel sat behind his desk, lit a cigarette, and leaned back in his chair, his hands clasped behind his head, the cigarette dangling from his mouth. His eyes never left mine.

"Doc, I think this one's for you."

"Sure, man. What do I have to do?" I said.

"Tomorrow, after Popeye's funeral. Fly out to Newark, New Jersey. Rent a car, and make the pickup for Dirty Dan. We sent him some crank from our lab in the desert. A couple of people in an RV who make deliveries for us on a regular basis. This one's gonna be made tomorrow night. The meet is scheduled for . . ." He spun around in his chair and turned on the computer. A late-model IBM PC sat on the credenza behind his desk. After a moment he punched a few keys. "Ten P.M. At the turnpike. A rest stop near Exit 14."

Very impressive. These guys had all their business down on computers. We had known they were organized, but we'd never dreamed they were this well put together. A central manufacturing lab and a mobile delivery unit that traveled the country, supplying all the other chapters with pure crank. All kept track of on Counsel's computer.

I must have looked visibly impressed, because Counsel seemed to eat it up. I could tell by the way he spun around in his chair and pecked away at the keyboard, as if to say "Wallah! Nothin' to it!" He worked hard in some respects to maintain the club's troglodyte image. Underneath, the club was being run by a very shrewd operator.

"I'll call Dirty Dan tonight, and give you the rest of the details tomorrow," said Counsel.

Little Vinney stood up. "But tonight is Doc's night. Let's get downstairs and party."

The four of us left Counsel's office and went down to the main floor. I had barely stepped through the door when Iron Man tackled me and threw me to the floor. His three-hundred-some-odd-pound frame nearly crushed my chest. He kissed me while the other members, women, and associates howled. His wet, foul-smelling mouth, redolent of stale beer and cigarettes, made my stomach lurch. He emptied his beer bottle on my face and rubbed the warm brew through my hair. Before I could clear my eyes, Iron Man placed Pam, the club's biggest, sluttiest mama, in front of him and on top of my face. I started to gag as she moved her raunchy-smelling crotch up and down on my nose and lips. The more I wondered about how many guys had fucked her that night, the sicker I felt. I was trapped. Any resistance would be a slap in the face to my new brothers. My brothers—who were hell-bent on showing me a good time to welcome me into the club.

After ten minutes I felt the relief of Iron Man's girth lifting from my body. Pam, meanwhile, continued with her attempts to suffocate me. Without losing a stroke, she began to unfasten my belt buckle. She took my prick into her mouth and began to suck vigorously. Despite my stomach's unsettled condition, my body began to respond. My prick hardened in her mouth as she continued her efforts. I started to forget her offensive smell, getting lost in the sensation. People started chanting: "Doc, Doc, Doc, Doc! Ride his face and suck his cock!" They kept it up until I finally climaxed. Pam, along with several other women who fell into the category of "common property," returned to whoring themselves with the other members.

I had barely gotten my fly zipped when Iron Man and Counsel lifted me to my feet and threw me across the room. Other members began punching and kicking me in the back, chest, and head. This wasn't a beating. Just a friendly welcome. The pounding stopped suddenly. Everyone's attention turned to Counsel.

"Now, my brothers. We officially welcome Dr. Death to the club." He held out a five-gallon metal bucket. "In this bucket is grease and oil from oh so many oil changes. But it's not yet complete, brothers. Gather round, gather round, and add to the mixture the missing, essential ingredient."

The other members huddled around the bucket that Counsel had placed on the floor. They took turns pissing wildly in the pail, half of them too drunk to aim properly. Iron Man helped me to my feet. I was dazed. A small cut had opened over my left eye. Iron Man held my arms as Counsel approached, bucket in hand. Counsel emptied the entire contents of the pail over my head and back. The place went wild. I was blinded for a moment by the mixture of grease and piss. *What the fuck am I doing here?* I wondered. *No operation is worth this shit.*

I wiped my eyes and stood there for a moment, dazed and confused. I figured there wasn't much else they could do to me, so I thought I'd better look like I was enjoying this horror show. I let out a big yelp, raced across the room, and grabbed a bottle of Scotch off the table. I guzzled a quarter of the bottle while my compatriots urged me on. If I was blind drunk, I would have a good excuse for not participating in any further bizarre actions.

Counsel interceded between guzzles. "Gather round, brothers!" he announced sonorously. "It's time to recite The Henchmen creed!" *Oh no,* I thought. *What's next?* Counsel, Iron Man, and about six other members started to recite:

"A Henchman is the ultimate biker.
A Henchman never backs down.
A Henchman is a great fuck.
A Henchman never gives up his colors.
A Henchman is always right."

Counsel put his hands on my shoulders.

"Doc?" he said, slurring his words slightly. "Do you swear to lif your life as a Henchman? Never backing down? Never . . ." He took another gulp of beer. "Never fucking over a brother? Always keeping the honor of the club's colors?"

"Fuck, yeah," I said, as I raised the bottle of Scotch

in the air, trying to figure out what having integrity and brains had ever done for my miserable life.

"Fuckin'-A-Yes!" added Iron Man sharply. "Henchmen forever! Forever Henchmen!"

I spent the next couple of hours getting as drunk as I possibly could. Around midnight Dog and Snake arrived. Word quickly spread that they had snuffed two Outcasts that afternoon, on a return trip from the truck stop in Brawley. They said they were certain these two Outcasts were the ones who had gotten to Popeye.

I felt almost pleased. Although it's rarely acknowledged openly, most agents feel a certain dark delight when one member of the underworld kills another. One less bad guy for us to worry about.

It wasn't long before Dog cornered me. "Congratulations!" he said heartily. He kissed me and gave me a hug. "Hey, Doc, what say we go downtown next week and get your Henchmen tattoo?"

"Sure, Dog. Whatever." I turned toward the mirror at the far corner of the clubhouse to get a look at the back of my vest. *Henchmen colors,* I thought. *Goddamn Henchmen colors.* Then I laughed to myself. *It's more like the colors of Judas. That's me, the Judas goat—accepted as one of their own, my only purpose to lead them to slaughter.*

"I'm gonna go find something to fuck. See you later, Doc."

Dog's comment made me think of Christy. I wondered about her, where she was, if she was all right. I figured it wouldn't seem strange for me to ask about her.

"Hold it a sec, Dog," I said. "There's a cute little chick . . . Chris or Christy. Know who I mean?"

"Too bad, Doc. You'll have to find a different cunt tonight. I heard she did herself a couple of days ago.

Jumped out a window or some shit." He shrugged it off coldly and walked away.

I was furious. It had meant something to me—to save her from this life, from The Henchmen's grip. There was nothing I could do for her now—except grieve. Grieve for someone whom I'd never really known. Someone whose life had never really gotten started.

I got absorbed into the party. We drank and carried on until about three-thirty. I slept on the floor.

Chapter 16

"Mr. Toritelli says everybody gets a bonus of five thousand dollars on this job," said Famantia to his troop of nearly fifty men. They were lined up inside the pier building on Front Street, two miles from Penn's Landing. Pier 20, owned by the Toritellis, was one of the last old piers slated to be renovated into waterfront condominiums. Today it would serve as barracks for a loosely-banded fighting force. A force with a mission. To destroy The Henchmen.

The men stood in rows of five. All wore black jeans, sweatshirts, and running shoes. All were armed with either 9-mm. pistols or Uzi submachine guns. All were hungry to impress the Toritelli organization and make a name for themselves in the underworld. They would be known as the hit squad that had brought down the Philadelphia chapter of The Henchmen. Calvecci stood in front, his own Uzi resting on his shoulder, barrel pointing toward the ceiling.

"Listen up!" ordered Famantia. "We make the hit in six hours. All of you designated Group A will go with Ricky Moose." Famantia motioned his weapon toward the burly, six-foot-nine enforcer. "You'll be hitting the building from the rear. There's a fire escape that leads to the roof. You'll pick off anyone attempting to leave the building by way of the escape or the back doors and windows." Eight men were assigned to Ricky Moose's team, twenty-four to Calvecci's.

Famantia would lead the remaining men in a frontal assault of the building. "Mario's group—Group B—will split up and enter the houses on each side. From this one"—Famantia pointed to a sketch of the structures—"he can blow a hole through the wall if there are problems getting in through their roof. They won't know what hit them. My group will assault from the front. Any questions?"

"What about cops?" someone yelled from the rear.

"Handled," said Famantia confidently. He thought about how easy it was to give instructions to the desk sergeant at the local precinct. Sergeant Barry, on the Toritelli payroll for the last ten years, would delay all calls regarding gunshots or disturbances in the area between nine and nine forty-five P.M.

"Now," Famantia continued, "report to the head of your team and review the attack plan. Remember, we're out of there by nine-thirty. The moving van leaves at nine thirty-five. Sharp. You miss the truck, you take your chances with the cops."

The men hurriedly grouped together to review the attack plans.

We rode two abreast behind the hearse. The twenty-minute ride to the cemetery was my first as a full patch-wearing member. The San Pagano, Riverside, Elmwood, Downey, and Culver City chapters were already at the gate when we arrived. Since Popeye was from our chapter, we rode behind the hearse and entered the cemetery first.

A canvas tarp was set up next to the grave site. Chairs for Popeye's immediate family were arranged next to the grave. All the motorcycles were lined up impeccably along the side of the road. Every wheel was turned to the right. Counsel, Dog, Monk, Snake, Smitty, and Popeye's brother John Burns were the pallbearers. John wasn't a member or associate of the club. Counsel permitted him to carry the coffin out of respect for Popeye's mom, who sat next to Popeye's wife and daughter, crying for her lost child.

I found it unsettling to watch this small, fragile woman gently dabbing at her tears with a tissue. Tears she shed for the child she had brought into the world, full of hopes and dreams for his future. I looked around at the hulking, raunchy-looking bikers. It was hard to believe that every one of these menacing figures, with their leather vests, their beards, their sinister reputations, had once been somebody's little baby. I laughed to myself as I remembered something Dog had said: "We come into the world from between a woman's legs and spend the rest of our lives trying to get back in."

When the eulogy had ended, the pallbearers lowered their brother into his grave. A colorful wreath, with a ribbon that read OUR BELOVED BROTHER POPEYE, lay on top of the coffin. Counsel shoveled in the first spade of dirt. The Henchmen strictly forbade anyone other than a Henchman to bury a brother. The local grave diggers union offered no resistance. After the funeral, all the attending chapters returned to the clubhouse in East Los Angeles. Once there, Counsel took me aside and led me upstairs to his office.

"I want to give you some instructions for the pickup tonight in New Jersey. Your flight leaves at three-fifteen. This will get you into Newark eleven-thirty East Coast time tonight. There's a reservation for a car at the National counter under the name Stewart Miller. Here, look at these."

Counsel showed me a set of phony ID's. A driver's license and two credit cards. They were some of the best I'd ever seen.

"Smile," said Counsel as he snapped my picture.

He took the photo to a cutter, the kind you see in passport photo shops, cut it out, and laminated it to the driver's license.

"We get about three hundred for one of these on the street." He handed me the license and the cards.

"Pay cash for everything. Only use the credit cards as ID if you need them."

"Who am I going to meet?" I asked.

"A dude named Sam, and his old lady Louise. They'll be there in the RV I told you about. New Jersey is their last stop."

"Where else do they stop?" I asked casually. I figured this would be a natural question for someone to ask.

"Several places," answered Counsel. "They left the lab with shipments for chapters in Houston, Philadelphia, New York, and New Jersey. A lab in St. Paul supplies its own chapter, as well as Chicago, Des Moines, and Detroit."

"Do we always do it through Sam?" I asked.

"No. Sometimes we fly it out if it's a small quantity. Or if it's an emergency. With Sam and Louise we can ship a lot, and they're reliable. They make the whole run in about six days."

It made sense. Keeping the manufacture of crank in just two locations gave them quality control. Henchmen didn't burn people in drug deals. They didn't sacrifice long-term customers for short-term profits. A philosophy some U.S. corporations would do well to keep in mind.

My instructions were clear. I was to drive the car to the turnpike rendezvous and pick up the crank. Then on to Paterson, and delivery to the clubhouse on 33rd Street. No need to check if someone would be there to receive. A Henchmen clubhouse is never left empty. There would be at least one prospect there.

Counsel and his wife, Elaine, drove me to the airport. I was surprised to see her, because he had never mentioned her before that afternoon. She was a nice-looking lady. Plump and light-skinned, with straight golden-brown hair. She had a beautiful tattoo of a rose on her left shoulder and another above her breast, which I couldn't quite make out under her sun dress. Elaine talked a lot about their two kids, Andy and Katherine. They were seven and five respectively. It all seemed so normal. Except for their biker-and-old-lady appearance it was as if I were talking to Mr. and Mrs. Middle America. They even talked about retiring one day to a ranch in Southern California. Either Elaine was unaware of The Henchmen's illegal activities or she simply didn't care.

They dropped me off in front of the terminal building forty-five minutes before my flight to Newark was scheduled to depart. Counsel had to drive on into Hollywood for a seven P.M. meeting with a producer who had approached him about a movie deal. Apparently they had a script all prepared for a film called *The Henchmen Ride*. In addition to a consultancy agreement, they were offering some minor parts to Counsel and other club members. Counsel was a bit apprehensive, but had decided to hear him out. I told him I thought it would bring too much national attention to the club. Elaine didn't offer her opinion.

I called Amy before I got on the plane. She was doing her best to sound calm and in control. I could tell she was worried as hell, with just a touch of pissed off and lonely. Alex was awake, and we had a little talk. He reminded me about my birthday promise to buy him the karate turtle with the orange mask. I assured him I would keep my promise. I hoped I would be able to.

I told Amy that the investigation was moving forward rapidly, and that she shouldn't worry. She said she'd seen a report on the news that an ex-member of The Henchmen had been murdered outside his home. I changed the subject, then told her I had to go. I didn't tell her I was traveling east, just that I had to get back to developing my reports.

"Martin, you don't sound like yourself," she said. I wasn't. I could never describe to her what I had been through. The feeling of guilt was strong.

"I'm fine. Really. Just a little tired." *I was raped by a biker slut the other day, and it's killing me not being able to say anything to you,* I thought.

"I love you," she said.

"I love you too, Amy. I'll call you soon. Bye."

"Bye."

Next, I called Base I. Molly Samuels was on duty. "Nice going on the McBright thing," I said.

"Hey, same to you, Martin. Dalton told me you used a double-barrel. Knocked McBright on his rear pretty hard," she said. I could hear the smile in her voice.

"Yeah. A last-minute change of plans, courtesy of our friend Counsel. Just between you and me, I wasn't a hundred percent sure I didn't kill him. How is he?"

"He's fine. A little difficult, but fine. We'll have them settled with their new names within a week or so. They're in a safe house for the moment. Dalton is staying with them until their case agents arrive."

"That's great," I said. "I've been given instructions from Counsel to go to New Jersey." I gave Molly the details of the drug pickup. She said she would arrange for a surveillance team to take photos of the meeting. Pictures of this Louise and Sam, as well as their vehicle, would prove to be useful after their arrest. Photos or videos of drug transactions always help support an agent's testimony in court. Atwood would have enough pull in the Bureau to get the surveillance done without bringing the team in on our investigation. They would photograph the individuals, then ship the pictures and reports directly to Atwood's office. I also told Molly that something was coming down in Philly. She said she would alert the desk sergeant at the local precinct.

I slept through most of the flight. As instructed, I paid cash for the car at the airport and followed the signs to the New Jersey Turnpike. It took me about thirty minutes to drive to the drop-off point. I spotted the RV parked near the east side of the lot, right where Counsel had said it would be. I parked in front of the RV. No one was sitting in front. I walked around the side and peered through the window. "How ya doing?" said a deep voice behind me, which startled me momentarily. "Say, you must be Dr. Death." He wasn't exactly what I had expected. His three-hundred-plus-pound frame took me a little by surprise. I'd been expecting some slick-looking drug-runner. Instead I got Baby Huey in a Hawaiian shirt.

"That's me," I said. "You must be Sam." He put his hamburger in the bag he was carrying, wiped his hand on his shirt, and offered me a handshake. "I was just getting a couple of burgers. Want one?" I shook my head no. "Glad to know you, Doc," he said. "The Mrs. is inside. Hey, Lou!" he yammered, as he pounded on the side of the vehicle. "We got company!"

I heard the click of the door being unlocked, and it slowly swung open. Sam motioned for me to enter. His wife Louise was sitting on one of the built-in couches opposite the door. Her girth took up most of the tiny seating space, and once Sam had squeezed his way in behind me there wasn't too much room left for me to sit. The camper smelled of body odor and rotten food. Louise was eating some sort of sandwich with melted cheese. Sam opened the bag and started to devour his hamburgers. This was almost as disgusting as having that biker chick sit on my face. I sat opposite the rotund couple, my back to the door. Sam finished a burger with two bites and a gulp and, while he shoved a second in his mouth, motioned toward two green plastic bags. "There it is, Doctor," he said, talking with his mouth full of food. Louise sat there, munching away. *God, these two were made for each other.*

"They told me in Philadelphia that you'd be here," Sam continued. "The Jersey boys had to go down there to help them out tonight. But I guess you know all about that, Doc."

"They're gonna kick some ass," said Louise. "If me and Sam were a couple of years younger," she said, patting her husband's belly, "why, we'd we turn 'round and head back there tonight. Wouldn't we, Sam?"

"Sure. Sure, Lou." Sam looked at me and rolled his eyes.

I stood up. "Look," I said. "It was nice meeting you folks, but I don't have time to chat. I gotta get this stuff over to Paterson and catch a flight back to L.A. tomorrow morning." I turned to grab the bags and froze at the sound of a knock at the door. I looked at Sam and Louise, as if to ask them if they were expecting anyone. They both looked surprised, and shook their heads no. *Better answer,* I thought. A second knock and I said, "Yeah, who is it?"

A young, male voice replied. "Excuse me, sir. I'm sorry to bother you. This is the New Jersey Highway Patrol. Would you please open the door?"

Sam reached under the cushion of the couch and

pulled out a .44 Magnum revolver. Louise, as fat as she was, reached quickly into the compartment above her and produced a MAC-10 machine pistol.

"Just a minute," I said to the cop outside. Then I whispered intensely to Sam and Louise, "Put those away, for crissake! Let's just see what he wants." To my incredible relief, they complied. The cop was getting impatient.

"I'm afraid I must insist, sir, that you open—"

"Yes, officer. What can I do for you?" I said as I opened the door.

"Just like to see your license and registration please."

I turned to Sam. "Uncle Sam?" *I hope to God that Sam is the name on his license and registration,* I thought.

"Sure thing, my boy." Sam huffed and puffed and finally managed to get his wallet out from his back pocket. He handed me the license and registration and I handed them to the young trooper. I could see Sam reaching under the cushion, ready to draw his gun. I was standing between him and the trooper, so his movements were concealed.

"Everything in order?" I asked. *I can't let this happen,* I thought. *I can't let this fat piece of shit kill this cop. Come on, kid!* I was screaming at him in my mind to get the hell out of here. *Just hand back the papers and get back in your patrol car, because I may not be able to stop these slobs from blowing your head off.* I must have been holding my breath without realizing it, because I let out a huge sigh of relief when the trooper handed me back Sam's papers and said, "Okay, sorry to bother you. Have a good night."

I said my good-byes to Sam and Louise and, after I was sure the trooper was long gone, loaded the two bags in the trunk of the car. I looked around, trying to make the surveillance team. There was a van parked about thirty yards away. It was hard to tell. If they were there, they were good. Two-tons-of-fun in the RV certainly wouldn't be able to make them.

I arrived at the Paterson clubhouse a little after two A.M. Two prospects met me curbside and took the suitcases. I returned to the airport, and after returning the car and taking a nap at the terminal building, I was back on the plane to California at six A.M. I figured that these drop-off points were located away from the clubhouse, because an RV would look suspicious coming into a run-down or low-income neighborhood. Also, if the clubhouse was too hot at the time of a drop-off, they could always bring the stuff to one of their associate's or woman's houses.

When I arrived back in California, Counsel was waiting at the gate. We hugged and kissed each other hello. People looked at us in startled disgust. To The Henchmen, kissing a brother on the lips was as common as shaking hands. It was also a hell of a lot of fun when it freaked out the citizenry.

"How did it go, Doc?" asked Counsel

"Smooth. Baby-ass smooth," I said. I didn't think it necessary to tell Counsel about the trooper. "Sam and his old lady are a trip."

"Ain't it the truth, brother." We walked outside and into Counsel's car. A skycap had kept an eye on it while Counsel went inside. He tipped him a ten.

"Hey, Doc," said Counsel, after about ten minutes of driving without much conversation. "Guess what?"

I shrugged.

"We're gonna be in the fuckin' movies."

Oh shit, I thought. I was in deeper than any agent had ever been in the history of undercover work, and these guys were about to go Hollywood.

"Counsel," I said, "that's great! Just great . . . By the way, man, I could use a drink."

Chapter 17

"It's eight-thirty, brothers," said Whitey, as he raised his gun above his head. "Let's get ready to take care of business."

With those words the bikers dispersed throughout the clubhouse. Each carried either an Uzi or MAC-10 machine gun. Bones, Stoned Eddie, and three of the Philadelphia Henchmen took positions in the back room. The back door was steel-reinforced and the three windows were bricked up, with a gun port in the center of each one. Whitey, Dirty Dan, and Zorro took their positions in front.

"See anything?" asked Zorro.

"Not a fuckin' thing," answered Dirty Dan. Dirty Dan was in position by the middle window, Zorro on his right, Whitey to his left. All three bikers had their gun barrels pointed through the steel openings. The fortification of the front of the clubhouse was almost identical to that of the rear. The only difference was a gun port built into the front door. From the outside, it looked like an oversized mail slot.

The rest of the bikers went to the rooftop. Fat Tom, The Philadelphia sergeant-at-arms, and his team set up positions on Mrs. Montali's side of the roof. Grease and his team watched the stairwell on top of Pablo Ramirez's house. They expected a lot of the action to take place on the rooftops, as Toritelli's men tried to make their way from the attached buildings.

The moving van arrived just before nine. The driver and helper would remain in the cab until the hit was complete. They wore uniforms with the name *FlagCo Movers* embroidered on the back. Using this Toritelli-owned business as a front, the hit squad could be easily transported to and from the target.

Few pedestrians were present as Calvecci's team scurried up the street toward the clubhouse. A man walking his dog and a woman listening to the radio on her porch quickly vanished at the sight of the armed men racing up the street. As was usual with the residents of this impoverished neighborhood, these two would not involve themselves in whatever calamity was about to take place by reporting what they had seen to the police.

Calvecci's team split up and piled into the two homes on either side of the clubhouse. The front doors had been left unlocked, courtesy of Calvecci's break-in men. They moved rapidly toward the roof. Ricky Moose's team cut through the fence behind the clubhouse. Ricky held back the mesh as the six men ducked through and entered the yard. Famantia's men took positions behind parked cars, aiming their guns at the front door and windows.

"We're through the fence," whispered Ricky Moose into his walkie-talkie. "Can you read me, Joey?"

"Yeah, I hear ya. . . ." Famantia turned the dial, increasing the volume slightly on his walkie-talkie. "As soon as Mario's team is on the roof, you go in. Wait for his signal."

"Okay, Joey. I don't see any lights on inside. Are you sure there here?" That question had barely been asked when a bullet ripped through Ricky Moose's skull. He fell to the ground face-forward, the walkie-talkie still in his hand. His team ran for cover while The Henchmen sprayed the yard with bullets. "What the fuck is that? Who's shooting? Moose . . . Moose, what the fuck?" came Famantia's voice over the receiver. There was no one in the yard still alive to hear it.

"Boss," Mario Calvecci's voice came over the airwaves. "We're near the stairwells to the roof. I hear shooting. What's happening?"

In a moment of fearful clarity, Famantia knew that his worst nightmare had come to life. *Oh shit,* he thought. He quickly turned his head, scanning the street in front of the clubhouse. *There's no fucking motorcycles parked outside. There's always fucking motorcycles outside. They know we're coming.* In a moment of panic, he stood up from behind the parked car.

"Mario, listen. Pull ba—" Famantia dropped the hand radio, clutched his chest, and fell. The rest of the team moved quickly toward the house in an all-out assault. Henchmen gunfire picked them off like ducks in a shooting gallery. Their bullets never entered the building. Cemented windows and steel-reinforced walls neutralized the attack.

Fat Tom motioned for everyone on the roof to stay low. The bikers were lined up on each side, their rifles pointed at the stairwell doors. The shooting at the front and rear of the building had subsided. Silence hung eerily for a moment, while the bikers waited for the anticipated attack. The silence was broken by the crashing sound of the stairwell doors being forced open. The hit squad began to emerge. The bikers waited . . . waited . . . then opened fire.

Within seconds, six of the attackers' bodies lay on the Ramirez roof, five on Mrs. Montali's. The rest, about fifteen men, retreated down the stairwells. Fat Tom jumped over the two-foot wall and scurried to the open door on Montali's roof. Two more bikers followed him. They lined up cautiously alongside the doorway. Four Henchmen did the same on the Ramirez roof.

Fat Tom took a quick look into the stairwell. He jerked back, to avoid a sudden outburst of bullets. He put his forefinger to his lips, signaling the rest of the bikers to be quiet. He then pointed to Grease, in position on Ramirez's roof, motioning for him to do the same. No shots were fired at Grease. The hit squad appeared to have retreated on the Ramirez side, while at least one gunman remained in the stairwell over Mrs. Montali's.

Fat Tom moved his head into the line of fire again. More shots into the air. Again he moved in and out. Again the shots. He pointed toward the floor and mouthed the word "lower" to his associate on the other side of the doorway. George "Goober" Hodge, also a member of the Philadelphia chapter, understood. He dropped to the floor and rolled out in front of the doorway. He fired, hitting his target dead-center. The force of the bullets from the MAC-10 knocked the man to the wall. His blood stained the white brick as his lifeless body slowly slid down to rest in a sitting position, eyes staring straight ahead at nothing.

Grease was starting to make his move over on the Ramirez side. "They retreated into the house," he said to his group. "Five of you"—he quickly pointed out five of the bikers—"go down through the club-house and come at them through the front doors. Tell the brothers in the rear of the clubhouse to watch for anyone trying to get out. We'll run them down through the top and squash the motherfuckers in the middle." Grease nodded toward Fat Tom, as the defenders now became the attackers. The bikers went down the stairwells shooting at anything that moved.

They had killed six more before they'd even reached the second floor.

On the second floor of Montali's house, Fat Tom cautiously approached the door to the bathroom. He could hear a slight scuffle as he neared the room. He slowly opened the door, to find Mrs. Montali lying facedown on the tile floor. She was gagged, and her arms and legs were bound. He sat her up and took off her gag. "Stay here. I'll be back when it's over." Her eyes widened suddenly, as Fat Tom turned and fired his weapon at the figure in the doorway. Chalk up another one for The Henchmen.

Near the stairway to the first floor of the Ramirez house, Grease and his team encountered two men preparing a charge of dynamite against the wall. A short, deadly burst from his MAC-10 interrupted their efforts. The bikers sandwiched the remaining men between the first and second floors. Bodies lay everywhere. In Mrs. Montali's house a similar scenario was being played out.

The victorious Henchmen returned to the clubhouse. It had the air of a pro football locker room after a Superbowl win. Players giving each other the high-five, popping beer cans open, and reliving the successful plays and exciting moments of the game. Or maybe of a fifteenth-century castle—triumphant knights drinking ale, comparing battle scars, patting each other on the back, and embracing in brotherly solidarity.

Dirty Dan kissed and embraced Whitey. The two chapter presidents were proud of their clubs. "Anybody hurt?" asked Dirty Dan.

"Stoned Eddie caught one in the leg, and I think Grease's arm is broken. Other than that, just minor shit." Whitey looked at his watch. Nine thirty-five. "Hey, brothers!" he shouted. "Who was on cleanup last party?"

* * *

It was slow that night at Mike's. Counsel and I had been drinking together for about two hours before Iron Man and Savage joined us. Most of the other members of the Los Angeles chapter were either out with their old ladies or home with their families. Some were at the clubhouse. Two bikers from one of the small local clubs were in the back room, playing pool with a couple of women who sometimes came into Mike's looking for action.

"You look pretty good for a guy who was recently shot," I said to Savage. His arm was no longer in the sling, but his shoulder and rib cage were still tightly wrapped.

"I heal quick, Doc. A Henchman's got to. Hey, I'm sorry I missed your party. After Popeye's funeral I had to take care of some business up north." I found out later that Savage was at the Glendale chapter picking up cash. All chapters give a percentage of profits to the mother chapter for the national coffer. These funds are used to buy real estate, finance expansions, and pay expensive lawyers to keep The Henchmen on the street and out of jail. From what I could gather so far, in addition to dealing in drugs and prostitution, each chapter had their own little specialty. Glendale's was loan-sharking, Philadelphia's, murder for hire. The Atlanta chapter made thousands of dollars planting bombs for various white supremacist groups in the South. Savage himself trained most of the Atlanta members in the use of plastic explosives and pipe bombs.

"You missed a good one, brother," I said. "We really partied hard." I slapped Iron Man a high-five. Under the play-acting, I was still wrestling with feelings of guilt. I had never been unfaithful to Amy, and I kept searching for reasons to justify my actions. It

certainly had been against my will. My life would have
been lost had I refused. Both reasons were valid. Neither gave me the vindication I was after.

"So what's up, Counsel? I got your message to meet
you here," asked Savage.

"We got a little situation," Counsel said quietly. We
had to move closer to hear him. "It's the San Pagano
charter. I'm gonna revoke it."

"Revoke it?" I said, surprised.

"Yeah, they really fucked up this time. They bagged
a couple of cunts after the Bobby Jones concert. Turns
out they did a real number on 'em. Those stupid fucks
have the heat on us now. Helmsford called me and
said the pressure on the cops is coming all the way
from the Governor's office."

"We fucking *own* Helmsford, that slimy pig," interrupted Savage. He winced slightly from the pain of
tensing his wounded body. I could tell his wounds still
hurt like hell. Most people who get shot up like that
spend a week or two in the hospital. Savage had spent
all of three hours in the doctor's office. I couldn't help
but admire something about this psychopath. The look
in his eyes would have scared Charlie Manson, but his
bravery and loyalty to his brothers were unshakable.

"Helmsford says he can't do nothing about it."
Counsel was irritated. He was acting like a disappointed parent. A mixture of anger and hurt over the
actions of an offspring he couldn't control.

Iron Man sat quietly, arms folded, occasionally
stroking his unkempt beard. Counsel finished his
drink, then continued, "They're too wild. They do too
much of their own crank and fuck too much with the
citizens. I fuckin' warned them a million times."

We were all silent for a moment. I made a mental
note of Helmsford's name. Again things were falling
into place. Having a cop on the payroll made them

virtually impervious to any surprise searches. If the cops were planning a raid on the clubhouse, Helmsford could warn them hours before. I thought to myself, *Shit, if every member of law enforcement was honest there would be no more crime. How many other cops, judges, or other officials does this club control around the country?*

"So what's next?" I asked.

"Next Friday. Six of us go down," Counsel immediately responded. "The four of us, Monk, and Dog. We'll go there during their regular meeting, pull their patches, and that will be that." He looked around the table. Everyone nodded their agreement. I was reminded of the scene in *A Clockwork Orange* where Alex and his buddies are sitting around the milk bar, and all the toadies are apprehensively saying "Right, right" to their leader's instructions.

The next morning I called in to Base I again. My Harley needed gas, so I made the call from a gas station near the highway. I told Dalton about Patrick Helmsford. Again, as with the police assistant, they would not move on him immediately. He would be watched and a case built against him. He might even be fed some disinformation to keep him from getting suspicious. When the operation was over, so would his life be as a free man.

When I'd hung up with Dalton, I took to the road for a thirty-mile solo trip down 425. With the wind in my face and The Henchmen colors on my back, I began to think about the ideal that had helped to forge the club in the late forties. That a man could ride free and do what he pleased, and never have to worry whether his brothers were behind him. As long as you wore those Henchmen colors on your back, you were respected and feared—two words that were synonymous in the world of the outlaw biker. Society's rules and morals meant nothing to you. You were part of a subculture that had its own laws.

I felt great. At that moment I wanted to be a Henchman. Living fast and furious and never worrying about tomorrow. My fantasy ended with the silencing of my engine in the driveway of my apartment. I was an agent. Trained and sworn to uphold the law. Integrity and brains. But now, a part of me was also Dr. Death, the Henchman.

During the next few days most of the activity centered around The Henchmen's movie. The documentary crew conducted several interviews with club members under Counsel's watchful eye. The members seemed to get a charge out of it all. Footage was even shot of an evening trip to an amusement park, where we rode roller coasters standing up, shot pellet guns in the shooting gallery, and rode bumper cars like twelve-year-olds during their summer vacation.

At one point six of us were playing the balloon-race game. The object was to fire a water gun into the mouth of a plastic clown head, thus activating a pump which filled the balloon on top of the head with air. Whoever's balloon popped first won. Dog led the conspiracy by tapping Iron Man with his elbow and motioning his head toward the attendant. Iron Man, in turn, did the same to me, and all the way to the end where Counsel was poised, ready to fire. As soon as the attendant rang the buzzer we fired at her, soaking the poor woman from head to toe.

She must have signaled for the park security somehow, because two security guards came running up to see what the commotion was all about. When the two young men turned the corner and saw us six grinning bikers, they looked like they wished they'd never gotten out of bed that morning. We teased those poor guys until they had tears in their eyes. Counsel grabbed one of their nightsticks and held it between his legs like a huge erect penis. Dog got on his knees and pretended to suck it off. The camera crew got the whole thing on film. A crowd started to form around us, and we knew it was time to end the little game before any real cops came on the scene. Before letting the guards walk, Iron Man took the handcuffs from one of them, a short, muscularly built guy in his mid-twenties, and kept them as a souvenir. I was troubled by how much fun I was having with the club. The renegade I-don't-give-a-shit attitude was infectious. I had to remind myself that I was here to put these guys away, not become one of the brethren.

The day before we were to strip the San Pagano chapter of their colors, The Henchmen threw a chili bash at the East L.A. clubhouse for the officers of the Paterson and Philadelphia chapters, to celebrate their victory over the Toritellis. Judging by all the boasting and backslapping that was going on, I guessed that the win had been a decisive one. I wondered what the hell could have gone wrong. I was sure Molly would have found a way to tip off the local police. Again, this was one of those times when I didn't actually regret that the incident had taken place, but was confused as to why. As far as I was concerned, if The Henchmen and Mafia wanted to destroy each other, so be it.

I also learned at the party that the New Jersey chapter was planning a huge rip-off of military equipment from the army base at Fort Dix. Dirty Dan, the chapter president, had cornered me. My back was to the wall and he had one arm over my shoulder, supporting himself.

"It's gonna be a tit . . . a fuckin' tit." He belched right in my face. I could smell the unsavory combination of chili and beer. "My ole lady," he continued, "she's been working as a sec'tery . . . sec . . ." He shook his head to clear his thoughts. He was slurring so badly I could hardly understand him. "Sec . . . re . . . tary." He winked at me, proud to have finally blurted out the word. He then turned abruptly away, walked over to a corner, and sat on the floor. I found out later that he was trying to tell me about his girl-friend, who worked in the records office at Fort Dix.

Before I left the party I wished him well on the heist.

Chapter 18

"Yeah?"

"This is Counsel. Who's this?"

"Yo, Counsel. How ya doin', bro? It's Slip. What's up?"

"You guys having your meeting tonight?"

"Sure as shit. Same time every week. Why?"

"I'm coming by. We have to talk about this Bobby Jones concert thing."

"Hey, man. Those babes wanted a good time and we showed them one. It got a little wild at times, but—"

"Wait a second," Counsel cut in. "I don't give a shit about the two cunts. We have to talk about handling the cops now. You brothers collect a lot of bread from the businesses in your neighborhood, and that's all going to dry up if the man turns up the heat." The San Pagano chapter had a flair for extorting money from local merchants. Fifty dollars each week bought them protection. Most of the merchants paid it enthusiastically. Once the word was out that an establishment was under Henchmen protection, robberies dwindled. San Pagano contributed an average of ten thousand dollars each month to the national coffer from this business alone.

"Sure, Counsel. Everyone'll be here. Later."

"What'd he say?" asked Iron Man

"They'll be there." Counsel walked from behind his

desk to the wall, where a map of the United States was displayed. He removed the pin from the area of San Pagano. Looking at it pensively, he recalled how six years ago eighteen members of The Commandos had approached him for a Henchmen charter. They prospected for the club for six months. Of the eighteen, only nine got their patches. Two were killed, and one was jailed when three bikers botched a bank robbery. The rest just weren't man enough to don Henchmen colors. Counsel had personally given Beef his Wild Bunch patch for taking out two Outcasts in Nevada. He tossed the pin in the trash.

"Who was on the phone?" asked Sandy.

"Counsel," said Slip curiously. "He's coming over tonight. Wants to talk about how we're going to handle the heat from the cops." The two bikers were sitting at a large table in the main room of the clubhouse. Slip was drinking a beer and casually flipping through the pages of *Iron Horse* magazine.

"Is he coming alone?" Sandy's sharp instincts caused him to feel uneasy.

"He didn't say." Slip's attention remained on the magazine.

Sandy picked at his tooth with his fingernail and looked thoughtfully at the floor. "You still got that little .25?" he asked, still looking down.

"Sure do, Prez. Right here." Slip lifted his boot to the table and pulled up his pant leg, to expose the handle of a .25 semiautomatic pistol secure in its holster. "You think something's coming down?"

"Nah. Probably not. Just a feeling, man." The shrewd biker thought for a moment about Counsel's visit. The chapter had been in bad situations with the law before. Counsel had never ordered a sitdown with the entire club. *What's on his mind?* he wondered. He looked at his Henchmen colors hanging across the back of a chair. "Would you die for that patch, Slip?"

"Hell, yeah, wouldn't we all?"

Twenty minutes east of St. Paul, Little Ferry is one of the most pleasant neighborhoods in Minnesota. Tree-lined streets, single-story ranch-style homes, and small-town hospitality give it the charm of a Norman Rockwell illustration. Frank "Dave" David, president of the Henchmen chapter in St. Paul, was working on the club's books in a small room in the rear of his home. Henchmen paraphernalia and trophies from his motorcycle racing days decorated the walls. An eight-hundred-pound safe, containing many years' worth of sensitive information, stood next to the desk.

An astute bookkeeper, with two years of business training, Dave did many of the duties normally reserved for the secretary/treasurer. He insisted that it be that way. The club's secretary could handle the files on members and associates. Bookkeeping and all other financial matters would be handled by the forty-four-year-old president. Partly gray and a little overweight, Dave was well suited to his white suburban surroundings. Although he didn't socialize with his neighbors, they all considered him a typical family man, albeit a rather reclusive one. While many men in the neighborhood sported Jaguars and Ferraris, a bright yellow Harley was Frank David's display of boyishness.

There was a timid knock on the door. "Come on in," said Dave with a sigh. He closed the ledger and pushed it to the side of his desk. His fourteen-year-old son, Mark, opened the door slowly.

"Dad, I'm sorry to bother you. Can I talk with you a minute?" Dave nodded and smiled at his first-born. Mark sat on the floor.

"I got a little problem," said the blue-eyed, red-headed youngster. "There's this guy. This big guy on the baseball team. Well, he's giving me a real hard time. You know, pushing me around and stuff. He's bigger than everyone else, and nobody's ever stood up to him. You know it really bugs me, because if I was allowed to tell him my dad was in charge of The Henchmen, he'd be real scared and—" Dave gently placed his finger on the boy's lips.

"Every man has to stand on his own, Mark. The members of my club would do anything I'd ask of them. That doesn't mean I don't have to stand up for myself. I've told you and your sister that under no circumstances are you to tell any of your friends about Daddy's club. Your mother doesn't even talk to her friends about it. Besides, even if you scared him with that you'd never get his respect, and you would never respect yourself."

"What should I do?" the boy asked forlornly. "This guy could kill me."

Dave chuckled and hugged his son, lifting him off his feet. Still sitting in his desk chair, he held Mark by his shoulders with his huge hands. "Mark, I love you. You know that. But if you don't stand up to this . . . What's his name?"

"Joseph."

"Joseph . . . Joseph will never respect you, and he'll continue to treat you like crap. I'm not saying you have to fight him, although you may. I'm saying that you've got to make him believe in his heart that every time he bothers you he's going to have to fight you, regardless of how it turns out. My guess is he's not looking for a fight as much as he's looking to intimidate people." Mark smiled. "Understand, son?"

"Yeah, I guess so. Hey, Dad . . . Will I lose self-respect if I kick him in the balls?" Dave laughed until he almost lost his breath. "No," he said, wiping a tear from his eye. "Whatever it takes."

"Thanks. Oh, I almost forgot, Mom told me to tell you Uncle Jimmy's here. He's waiting for you outside. Bye." The youngster left his father's office. The Henchman put the ledger in the safe, locked the office door, and left the house. He walked to the curb, where James "Jimbo" Hill was standing next to his blue Chief Cherokee jeep.

"Hey, Jimbo! How ya doin'?" The two bikers shook hands.

"I'm good. We got a new shipment of merchandise. It's a lot larger than we expected. I think the guys need a little help on the distribution of this one. You ready to go?"

"Yeah. Let's take my car. I don't trust that piece-of-shit jeep of yours."

"Fine with me, man. Use up your gas, fine with me. You got a smoke?"

Dave handed Jimbo a pack of Marlboro cigarettes from his shirt pocket. Jimbo took one and handed the pack back to Dave.

"Got a light?" asked Jimbo.

"Christ, you want me to smoke it for you too?" Dave lit the cigarette with a small yellow disposable lighter. "It was the same shit when we started out in '72, you were always grubbing stogies." Dave's mind quickly returned to the days when he and Jimbo had started the Iron Riders together. Broke, owning only their clothes, boots, and motorcycles, Dave and Jimbo had gone to work recruiting bikers and building up the club's business. They'd built the club into a force of almost fifty members by 1977. By that time the two founders had amassed a fortune selling drugs, and running one of the largest fencing operations in the northern United States. It was that end of their busi-

ness that had caught Counsel's attention. Using the
club's women, they would lure unsuspecting truck
drivers with smiles and promises. What the truckers
received were beatings and the loss of their cargo. It
didn't matter what—electronics equipment, clothing,
even produce.

Dave remembered how he had built up such an
elaborate network of contacts around the country that
he could unload anything his people could highjack.
He also remembered how The Outcasts had become
interested in his club as well. For months both The
Outcasts and The Henchmen had competed for the
assimilation of The Iron Riders. Finally, to thwart off
a "hostile takeover" from The Outcasts, The Iron
Riders buried their colors and put on the hooded executioner insignia of The Henchmen. Dave smiled as
he thought about the contrast between his life in the
early seventies and his life now, almost twenty years
later. He had gone from sleeping on the clubhouse
floor to a three-hundred-thousand dollar home in
suburbia.

As the two men walked toward the garage, Dave
suddenly put his arm out, stopping Jimbo. "Wait,
Jimbo. Somebody's been in this fucking garage."

"How do you know?"

"Look." Dave pointed to the top of the door frame.
"See that broken piece of masking tape? Every time
I close the garage door, I place a small piece of masking tape between the door and the frame. It's a habit
I got into when Mark was younger and always wanted
to get in to fuck around with the bike. The only way it
could get broken is if someone has opened the fucking
door."

"Maybe it was Mark," Jimbo offered.

"No way. Look at this." Dave pointed to the lock

on the center of the door. Tiny scratches, evidence of a picked lock, were very barely visible.

"Get Mark and Gloria out of the house," Dave ordered, and Jimbo immediately moved off to comply. Moments later he emerged from the house with Dave's wife and son. He told them to get into his jeep, then joined Dave by the garage door.

Dave slowly opened the overhead doors. Jimbo stayed at Dave's side, holding his breath until the door rested in its open position. "Look over the bike, Jimbo. I'll check the car." Seconds later, Dave found it. "Jimbo, it's fucking wired." Both men examined the bomb, which was taped to the car's steering column. Four sticks of dynamite, armed with an electronic blasting cap, were wired to the spark plug. Dave would have been killed as soon as he turned the key.

Jimbo carefully disarmed the bomb, first clipping the wire to the spark plug, then separating the blasting caps from the dynamite sticks. He handed the caps and the sticks to Dave. He then locked the sticks of dynamite and the blasting caps in the trunk of his car.

Dave walked over to the jeep to speak with his wife and son.

"Babe, I'm gonna have Jimbo take you and Mark to your mom's. Stay there until I tell you it's safe to come home."

Gloria said nothing. In the sixteen years she'd been together with Frank David, she had learned to expect disruptions in her life. She looked over at her son. Mark was busy tuning the jeep's radio and playing with the steering wheel. The thirty-eight-year-old wife of the Henchmen leader remembered vividly the day she'd married Dave, ten years ago. It was the same day the club threw a party to celebrate the second anniversary of their Henchmen charter. They had rented a boat, packed over three hundred people in it, and cruised Lake Superior for ten hours. She thought about how she'd stood next to a smiling, slightly drunk husband-to-be, while Counsel performed the ceremony.

"Do you, Gloria, take Dave, to be your husband . . . promise to polish his bike . . . not question his every move?" asked Counsel, reading from a book of Henchmen law that he had authored.

"I do," she said.

When the boat docked, Frank David and four other Minnesota Henchmen were arrested for having beaten a trucker in a bar the night before. The Henchmen were out of jail in twenty-fours hours, and the charges were eventually dropped.

Now Gloria stared out the window as Jimbo drove them away.

Dave called the clubhouse and spoke with his security officer, John "Jack The Ripper" Kendall.

"Jack? Dave. Listen, I found a bomb in my fucking car. It could have been The Outcasts. They killed a brother from the Los Angeles chapter a week ago, and they may be launching a new offensive. I want the word put out on the street that The Henchmen are to be notified of any sighting of an Outcast or associate club member." At least five other motorcycle gangs in Minnesota were Henchmen affiliates, with another two hundred or so people working for them in various capacities. If The Outcasts were responsible, Dave would find out.

Dave hung up the phone and sat silently for a moment in his black-leather armchair. He stared at the dust particles floating amidst the rays of the afternoon sun, like tiny snowflakes. He took a deep breath, held it for a moment, then let it out sharply, disrupting the pattern of dust flakes. *This could all be gone in a second,* he thought. *My home, my family. All gone.* He quickly reminded himself of how he had come to own this expensive home. *How many bones have been broken? How many widows and fatherless children have I and The Henchmen been responsible for producing over the years? He who lives by the sword, dies by the sword, Dave.* This rare moment of soul-searching was interrupted by the sound of Jimbo's Cherokee jeep pulling into the driveway.

The two bikers left in Dave's blue Mercedes, leaving the jeep parked in front of the garage door. As they pulled away, Dave began to sweat. The calm he had experienced during the crisis was now replaced by anger. "Goddamn motherfuckers!" he yelled, using his right hand to punch the roof of his car. His left hand remained steady on the steering wheel.

"My family could have been killed by that fucking bomb! Christ almighty, Jimbo, how the fuck do they know where I live?"

"Take it easy, man. We'll get the motherfuckers. Red light, Dave." Dave quickly and smoothly applied the brakes.

"It's all gotten so crazy," said Dave, his emotions starting to even out. "We used to brawl all the time with other clubs. They would throw us a beating one week, we would get them the next. You took your lumps and you didn't complain. Now, man . . . Shit, it's just getting fucked up, that's all." Dave slowly accelerated as the light turned green. They drove without conversation for about ten minutes. Calmer now, Dave leaned over and opened the glove compartment. "Look in there, Jimbo. With all this shit I forgot to tell you. The newsletter. It came yesterday afternoon."

The newsletter came irregularly. However, Counsel always managed to produce at least three issues a year. Every chapter president received a copy. It then circulated among the members. Only patch-wearing brothers were permitted to read it, although it seldom contained anything compromising or confidential. It was always returned to the chapter president. No one was allowed to photocopy it.

"Well, look at *this* shit," said Jimbo as he began to skim through the document. "Counsel got a request from a club in Australia for a charter. Fucking *Australia,* man. You think Counsel will do it?"

"He might. First he'll send a couple of brothers to check them out. If they make the grade, why not?" Dave shrugged, both hands now firmly on the wheel.

"Whoa," said Jimbo, surprised.

"What is it?" asked Dave, turning his eyes from the road to look at Jimbo.

"My brother probably knows this guy."

"Who?"

"The new member in L.A.," said Jimbo. "Johnny lives up in Hallock. He's about an hour from the Canadian border. He used to party with the Satan's Saints all the time. Shit, I'll have to give him a call and tell him Doc Death is a Henchman now."

"Maybe your bro can come with us when we make the run to Eureka Lake next month. He can say hello to Dr. Death personally."

"Yeah. Won't *that* be a piss!"

Chapter 19

I stopped at a phone booth on my way to the club-house to call in to Base I. Although I was a member, I wasn't about to take a chance using the phone at my apartment. For all I knew the club tapped the phones of all members, just in case. Fred Parkins was on duty when I called.

"Walsh, how are you, buddy?" he said insincerely. "Your boys did some number last week in Philly."

"They're not my boys," I said. Of course I could never share with anyone in the Bureau, especially this dick Parkins, that I was pleased The Henchmen had won the fight with the Toritellis. They had managed to accomplish what years of law enforcement had failed to do. The only problem now was how to deal with a more powerful, more brazen Henchmen chapter.

"Is Leverick around? Or Atwood?" I asked.

"No, sorry, bud. Just me."

"Lucky me," I mumbled sarcastically. "I may need some assistance."

"Shoot!"

"We're driving down to San Pagano in a couple of hours. Six of us. Counsel wants to shut down the chapter. He plans to take their colors and suspend their membership indefinitely."

"So, that's good. That's one less Henchmen chapter for us to deal with."

"Yeah, but I'm afraid there might be trouble. You

don't know what these colors mean to these guys. It goes deeper than we ever thought," I said with a sense of urgency.

"I don't think we want to spook them now. What if they pick up the other agent's presence? We'd blow a major investigation for nothing. No. You've been in too long . . . too deep."

"Parkins, I'm telling you! This could be *serious,* man!" I started to get angry. I was almost yelling.

"I'm telling *you,*" said Parkins sharply. "Everyone of us on this team is a supervisor. We have to make decisions based on what we feel is best for the investigation, as well as for the people in the field. And I say you won't need backup on this. We all have the files on The Henchmen. Counsel is legendary among all the chapters nationwide. He's shut down chapters six times since 1970. No one's ever gotten killed. A couple of beatings maybe, but no homicides. After what you and that guy Monk did to those boys in the pizza shop, you should be used to this shit by now."

"God damn it, Parkins!" I was heated. "You'd better pray this comes off smoothly, or I'll file the biggest grievance against you the Bureau has ever seen!"

"Fine. You do that. Anything else you want to report before I take my dinner break?"

You fuck, I thought to myself. *Here I am risking my life and you're concerned with your dinner break.* I knew I didn't like this chickenshit the first time I met him. He's the type of guy that agents in the field refer to as a real "suit." Someone who has no idea what the real world is all about and doesn't give a shit about anyone's life. The only thing that matters to suits like Parkins is their own careers. Fuck everybody else. He wouldn't last five minutes rubbing elbows with these guys, but *he's* the one calling the shots right now. Integrity and brains? Not this one.

"One more thing," I said. "In Jersey. They're planning to hit Fort Dix. I couldn't find out exactly when, but they got a woman inside. A secretary in the records department. Is *that* worth some manpower?" I made no attempt to hide my sarcasm.

"I'll take care of it. Call in first opportunity tomorrow."

I must have seemed a little pissed off when I arrived at the clubhouse. Dog ribbed me a little about my mood.

"Hey, shitface. You look like you just tongue-kissed your grandmother," he said.

"It's that fucking . . . parole officer. He's a fucking ballbuster. Fuck him." I figured since I was pissed off and it showed, I might as well add credibility to my parole officer story.

"You got that right. You know, maybe we can take care of your PO problem."

"How so?" I asked.

"Depends. Let's say he's married or some shit. We send one of our cunts to scope him out, get him to go to bed, then photograph him. We tell him we'll give the photos to his old lady if he doesn't do the right thing by you. Or maybe we just slip him a few bucks, or threaten to kick the shit out of him. We've done it before."

"I'll let you know, man. It's just a bad fucking day, that's all." I actually began to visualize Dog and Iron Man beating the shit out of that asshole Parkins, and I liked what I saw. It was strange. I felt more camaraderie with Dog than with one of the men on my own team. I decided at that moment that the next time I spoke with Atwood I was going to insist that Parkins be kicked off the team.

We rode to San Pagano in the blue van. Counsel

drove. Dog sat on the passenger side. Savage and Iron Man were sitting in the rear. I sat opposite Monk near the middle. Most of the conversation was light during the trip. Dog would occasionally offer one of his many tasteless jokes.

"Hey, what's the difference between quiche and pussy?" he asked.

"What, Dog?" the rest of us answered simultaneously.

"Real men don't eat quiche." Dog laughed loudly, almost losing his breath. The rest of us rolled our eyes and chuckled, more at Dog's reaction than at the joke itself.

Counsel pulled into the driveway of the San Pagano clubhouse and turned off the engine. He motioned toward Iron Man, who lifted a metal box from the back and placed it in the middle of the van. The toolbox-size case contained three nine-millimeter pistols, two sawed-off shotguns, and one .357 Magnum revolver. Counsel reached over and grabbed one of the sawed-offs. I took the Magnum. Savage got the other shotgun.

"Why so much hardware?" I asked.

"Just a precaution," said Counsel. Monk was quiet. He had hardly said a word since we'd left the clubhouse. Of course, Monk didn't say much anyway.

"Let's go," said Counsel. He looked over at Iron Man and nodded. Iron Man returned the nod and stuffed the pistol in the back of his belt. Savage did the same and we all followed his lead. We approached the house slowly. Counsel had his hand behind his back, ready at the trigger. Monk walked beside me. He looked cool, confident that there would be no trouble. "They fucked up," he said to me earlier, "so they lose their charter. No big deal. Counsel took other charters away before."

Counsel stopped a few feet short of the door to let Savage and Iron Man overtake him. They knocked at the door and waited. Counsel stood behind them, Dog behind him. Monk and I looked from right to left, scoping out the surrounding houses. "Seems pretty quiet," said Monk.

The door was barely open an inch when Iron Man kicked it in, knocking the man behind it to the floor. I recognized him when I got closer to the doorway. It was Slip. I remembered him from Popeye's funeral.

"Hey, man! What the fuck . . . ?" complained Slip. His complaint was abruptly silenced by a shotgun blast to the face. I looked on in disbelief as Counsel, Iron Man, and Savage entered the house shooting. One of the bikers, seated behind a large table, began to fire a small-caliber handgun. Iron Man took him down. I fired the Magnum at the walls a few times, giving the impression that I was taking part in the slaughter. Dog followed along, too. I wasn't sure if he'd shot anyone or not. Monk never fired a shot.

It was all over in less than a minute. We had murdered the entire chapter, massacred them. No chance to even give up the colors. Just *boom!* I couldn't believe it. We stood there silently for a moment. "Savage!" said Iron Man. He crossed the room and knelt beside him. "Shit," he said. "He's fucking dead." Savage had a bullet hole dead-center in his forehead. Someone had managed to take one of his murderers with him.

"Peel the colors!" ordered Counsel. "Savage, too."

"Counsel, we can't, it's Savage!" pleaded Dog.

"I said peel the fucking colors!" Counsel shot a hard look at Dog. "He bought it. Them's the breaks."

We took the colors off all the bodies. Iron Man

placed the sleeveless vests, all soaked with blood, in a plastic bag. Counsel reached down and removed a knife from his boot. He walked over to Sanford Collins' body. Collins, the chapter president who was known as "Sandy," was lying facedown, his legs on top of one of his dead comrogues. Counsel flipped him over and carved the letters OR on his forehead.

"What was that for?" inquired Dog.

"The Outcasts' calling card," said Iron Man. "As far as the man is concerned, as far as the rest of our club is concerned, they're just more victims in the ongoing biker war. Let's get the fuck going." I found out later that the initials OR, which every member of The Outcasts had tattooed on his body, stood for "Outcasts Rule." The news of that mutilation would be enough to convince other Henchmen chapters that this had been an Outcasts hit.

The ride back to the clubhouse seemed to take forever. Iron Man sat alone this time, Monk and I opposite each other again. I looked in his eyes, trying to read him. He hadn't spoken a word since we'd left for San Pagano. "Monk, you okay, man?" I asked. He nodded slightly, then closed his eyes and leaned his head back, obviously not wanting to talk with anyone. At my first opportunity I had to call into Base I and let them know what had happened. A goddamn slaughter. *That fucking Parkins*, I thought. I had told him this was going to be bad. Now we had to shut down the operation because of my witness to the homicides. At least we would have Counsel and Iron Man on Murder One. It was obvious now that the three of them had planned all along to gun the other bikers down. Me, Dog, and Monk were just backup for their assassination team. Within twenty-four hours I would have warrants issued for Counsel's and Iron

Man's arrest. I would have to include Dog and Monk in the arrest, but I planned to testify on their behalf to get the charges reduced. *Too bad,* I thought. *All these months of preparation. Becoming a patch-wearing member of a motorcycle gang, for the first time in the history of law enforcement's battle against them. All coming to an end.*

Monk was the first to leave the van, practically knocking Iron Man down in his haste to get out.

"Yo, Monk!" said Iron Man, beckoning to him. "What's up, man?" Monk didn't acknowledge him. Moments later, when Counsel and Dog got out, we all turned at the sound of Monk's bike kicking over.

Iron Man volunteered to chase after him in the van. "No," I said, thinking Iron Man would probably shoot him. "I'll bring him back." I hopped on my Harley and raced down the Avenue. I spotted Monk heading toward the freeway. I must have run a dozen lights by the time I caught up with him. I motioned for him to stop. Monk just cranked his hog up full throttle. We must have been doing close to one hundred mph, Monk always managing to stay just ahead of me. After about ten minutes, Monk turned off toward the beach. He drove his bike right up the steps of the boardwalk and down into the sand, until the wheels spun the Harley too deep to move. I left my bike on the board-walk and took off after him as he ran down the beach.

"Monk! Monk!" I called, panting and straining to keep up with him. I finally caught his shoulder and slowed him down. He turned and punched me in the jaw. I fell back to the sand and he stood above me, pointing his finger. "You get the fuck away from me, man!" he said, with fury in his eyes. He turned and ran again. I kept after him. My jaw was swelling and I had a pain in my side from running. We must have continued for a half-mile down the beach. Monk, about ten yards ahead of me, fell to his knees, grabbed two handfuls of sand, and began squeezing them with clenched fists as he cried out: "Motherfucker! Goddamn motherfucker!" He began punching furiously at the sand.

I approached him slowly, in part to catch my breath so I could speak. I crouched down beside him.

"Monk . . . Monk . . . listen . . . man . . ."

"No!" Monk interrupted. "*You* listen!" He turned to face me. "It's all fucked! What the hell do you know? You've only been a brother for a couple of weeks. I've been with the club fifteen fucking years. It's all fucked now. We used to have the strongest brotherhood on the fucking planet. We fought, rode and drank together. We stood by each other no matter what. Now it's all measured by what's good for fucking business. The motherfucking pursuit of cash is all that matters now. Shit! God damn it! It's all fucked up!"

He put his hands on his head and started to get his breathing under control. I wanted so bad to tell him who I was and that I was going to arrest those bastards, but that was a chance I couldn't take. Far worse than brother killing brother was brother turning rat. Or brother being the law.

"Monk, nobody liked what happened tonight. We had no choice. That chapter was too wild. They wouldn't have let us leave there alive tonight. As it was they managed to kill Savage. Counsel was only thinking of the good of the club."

"It's fucked, Doc. It's just fucked, that's all." Monk was a little calmer now, his breathing even. I continued to try to bring him around.

"Everybody misses the way it used to be, man. It was that way with my old club, the Saints. The Henchmen are big now. The biggest and most powerful bike club in the world. The old rules just don't work any-more." I extended my hand and helped him to his feet.

"I don't know, Monk. Maybe we can bring it back. You just gotta hang on and see." Sometimes I wasn't quite sure exactly who was talking. Dr. Death himself couldn't have been more convincing. When you're in deep cover you make up so much of your own reality that, at times, you start to believe it. At times you *must* believe it. Dr. Death had become my alter ego. He would be hard to let go.

Monk wiped the sand from his clothes. We stood there silently for about fifteen minutes, listening to the sound of the surf breaking and smelling the aroma of the salty air. It had a calming, hypnotic effect. Monk turned to me and half smiled.

"Thanks, Doc. I love you, man." We gave each other a bear hug and then trudged back to retrieve the bikes. We rode back toward the clubhouse, two abreast, at a leisurely thirty-five miles per hour. I kept asking myself, *Why did you go after Monk?* Opera-tionally, it made absolutely no sense. Had it been some instinctive move to keep all my quarry together for an arrest? Was I afraid Iron Man would have shot him? Did I do it out of brotherly love? I would never know.

Chapter 20

There was no getting away. Counsel strongly suggested that we stay together at the clubhouse and listen for details of the shooting on the morning news. He also wanted to make sure that everyone was cool. Dog and Monk assured Counsel they stood behind the club.

"Okay, bros," said Counsel. "We got to keep what happened tonight to ourselves. Let the rest of the chapters and the cops believe it was The Outcasts that got 'em. Tomorrow, me and Iron Man will go down to the sheriff's office in San Pagano. We'll raise a little hell about how much we'd prefer to take care of it ourselves."

Counsel was smart. Had this been a real hit on one of his chapters, that's exactly what the police would expect him to do and say. This would push suspicion further away from the club.

"Tomorrow morning I need you two," Counsel said, addressing me and Dog, "to go to Pedro's and pick up a shipment for Beverly Hills. The rich kids are starting to run dry. Mitchell called me yesterday. Says he'll be completely out by tomorrow night."

Mitchell . . . Joseph Mitchell. I knew that name. I remembered hearing it many times around the police station. All the cops knew he was the biggest supplier of crank in the Hills and surrounding areas. He had so many friends in movies, publishing, and local politics that no one was ever able to catch him cold. But all the Hollywood brats stayed high thanks to Mitchell. I was going to love putting this guy out of business. The beautiful people would have to find another source for their thrills. This was one aspect of the drug problem that really pissed me off. The same people who are the first to condemn drug-related violence on the streets of America keep the dealers in business with their so-called "casual" use of speed and cocaine.

It was about six A.M. by the time I fell asleep. There were always places to crash at the clubhouse. Iron Man went on guard duty upstairs and sent Snake home. He had been there since I'd returned with Monk, but wasn't hip to what was going on. Monk was still watching TV when I fell out.

"Come on, Doc. Rise and shine," said Dog, kicking me in the leg. A redhaired, bearded Hun with auburn-tinted sunglasses is an ugly first thing to see after only three hours sleep. "We got a long ride, Doc. Let's roll, man."

I struggled to my feet, went to the bathroom and splashed water on my face, then left the clubhouse with Dog. We left Monk sleeping in an old armchair, the television still on.

We had been riding in the van for a half-hour without saying much. I had to get to a phone. At this point I regretted having given Dog the story about calling my parole officer the day before. It would arouse too much suspicion if I asked him to stop the van so I could call again. Atwood must have heard about the murders by now. If I continued the operation, I would be in violation of both Bureau policy and federal law. What the hell. I'd come in at my first opportunity. I guessed that would be shortly after we made the delivery in the Hills. The location of the lab and the busting of Mitchell would be gravy.

Dog broke the silence.

"Hey, Doc. You think Counsel was gonna do them all along? I mean, it happened real fast. Before I knew it we were shooting them down like pigs. What do you think?"

"I don't know, Dog. Counsel and Iron Man both have good instincts. Could be they just read the situation immediately and did what they had to do. Who the fuck knows?" The lies came so easy. It was as if three people were riding to the desert in that van: Dog, myself, and a ghost called Dr. Death. A man who'd been dead for over five years. I actually enjoyed the role I was playing. The danger of deep cover I had always feared and avoided had now become something I reveled in. At that moment I felt that I was going to miss this assignment, which means I should have ended it right there.

"There it is, up there," said Dog, as he pointed down the road to a beat-up old service station sign.

"A gas station?"

"Why not, Doc? It's the perfect cover. Not many cars come this way, and nobody complains about the smell of the cooking."

Dog brought me inside the store. Inside, it smelled like cat piss, a telltale sign that crank is being cooked up. Dog said hello to an old Mexican who was sitting behind the counter smoking a cigar. He then led me through a secret door in the floor of the back room and down a set of stairs.

The lab was a drug dealer's dream come true. A hundred miles from nowhere, and plenty of time to cook and package the stuff for pickup and distribution. Dog introduced me to an Asian named Kim who was the chemist, and Billy E., the Henchman in charge of overseeing the lab. We were in and out of there in less than twenty minutes. We left with about thirty pounds of crank in the back of the van. Dog placed it in the compartment usually reserved for weapons. About an hour into the return trip Dog reminded me of my obligation to get the club tattoo within one month of getting my colors. "You know, Doc, we have to get that tat before too long." He held out his arm, displaying his own tattoo. A hooded executioner with an axe in one hand and a rope in the other, with the month and year of Dog's initiation into the club, filled most of his huge forearm. "Counsel says the movie company is gonna finish up this week. Why don't we have them shoot you getting yours? Good idea?"

"Yeah, great idea," I said, slightly distracted. I had spotted some movement on the road in my side-view mirror. "Dog, does that look like a couple of bikes in the distance?"

"Might be." Dog looked in his side-view. "Yes. Definitely. Coming up fast, too. I can't tell if they're Henchmen or not." Dog's eyes widened as the bikers came within thirty feet of the van. "Doc, get the twelve-gauge! Shit, man! They look like fucking Outcasts! Quick, Doc! They're coming up fast!"

I climbed in the back, trying to steady myself against the sides of the van. The two bikers pulled along the passenger side.

"Dog!" I yelled. "They're coming up on the side! Watch it, man!"

Dog was frantic, turning his head from side to side. "Where? I lost them! I don't see them!"

The sound of the gunshot echoed in my brain. I tried to reach for Dog, who lay dead on the wheel. I felt myself move, as if in slow motion, reaching for him as the van veered to the side of the road. My head smashed into the side of the van as it spun out of control and flipped over. The pain and confusion were intense. I felt like I was falling into a bottomless pit.

Atwood was late. The team had been waiting for over an hour. Molly Samuels was reviewing case details with Dalton Leverick. Fred Parkins was disinterested. He chain-smoked and drank coffee, while he nervously awaited the commencement of the emergency meeting that had been called four hours earlier.

"Sorry I'm late," said Atwood matter-of-factly, as he came breezing through the door. He sat down at the white marble conference table and opened a file marked FBI, CONFIDENTIAL. "Parkins, please thank your father for the use of his conference room. I thought it best we not meet at Bureau headquarters until we'd figured out our next move. I've been avoiding the Director's calls. I'm sure he would have insisted on attending this meeting had we met there."

Atwood picked up a pencil from the table and tapped the eraser on his lips.

"First of all, has anyone heard from Martin?"

Samuels and Leverick shook their heads—their concern obvious. Parkins looked down at the table. Atwood continued to view the file.

"From the updates in the file," Atwood continued, "I see that the last time Martin checked in was six days ago. He was going with several members of the mother chapter to discuss some business in San Pagano. What kind of business, specifically? Parkins?" Parkins hastily returned his coffee cup to its saucer, spilling some on the table.

"Well, sir . . . er . . . they were on their way to discuss some internal problem . . . with the San Pagano chapter. Something about their charter being revoked."

"Their charter was fucking revoked all right," said Atwood sharply, snapping the pencil in half between his fingers. Parkins immediately offered him a replacement. "It's been two fucking weeks, no cigars! I don't need this shit in the middle of trying to quit smoking! Molly, anything new?"

"No. The seven bodies have been identified. All six members of that chapter were killed." Samuels flipped through some of her papers. "One . . . a Henry Rivers, a.k.a. 'Savage,' was also killed. He was from the mother chapter. The rest were all from San Pagano."

"The police say he was the only one killed with a .25-caliber gun," said Leverick. "The rest were either buckshot or nine-millimeter." He handed the police report to Atwood.

"What else?" asked Atwood.

"They believe it was the work of a rival club, The Outcasts. Their calling card was left behind, the letters OR carved in one of the biker's heads. Kurt Benson— the one they call 'Counsel'—told the sheriff's office that Rivers went there to discuss the upcoming bike run to Eureka Lake."

"What do you think, Dalton?" Atwood spit pieces of the eraser into the ashtray.

"I think it might have been a way for Counsel to get rid of a problem. He's been under a lot of pressure from the police since the girls' abduction from the concert. I'll bet they went there specifically to murder them."

Atwood leaned over the table and stared directly into Parkins' eyes. "Parkins, what exactly did Martin say when you spoke with him last week?"

Parkins took a deep breath and, hesitating only a

little, did what drug dealers and presidents alike do when they feel their survival is threatened: He lied.

"Martin said it was a done deal. Counsel was going to suspend their charter and take their colors until they got their act together. I offered him backup, but he insisted that he go it alone. Said it would be no sweat. Then he told me about the Fort Dix thing. It's all in my report."

Atwood looked over at Leverick. Leverick shrugged and turned to Samuels. "Maybe Martin was hurt," she said. "Except for a cache of weapons in the basement of the house, no guns were recovered at the scene. The ballistics report shows no .25-caliber bullets in the walls or furniture."

"Which means?" inquired Parkins.

"Which means the .25 was probably returning fire. Which means we have no idea whether or not the guy who fired that weapon hit anyone else besides Rivers."

The room became silent for several minutes. The agents flipped through paperwork, drank coffee, and tapped pencils nervously on the conference table. Molly Samuels broke the silence. "We have to go in," she said.

"What?" asked Parkins.

"Someone has got to go in and try to make contact with Martin. He may be hurt. He may have tried to intervene when the killing started, and is being held. Who knows? Something is definitely very wrong."

"Dalton, have you gone over the photos again?" asked Atwood.

"Several times. We had surveillance teams at both cemeteries. We got shots of every person coming in and out. Everybody, whether they were bikers or not. Martin wasn't at the funerals. Since the only excuse for a club member not attending is hospitalization, death, or jail, I'd say we've got a problem."

All eyes turned to Atwood. He had more undercover experience than all of them combined. He nodded his head. "I agree. We have to find him, bring him in, and shut this operation down. We'll take what we got so far and call it a day. Any suggestions?"

"I could go," volunteered Samuels. "I worked vice for a joint task force in Hollywood two years ago. I could hang around and make contact with some of the women who work for the club. Maybe some of them have seen Martin."

"Too risky." Atwood shook his head. "The club may take notice of you and try to induct you into their stables. We would have to move in. That would place Martin further at risk if they're holding him. No. I'll go in."

"You?" questioned Leverick. "How?"

"The Henchmen meet and hang around Mike's, right? I'll stop there a few times on the way fishing or something. Get to know some of the regulars. It's not much, but I think it's the safest way to get close to the club right now. If we act too aggressively and Martin is holed up somewhere, injured, we could blow his cover and jeopardize his life."

"If it hasn't been blown already," said Leverick.

"Right, if it hasn't already," responded Atwood.

"Sounds good to me." Leverick looked at Samuels and Parkins. They both nodded approvingly.

"It's set then. I'll give the Director a briefing this afternoon. Tomorrow I'll pay my first visit to Mike's. I hope to God Martin is still alive."

"What about the rest of the team?" inquired Samuels, holding her arms out, palms turned up. "Give us something to do here."

"Yeah, Richard," added Leverick. "We can't just sit around."

"All right." Atwood tugged at his lower lip, his eyes looking upward. "Start checking all the hospitals within a hundred-mile radius of the clubhouse. Get descriptions of anyone who was treated for a gunshot wound during the last week. Make sure the hospital records correspond with all police reports. I don't care how you split it up. Decide that among yourselves." Atwood looked over at Leverick. "Dalton, call me later this afternoon." Leverick nodded as Richard Atwood picked up his files and left the conference room.

"Any preference, Fred?" asked Leverick. "Fred!" Leverick snapped his fingers in front of Parkins' face.

"Oh . . . sure, whatever. After lunch. I made an appointment with my father for"—he glanced quickly at his watch—"one-thirty. I'll meet you two downtown at about three P.M. Okay?"

"Sure, Fred. Enjoy your lunch."

Samuels and Leverick gathered their things and left the room.

Parkins sat by himself for a moment, contemplating the seriousness of his situation. *If Walsh is dead,* he thought, *I'll have to live with the knowledge that I could have saved him. If he isn't, my career as an FBI agent is over.* He imagined his father, having heard the news, summoning him to his office. He would sit in the old burgundy leather chair, opposite his father's antique oak desk. Just as he had done when he was six years old, facing his father's wrath because of a below-average report card. He could picture his father pointing an accusing finger at him.

"You loser!" he would say. "I used my best political and business contacts to get you into the Bureau, and you get kicked out?"

"Dad," he continued the conversation in his mind.

"You *pushed* me into joining the Bureau. I would have been happy joining the firm."

"Damn it, Frederick! If I didn't have this damn heart murmur, I would have been able to pass the physical exam. I would have joined the Bureau myself. I placed all my hope in you."

Parkins could see his father shaking his head in disgust, arms folded, and then saying, "Get out! Get of my life! There's no place for you in here!"

No, thought Parkins, *that cannot happen. Walsh* must *be dead. He must* never *come in.*

Chapter 21

"Who's there? Identify yourself!"

"Who's there? Identify yourself!" the female voice said mockingly.

The young enlisted man relaxed, placed the M16 back on his shoulder, and lit the cigarette he had been carrying behind his ear. "Shit . . ." He blew out the smoke as he spoke. "What the hell's wrong with you, Carol? It's after midnight. No civilians are supposed to be on the base. I could have shot you."

"Oh, did the big, bad soldier almost shoot me?" she said in a babyish tone. "Give me a kiss, Rambo."

The private enthusiastically complied. He complied as he had four other times during the last week. He remembered the first time, in his car, as he'd prepared to drive the new secretary from the recruiting office to the bus stop. The next day she'd seduced him in the men's room just off the southside barracks. He gladly drove her to the bus the next two nights. If he hadn't pulled guard duty two nights in a row, he would have had a go at her again.

"Well, I'm glad to see you anyway, Carol. How's the job going?" asked the private, after a prolonged kiss.

"It sucks. But at least I met you, baby." She dropped slowly to her knees and unbuckled his belt. The private leaned back against the railing to the sentry booth. *How wonderful*, he thought. *This experi-*

enced, sensual woman is attracted to me—a nineteen-year-old kid with pimples. Except for a couple of whores, and one fling with a divorcée in his hometown of Harrisburg, Pennsylvania, he hadn't had much experience with women. The promise of easy sex had made him the perfect victim.

She buckled his belt and stood up.

"What'd you stop for?"

She pouted, then resumed the babyish tone: "I want to see all the weapons and guns and stuff. I could be a real naughty little girl with all those big, big guns around." She gently squeezed his testicles. He moaned approvingly.

"I don't know, Carol, I—"

"You promised, Danny. You said you would show me someday. Well, someday is here." Her voice became cold, more like a scolding mother's now than a baby girl's.

"Yeah, but things are different lately. Security has been beefed up. Lots of MP's coming and going all the time. It may not be safe."

"Come on now, honey, you ain't no scared little boy, are you?" Again she placed her hand between his legs.

"All right, all right," he said, surrendering. "Hop in the jeep. Let's go."

It was a five-minute ride to the stockade. The private didn't notice the truck following them. A two-ton delivery truck, stolen earlier from the parking lot of Chairs and Stuff Party Rentals in Paramus. It would not be missed until the owners opened up shop in the morning. The five Henchmen inside would have completed their task by then and have abandoned the truck somewhere near the Secaucus swamps.

"I'll have to ask you to look away while I open the door." The door to Stockade C had an electric lock that could be opened only by depressing a series of numbers on the dial pad, then using a key. The auxiliary stockade contained twenty rocket-launchers, twelve bazookas, forty M16's, two hundred sticks of dynamite, sixteen cases of hand grenades, and four hundred .45-caliber handguns with over ten thousand rounds of ammunition.

Danny turned to speak to Carol, "Okay, babe, let's—" The barrel of a .22 was aimed right between his eyes. "Carol, what the hell is this?"

"Just stay quiet, soldier boy." He instinctively raised his arms above his head. The Henchmen quickly appeared from the shadows.

"Good work, baby," said Dirty Dan, giving Carol a kiss. "Go wait in the truck."

Stoned Eddie removed the private's weapon from his shoulder and tossed it to Grease. They tied the young man's hands behind his back.

"You guys are nuts! You can't rip off the Army!"

"Shut up, faggot! There's nothing we can't do!" said Grease, pressing the barrel of the M16 against the boy's temple.

"Let's get inside," said Dirty Dan.

The five Henchmen entered the building with their prisoner. The moon shone through the wire-mesh windows, but provided little light.

"Where's the light, shithead?" demanded Bones Blackwell.

"There a timer on the inside of the door frame. Just turn it a full turn to the right."

The lights came on brightly, causing everyone to squint. Before The Henchmen's eyes could adjust to the light, the sound of over thirty M16's being bolted into firing position echoed through the room like a thousand pairs of tap shoes. The bikers found themselves facing a group of heavily armed military policemen.

"Oh, shit," said Dirty Dan. "There goes my vacation at the lake."

The phones were busy at the downtown St. Paul office of The H.F.F.H. Trading Company. The operation was moving two trailer-loads of stereos, seven brand-new Lincoln Continentals, and a small load of blue jeans intended for a major department store chain. Dave was having trouble unloading a trailer of produce that had been highjacked the previous day.

"We gotta find a fucking buyer for this goddamn lettuce, or we'll wind up dumping the shit in the river." Dave's breathing was heavy, his pulse rate high.

"Dave, take it easy, man, we're working on it." Jimbo offered him a cigarette.

"Thanks, man. Light?"

Jimbo flicked a small yellow lighter under Dave's cigarette.

"Dave!" said a small, pudgy man in his late thirties. Balding, with thick glasses, he held the clipboard close to his face as he read. "The guy at Vintage Appliances says he'll take fifty of the receivers, but he only wants to pay thirty-five dollars each."

"Tell him he'll pay fifty or he can suck my fucking dick. That scumbag is always looking to screw us."

The man scurried back to his desk and resumed his telephone conversation. Dave took a puff on his cigarette as he looked over the paperwork on his desk.

"You know, Jimbo, this is going to be the last time I deal with that creep Louie. He fucking told me he'd have a buyer lined up this morning. The shit is gonna rot if we don't move it right away."

"Yo, Dave!" shouted Ron "Pervert" Hawkins from

the far corner of the room. "I got Louie on the phone, line one."

Dave picked up the receiver and depressed the first button.

"Lou, you scumbag. I think—"

"Dave, listen . . . listen. I got the buyer, man. Just like I said. Twenty-five cents a head."

"When?"

"One hour. They'll take the whole fucking trailer. They think they can move the truck, too. They're offering five thousand for it."

"Take it. Just get the trailer the fuck out of the warehouse right now."

"You got it, Dave. I told you I'd come through."

Dave stood as he hung up the phone, stretched from side to side, and threw on his colors.

"Let's take a break, Jimbo."

Dave was stopped by a short, fair-skinned woman as he and Jimbo walked toward the door. "Dave," she said. "The buyer at J.R. Goodman says he needs an answer right away on the minks."

Dave sighed, placed his hands over his face, and rubbed his eyes. "Thursday; the shipment will clear customs on Thursday. Check with Sam to be certain, okay?"

She nodded and returned to the office. Dave and Jimbo left the building.

The two bikers rode forty minutes north on Highway 11. They stopped at a greasy spoon to grab some lunch before returning to the trading company office. Dave always found a quick trip on his bike invigorating. He would return to the office ready to wheel and deal in the moving of merchandise.

When they returned, Dave stopped before the doorway and looked up at the sign hanging over the door-

way of the old concrete-and-iron building. It read
H.F.F.H. TRADING COMPANY. Incorporated six years
earlier, fifty percent of the company's activities were
related to legitimate businesses. The legal activities
included shipments of furniture and fur products from
Canada. The office supplied distributors in North Dakota, Iowa, and Illinois.

"It may be time to replace that old sign, Jimbo,"
observed Dave.

Jimbo laughed. "Let's see if we got money in the
budget for it."

Dave laughed as well. He thought about how last
year H.F.F.H Trading had posted a profit of thirty-
five thousand dollars, although he personally had
made bank deposits in excess of one million dollars
into various accounts. To hide their wealth, the bikers
deposited money and registered houses in the names
of girlfriends or club associates. Although four members of the St. Paul chapter were worth over two
million dollars, the IRS would never find more than
fifty thousand dollars traceable to the whole chapter
combined.

Dave open the door and motioned for Jimbo to
enter.

"Let's get back to selling merchandise, Jimbo. We
got a lot of work to do before we leave for the lake."

"Yeah. Eureka Lake, brother. A fourteen-hundred-
mile run to three days of bikes, beer, and tits."

The two men returned to their desks.

"Hey, Jimbo, you talk to your bro yet?"

"Oh yeah. He's coming on the run. He can't wait
to see Dr. Death again. He thought the fucker was
dead."

It took two hours for Amy Walsh to get Alex to
bed. At least five times, he had come out of his room

with a request for a glass of water or another story. Finally he cried himself to sleep, and Amy went up to his room for a final look at her young son before turning out his light. She remembered how she and Martin would often stand and watch Alex sleep, their arms linked together, and she felt saddened. Sadness quickly changed to anxiety as she reminded herself that it had been over two weeks since she'd last spoken to Martin.

Martin had gone this long without calling before. Only this time she felt afraid. Something wasn't right. She couldn't put her finger on it, but in her heart she knew. She tried to relax by calling a friend, but failed to reach anyone. "*Someone's* got to be home at nine-thirty on a Saturday night," she muttered, as she hung up the phone for the fourth time.

After rummaging through some bills and reading a letter from her mother, she turned on the ten o'clock news. She'd been out of touch lately and needed to catch up on world events. Amy was beginning to doze off when the anchorperson spoke a familiar name, causing her to sit up attentively. "Officials believe last week's killing of members of The Henchmen motorcycle gang could be just the tip of the iceberg in what's been described by some as 'a biker war.' Residents and shop owners in Eureka Lake aren't worried. They say the yearly event, scheduled for two weeks from now, hasn't seen any serious violence since the late sixties, and they don't expect any this year." Frantically, Amy began to search through her purse and telephone directories for Richard Atwood's telephone number. He had told her to call if she needed to talk, and that if he wasn't available, Mrs. Atwood would be glad to lend a sympathetic ear.

"Hello," said a warm, mature female voice.

"Is this Mrs. Atwood? This is Mrs. Walsh! Can I please speak with Richard Atwood?"

"Honey, what's wrong? You sound frantic," said Mrs. Atwood concernedly.

"I must speak with him. My husband is on assignment for him and I'm afraid—"

"He's not here, dear. I can page him, though. Let me have your number, and I'm sure you'll hear from him within the hour."

Forty-seven minutes later, the telephone rang. Amy had never taken her eyes off the clock.

"Mrs. Walsh? This is Richard Atwood," he said formally.

"Where's Martin? I mean . . . have you heard from him? I just learned about this 'biker war' thing, and I've got to know if he's all right."

"Everything is fine, Mrs. Walsh. Martin is at a critical point in the investigation right now. I have a strong feeling that it will all be over soon."

"When was the last time you heard from him?"

"Now, Mrs. Walsh, that's proprietary information. An agent's contact dates cannot be disclosed to anyone outside the case."

"He's my *husband*! God damn you and your fucking case!" She could picture Atwood moving the phone away from his ear as she exploded furiously into the handset, all the frustration of the last few months pouring out. After five minutes of angry abuse, Atwood was able to get some words in.

"Mrs. Walsh, I assure you that the next time I speak with Martin, I'll instruct him to call you immediately. You must remember that it's hard for him. It's not just a matter of logistics. I've worked undercover for many years. I've put my wife through the same pain, the same worry, dozens of times. It can sometimes be very difficult to get to a phone to call your spouse.

It's even harder emotionally to prepare to speak to someone you love, after you've been working so hard to maintain the character you've assumed to make your case. Everything will be fine. Okay?"

"No, it's not okay. But thanks anyway, Mr. Atwood. I'm sure he'll call. Good-bye."

"Good-bye."

Amy Walsh slammed down the phone.

"Bullshit." She walked over to the oak wall unit and opened the bottom drawer. Unfolding a map of California and spreading it out on the coffee table, she quickly traced a route with her finger. "Eureka Lake. Twenty miles south of Riverside." She returned the map to the drawer and went to bed.

Chapter 22

I thought I was blind when I first opened my eyes. Then, little by little, I could make out the dark shapes of the objects in the room. There was a lamp on an end table next to the bed. I reached for it to turn it on, and my head exploded in pain. I must have blacked out, because the next thing I knew I was lying on the floor, the lamp on top of me.

I got myself up to a squatting position, my head still pounding like someone was beating me with a sledgehammer. I touched the side of my head and could feel the bandages. What the hell had happened to me? It seemed like hundreds of images and as many voices and sounds were spiraling through my mind.

Hearing the sound of footsteps outside the room seemed to calm the noise in my head. As the steps drew closer to the door my heart began to pound and my pulse rate must have soared, because I sprang to my feet as if I'd just been given a shot of adrenaline. Whoever it was now stood right outside the door. As the door opened and the outline of a massive person came into view, I was suddenly hit with a wave of paranoia. Whatever had happened to me, I was sure someone was now coming to finish the job. With all the strength I could summon, I kicked the hulking figure in the chest.

The kick had little or no effect, because before I

knew what had hit me I was in a headlock and pinned, facedown, to the floor.

"Who the fuck are you? How the fuck did I get here?" I blurted. To my surprise my attacker spoke in a low, soothing tone.

"Doc, Doc. It's Jack, brother. Calm down," he whispered intensely into my ear. "You've been out cold for days, man." I was breathing heavy, and my eyes felt like they were darting about in a frenzy, for the rush of images had once again returned to torture and confuse me. "Do you hear me, Doc? You and Dog were on your way back from the desert. Dog got wasted. Think, man. Remember!"

My attacker loosened his grip on my neck. I started to relax, and after a few moments he let go completely. He helped me to my feet, and I started to feel dizzy.

"I'd better sit," I said, holding my hand to my head. I sat on the edge of my bed, and my mystery host placed the lamp on the end table and turned it on.

"Dog . . . he's dead. The Outcasts . . ." I said. It was coming back to me.

"I know, man. We buried Dog three days ago. They brought you guys to a hospital near Keeler. Dog was DOA. Counsel says they thought you were gonna buy it too. Soon as the doctors got you stable, Counsel and Snake brought you here and asked me to look after you. I don't hang much with the club anymore— just some parties and the funerals and runs—but my door is always open when my brothers need me."

I sat there on the side of the bed, rubbing my temples. Fat Jack! Yes, I remembered seeing his picture. The full white beard and wavy white hair. The jolly, Santa-like face.

Fat Jack leaned over and placed a hand on my shoulder. "You've been out for almost five days, except for some moaning and talking in your sleep. Who the hell is 'Amy,' anyway?"

"I don't know. I mean I know. I know the name but I don't know who she is, you know?" *That's it, Walsh,* I said to myself. *Think fast, and pray you didn't say too much.*

"Whoa, slow down, Doc! Now you're making *my* head spin."

"I think I know you, too," I said.

I squinted, as if I were trying to get a better look at him. In case I'd said something that might have aroused suspicion, I thought I might as well play up the "dazed and confused" routine. It wasn't far from the truth. There was still a lot that wasn't coming in loud and clear.

"Yeah, I *do* know you," I said. "You've been with the club since '69, got your own vending-machine business. Two kids, right?"

"Right. My son Billy and a daughter, Alice. She's away at school. Studying in France to become a teacher. Billy lives in New York City. Christ, Doc, how the hell do you know so much about me?"

I shrugged my shoulders.

"I couldn't tell you, I just know. It's *me* I don't know much about. Things are real blurry. Names, faces, things coming back then fading away again."

I opened my eyes wide when it hit my mind like a freight train.

"The Henchmen! I just got my Henchmen colors. Used to ride with Satan's Saints in Canada. Randall . . . my name's Randall. Right?"

Great. I'm reminding myself as much as I'm convincing him. Man, does my head hurt.

"That's right," said Fat Jack. "Better known to his brothers as Dr. Death. Look, try to relax, brother. I'll let Counsel know you're all right. You gotta rest up, Doc. The Eureka Lake run starts in three days, and you gotta be able to handle your hog. Want a sandwich or something?''

"Sounds good," I said. Now that he'd mentioned it, I realized I was starving.

After wolfing down two sandwiches, I walked around the room a bit to try to work out some of the stiffness in my joints and muscles. I looked out the window. From the view here it seemed that the house was pretty well secluded. Through the thick trees I could just make out another house about a quarter-mile away. I would have to rest. Maybe another day. Then I would get the hell out of here, go down to that house, and call in this goddamn operation. I was much too cautious to take the chance of using Jack's phone. If he or anyone in the club overheard me, I would hardly get the phone receiver back in its cradle before I'd have a bullet in my head. As I lay there drifting off into sleep I thought, *What the hell was that number to Base 1? Boy, does my head hurt.*

Staring at the telephone, he poured his fourth Scotch. For more than an hour Fred Parkins had been drinking, pacing the floor, and playing a game of mental ping-pong. What should his next move be? He looked at the clock. Seven forty-five A.M. In fifteen minutes Helmsford's shift would be over, and he would lose the opportunity. Another day would be spent wondering about the end of his career in law enforcement. And the end of his relationship with his father. Taking a deep breath, he grabbed the phone and dialed the number.

Patrick Helmsford stacked the piles of unfinished work neatly on his desk. It would all keep until tomorrow's shift. A few arrest reports, a proposal from a local plumber to fix the sink in the rest room, assorted letters and requests for information from family members and news people concerning recent cases. His plan to leave ten minutes early was thwarted by the ringing of the telephone.

"Helmsford." He made no attempt to hide his annoyance.

"Patrick Helmsford?"

"Yes . . . yes. Who the hell is this?"

"Who I am isn't important. What is important is that I have some critical information for you and your buddies—The Henchmen."

There was a long silence, as thoughts flew through Helmsford's head. *What can this be? A joke? Maybe an investigation. Maybe it's a test. That's it. Someone suspects me of having close ties to The Henchmen and is trying to trap me.*

"Henchmen. Yes . . . the motorcycle gang. Not exactly my buddies. You ought to be speaking with Detective Ross. He's our expert on the biker gangs."

"Sure, tell me about it." Parkins' tone was antagonistic.

"Now wait a fucking minute, asshole! Who the hell *are* you?"

"The biker who calls himself Dr. Death is a fed. He was brought in to shut them down. The only reason you're still in business is the feds can't get a triple shift authorized to monitor your phone calls. It's just a matter of time."

Sweat ran down Parkins' face as he hung up the phone, suddenly panicked by his own actions. The enormity of what he had done dawned on him as his stomach tightened and his head began to ache. He poured his fifth Scotch and walked over to the mirror. A sad, pathetic drunk looked back at him.

"You had to do it," he assured his image, taking

another drink. "Besides, he's probably dead anyway, so it won't matter. You did the right thing."

He held the empty glass up to the mirror, dropped it on the floor, then fell back on the couch. He would sleep until noon, when Dalton Leverick, concerned that he hadn't shown up at the office, would call him.

Helmsford was at his wit's end. *Who was that? How had he known to contact me?* He asked himself these questions repeatedly during the forty-five-minute ride to his apartment. Each time, no answers. Each time he was no closer to a decision. If he didn't say anything to Counsel, and the information turned out to be true, he would be finished with The Henchmen. Maybe finished with living. That would be so only if Counsel knew he had the information. How could he know? Unless Counsel was testing his loyalty to the club. And if not Counsel, then someone else knew of his Henchmen connection. But who?

He fumbled with the keys to his apartment door, dropping them three times before finding the right one. Once inside he headed straight for the kitchen, the cabinet over the sink, right-hand side.

"Shit," he said, disappointed. "No Scotch. I guess it'll have to be vodka." He sat in front of the telephone. Drinking straight from the bottle, he looked at his watch between gulps. Nine-thirty A.M. Too early to call Counsel at home. He took another gulp from the bottle. "Fuck it." He depressed the digits hesitantly.

"Counsel? It's Helmsford."

Snake and Iron Man were making the rounds along the strip. They would park their bikes at one end of the street and walk together from shop to shop, making their weekly pickups. Establishments under Henchmen protection would pay them the weekly fifty.

Shops owned by the club would simply open their books for a quick review. No need for a cash payment. Counsel controlled the bank accounts, and would make regular transfers electronically through the club's computer. The businesses were legitimate. None was registered in the name of the club or any of its officers.

Snake went right to the novelty section of the Hole In One books and novelty shop, while Iron Man went to the main counter.

"Evenin', Sally," Iron Man politely said.

Sally was a short, fifty-six-year-old woman with rotten teeth and a bad left eye that was always half-closed. She had worked in the pornography business for over forty years. She and her boyfriend had started one of the first shops on the strip.

"You're not on rounds this week, are you, sweetheart?" she asked, surprised to see him.

"Sure am, Sally. Me and Snake."

He gestured toward Snake, who was looking perplexed as he studied a double-headed penis, hearing none of their conversation.

"Well, I done paid a young feller no more'n an hour ago." Sally picked her nose and nonchalantly rubbed her fingers on her blue polyester sweater.

"*What?* Who?" Iron Man's eyes bulged like they were about to pop out of their sockets.

"Never saw him before. He had a Henchmen tattoo on his forearm, just like you boys. He says he was comin' to collect, so I gave him his fifty."

Iron Man slammed his hand on the counter. "What the fuck did he look like?"

"He looked like most of you boys. Long hair, scraggly beard. A little on the skinny side, though. Not like you . . . No, not like you at all." Sally leaned over the counter and patted him on his belly.

"Sally, you don't pay nobody you don't know!" Iron Man turned toward the novelty aisle. "Snake, let's go, man. We're gonna find that motherfucker."

"Who? Hey, I want to get one of these!"

"Not now, dipshit. Come on, I'll explain along the way."

"You don't pay nobody you don't know!" Iron Man repeated, pointing his finger at Sally as they exited the shop. She shrugged, scratched under her armpit, and sat back down to a copy of *Bestiality* magazine.

The two bikers spent the next three hours riding up and down the strip in search of the imposter. Stopping in all the bars and strip joints in the area, they questioned over fifty people. Finally, at almost two in the morning, a hooker named Jinx told them a guy with a Henchmen tattoo had tried to talk her into a free blow job.

"I said Henchman or no Henchman, you gotta pay if you want Jinx to swallow your salami, baby," she had told them. "I'd seen that boy before. I think he regulars over at The Crossbow, on 10th Street."

The bikers rode over to 10th Street. They noticed a Japanese motorcycle parked outside The Crossbow bar. Iron Man and Snake pulled over about fifty yards down the street.

"If this guy did this while riding a rice wagon to boot, I'll rip out his eyes and fuck his skull," said Iron Man as he dismounted his Harley.

They entered the bar and began to walk from table to table, looking everyone up and down as they made their way through. Suddenly, a man stood and ran toward the back of the bar.

"The back door!" shouted Snake, as he darted after him. The imposter ran across the yard and started to climb a chain-link fence. Snake leaped and caught him by his ankle, shaking him loose. He fell on his back, his head hitting the ground hard. Snake picked him up by the jacket, spun him around, and held his arms, while an out-of-breath Iron Man confronted him.

"You little shit!" He tore the sleeve from his jacket, exposing the phony Henchmen tattoo on an arm covered with needle marks. "Where'd you get this?"

"I d-did it myself, man! Honest! I thought I could get a couple of fast bucks. P-please, man! I'm sorry! I'll have it removed! I'll give you guys back all the bread!"

"Shut the fuck up, dickhead!"

Iron Man slapped him across the face, opening a small cut on his lip. He punched him in the stomach and kicked him in the groin, causing his knees to buckle. Snake still held his arms as the junkie quivered and gagged.

"You're goddamn right you'll have it removed."

Iron Man held the man's wrist and pulled an eight-inch buck knife from its boot strap. With one stroke he sliced off the tattoo, along with most of the man's forearm. It fell to the ground like a slab of raw steak. A look of shock and disbelief appeared on his face, then screams that didn't sound like anything human followed. Snake loosened his grip and the man fell to the ground, writhing in pain and still screaming his inhuman cry.

The two bikers pushed their way through the crowd that had gathered at the back door, every one of them too scared or too indifferent to offer any assistance to the victim. Snake and Iron Man could still hear the screams as they mounted their Harleys.

"Hey, Iron Man, let's go back to Sally's!" suggested Snake. "I want to get that dildo for the run to the lake!"

Chapter 23

The coffee was bitter. Atwood took small sips, hoping to get used to it. He placed the cup on the edge of his desk, careful not to disturb the mounds of paperwork and reports relating to the biker case. He looked at his watch, reached again for the cup, then abandoned his decision to try again.

"Susan, order me some coffee from outside, please. All that machine can make is mud."

"Right away, Mr. Atwood. Shall I order some for Mr. Leverick too, sir? The receptionist says he's on the way."

"Yeah, sure. Although I should make the bastard pay for his own," he mumbled playfully.

"What was that, sir? I didn't understand."

"Nothing, Susan. Send Dalton in when he arrives."

Atwood returned to making notes on a yellow pad. He had set up a list of arrests that he felt they could make stick—if Martin Walsh was still alive. If the worst had happened and Martin was dead, there was little they could do. Most of the crimes had either been witnessed by him or confessed to him. They did have some signed 302's that implicated the club in dealing firearms. That might be enough to invoke the RICO Act. Then again, it might not be.

He broke the point of his pencil as Leverick walked briskly through the door.

"Walsh is alive!" said Leverick. His smile was broad and vibrant.

"How? When?"

"You know we were working the hospital angle, checking for gunshot wounds? Well, it turned out that a hospital outside of Keeler took in a DOA from a gunshot wound, and another guy fitting Martin's description. The DOA was Henchman Jerome Fenway, known to the bikers as 'Dog.' "

"The guy from Boldero Prison?"

"One and the same. Get this: Four bikers come in to the ward the next morning, intimidate the shit out of the entire medical staff as well as some deputy kid from the sheriff's office, and take Martin out. The doctors say he was unconscious when they took him. It was definitely Martin. We ran a check on the fingerprints taken from the van."

"Van?" inquired Atwood, still smiling at Leverick's keyed-up explanation.

"The sheriff's office hauled in a van that had crashed in a ditch along Highway 190. A passerby told the sheriff that before he'd called in the crash, he saw two bikers taking something out of the van."

"What was it?"

"We don't know. My guess is either drugs or weapons. Sounds like part of the biker war to me."

"Me too." Atwood's face became serious. "Was Martin shot?"

"No, the assailants must have left him for dead. The doctor said he had a bad concussion. No broken bones."

Atwood stood up and walked over to his bookcase to get another pencil. "Do we know were he is?"

"No. Molly checked his apartment last night. She gave his landlady a fifty. Said she was an old girlfriend, and wanted to surprise him with a visit when he came home. It didn't look like anyone had been there for days."

Atwood and Leverick both stood silent for moment. Then, as if prompted by the same thought, both men solemnly seated themselves.

"Why hasn't he called in?" asked Atwood.

"Precisely, *precisely* what I'm asking myself." Leverick rose to meet Atwood's secretary in the doorway. "Thank you, Susan." He took the brown paper bag and removed the two containers. Susan left silently. "They never put enough milk in these, you know?"

"Don't complain. It's free, isn't it?"

"So what do we do, Richard? Bust them? Then ask where the hell Martin is?"

"No. Too risky. Martin could be laid up somewhere, and he'd be a sitting duck if a mass arrest were to suddenly take place and questions were asked about him. I think we have to get near the bikers, scope it out."

Leverick sipped his coffee. "A visit to Mike's?"

"Yeah. Tonight. Get the jeep from the garage and pick me up at nine o'clock."

Leverick looked at his watch. Five-fifteen P.M. "That doesn't leave me much time. I'd better run." He picked up his coffee container and headed toward the door. "Oh, one more thing. I'm worried about Parkins. He's been acting real strange." Leverick waited for him to add something. Atwood just nodded. "I can't quite put my finger on it, but something's not right. What do you think?"

"I think we have to get to Martin. Tell Parkins nothing. I'll arrange to have him taken off the case until we can find out what's wrong."

It was daytime. What time, and exactly what day, I had no idea. I felt stronger now; still a little dazed in the head, but definitely stronger. Strong enough to leave the house and put this nightmare to rest. I still wasn't sure exactly what the number to Base I was, but I was confident that when I started dialing it would come to me. I figured the team had to be out of their minds by that time, wondering what the hell had happened to me. And Amy. My dear, sweet Amy. At least it would soon be over. Or so I thought.

I was surprised when I opened the door to see Snake standing outside the room with an M16 in his hands.

"Hey, Doc. How you doin', man?" he said.

"Great, Snake. Feeling great." Sure I was. "What's with the hardware? Where's Jack?"

"Jack's out. Counsel wants to talk to you. He'll be here soon, Doc. He told me to make sure you didn't leave the house."

"What the fuck is that shit?" I had to show Snake I was pissed. Compliance would have shown I was hiding something. "If he wants to talk to me, he could just come over and talk to me. He doesn't have to put a fucking guard at my door."

Snake became defensive. "Look, Doc. The prez said you wait, and that means you wait." His eyes displayed cold determination. He would shoot me if I tried to leave. I was certain of this. I moved closer to him.

"Look, Snake, we don't have to—"

"Sorry, Doc." He pointed the M16 at my head. "Just go back inside until Counsel gets here. I'm sure it's nothing, man. Just don't fuck up, okay?"

I put my hands up, almost mockingly. "Whatever you say, Snake." I returned to the room. I looked out the window and saw another Henchman, I wasn't sure who, standing below with a shotgun propped on his shoulder. I was stuck. I sat on the edge of the bed and waited.

About an hour later the door opened and Counsel walked in.

"Doc, we have to talk, man," he said without a greeting. Another man whom I had never seen before followed Counsel.

"This is Pat Helmsford. I'll cut right to it, man. He says somebody tipped him off that you're an agent. He says your real name is Martin Welsh or some shit." Counsel turned toward Helmsford. Helmsford was looking at me menacingly.

"Walsh," said Helmsford. "You're a fucking plant, aren't you, scumbag?" Helmsford took a step closer to me, accusing me face-to-face. "I did some checking. There *is* a Martin Walsh working for the FBI in California. I called, and they declined to comment on his whereabouts. I think you're him." He poked me in the chest.

I knocked his arm away. *Think fast, Walsh. Integrity and brains. Now more than ever.*

"Get your fucking hands off me, motherfucker!" I said.

"Hold it," said Counsel, pointing a snub-nosed .38 at my head. "I gotta make this call, Doc. I don't know. . . . I just gotta make the call."

Christ, this is bad.

"He's full of shit, Counsel! Don't you see? Someone's trying to turn us against each other!" Counsel lowered the gun. I continued talking rapidly. "They feed some name of some retired agent to this asshole and create a fucking war inside the club." I turned back to Helmsford. "I should kill you, you stupid fuck! You don't know what the fuck you're talking about!" *This better be working, or I'm going to die today,* I thought.

Counsel also looked at Helmsford, who was beginning to look uneasy. He flipped the gun around and
handed it to me. "Here's your chance, Doc. Blow him
the fuck away."

Helmsford looked at Counsel in disbelief. "Are you
crazy? Counsel, please, stop this shit!" He placed his
hands in front of his face. I stood there, almost frozen
with fear, forcing myself to raise the gun and point it
at Helmsford. I could practically feel Counsel's piercing gaze as I fought with all my will to keep my hand
from shaking. *Oh my God,* I thought, *I'm losing it—
got to hang on!* Then, as if my instinct for survival had
set my brain on automatic pilot, I told myself that it
was going to be him or me. *He's a crooked cop. Fuck
him.*

I pressed the snub-nose against Helmsford's forehead and squeezed the trigger repeatedly. Four successive clicks. No blood. No bullets.

Helmsford sank to the floor. He placed his head
between his knees and started to cough. "God damn
it, Counsel!" he said, panting. "You scared the fucking shit out of me!"

I stood there in a daze. Counsel carefully took the
pistol out of my hand. Helmsford, regaining some of
his composure, rose to his feet and scurried out of the
room like a scared rabbit.

"Sorry, Doc. I had to be sure." Counsel hugged me.
"You gonna be able to ride your hog on Sunday?"

"I'm ready to ride it now," I said. "Let's go." I
started to walk toward the door. Counsel stopped me.

"Wait here, Doc. We still don't know who's trying
to fuck us up. You'd better stay here. Fat Jack will
drive you to the clubhouse to get your bike right before the run."

This was bullshit. Even though I'd passed his little
test with Helmsford, Counsel obviously didn't want to

take the chance that I would disappear. There was tension between us, and I didn't want to push my luck. *Fine,* I thought. *I'll play it out. I'll wait until the run, and when hundreds of bikers are partying and raising hell I'll slip out and be on my way. It should work out. Unless Counsel's got another test planned for me. One that I can't pass.*

"You should have let me waste that creep," I said as Counsel was leaving.

He turned around and smiled. "He is a creep, but a useful creep. Saves us a lot of grief having a cop on the payroll. But I still wonder who the fuck told him that bullshit." Counsel shrugged it off and left the room. *Whichever way you look at it,* I thought, *this is all coming to an end soon.*

Leverick waited outside the Federal Building. The jeep's engine was running, and he had the air conditioning turned up high to combat the odor of dying fish. He spotted Atwood coming down the steps dressed in a khaki-colored fishing outfit. Lures and hooks decorated his vest and hat. He was carrying a rod-and-tackle box, which he threw in the back of the jeep.

"Don't you think we're carrying this cover a little too far?" asked Leverick. "I can understand looking like something from the pages of *American Fisherman,* but making me buy a load of fish, too?"

"Did you ever run into a man on his way home from two days of fishing in the mountains? It takes about three days to get the smell of fish off him. If I'm going into that bar pretending to be coming from a fishing trip, everything is going to be just right. Right down to the fucking stench of fish. Hell, maybe I'll offer the bartender a couple of fillets."

Leverick tapped his lip with his forefinger, remembering Richard Atwood's reputation for paying attention to detail.

"That's right," said Leverick. "You're the one who organized the surveillance a few years back of that fruitcake killer. What'd they call him?"

"Jaws."

"Yeah, Jaws. They still talk about how you made two of the decoy agents douse themselves in that ammonia mixture, so they'd smell like street people. Always thorough."

"Damn right. When a bad guy smells a rat, it's usually because his senses are telling him that something ain't right. These Henchmen are shrewd operators. Some of them, at least. They rely on instinct for survival, just like you and me."

Leverick nodded.

"Let's get going," said Atwood.

Leverick drove the four-by-four jeep into the parking lot at Mike's. He wore a green windbreaker, jeans, and an Oakland A's baseball cap. Atwood handled the fish, then threw them in the back of the jeep with his rod-and-tackle box. "Sit on the passenger side," he instructed Leverick.

"Good luck, Richard. How will I know if things go sour?"

"If you see a Henchman come flying through the window, that's your signal."

Atwood tapped on the hood of the jeep and then made his way past three rows of motorcycles, lined up in perfect order, creating a walkway to the door. Inside it was crowded, noisy, and filled with smoke. Henchmen colors were everywhere, with a few patches from local clubs popping into view from time to time. Atwood noticed members of The Road Stompers, Dead Heads, and Dark Knights motorcycle gangs mingling amongst the crowd of almost one hundred Henchmen. Nationwide, The Henchmen influenced or controlled over forty different motorcycle clubs. Each year at least five of those clubs from the Southern California area got invited to the Eureka Lake run.

Some of the locals sat quietly by the bar while country music played loudly from the jukebox. The occasional cracking of billiard balls could be heard from the back room. No one paid attention to Atwood as he casually made his way to the only empty stool at the bar.

"What'll it be?" Sam the bartender placed a paper coaster and napkin on the bar.

"A beer. Don't matter what kind," said Atwood, as he turned his head and scanned the room.

"Not usually like this. Big run coming up." Sam opened a bottle of Budweiser and placed it on top of the coaster.

"Thanks." Atwood placed a ten-dollar bill on the bar. Sam quickly replaced it with seven singles.

"How's the fishing?"

"Not bad. Got about two dozen blues, almost as many bass."

"Pretty good. Give me a shout when you want another beer." Sam left to tend to another customer at the end of the bar. Atwood swung around on his stool to get a better look at the crowd. He thought he saw Walsh a few times, but he didn't want to strain to see through the crowd and draw attention to himself. After ordering another beer, he walked to the back room to watch the pool game. A wiry-looking man with red hair and a long red beard was making a shot with the pool cue behind his back. His leather vest displayed the colors of The Dark Knights.

"Seven ball. Straight-up." He missed the shot.

Atwood raised the bottle to his lips and continued

to look for Walsh. The noise level in the bar increased suddenly, and many of the bikers turned toward the door. Counsel and Iron Man had entered the bar, and many of the other bikers, who had not seen them since last year's run, surrounded them to shake hands, embrace, and exchange a few words.

Atwood returned to his seat at the bar, his eyes and ears wide open. Counsel stood next to him and ordered a beer.

"On my tab, Sam," said Counsel. Sam laughed as he handed Counsel the bottle.

"I'm real sorry Dog can't be here, Counsel. I used to have to order extra beer just for him."

"I know, Sam. It's been rough." Counsel gulped down the beer and handed the empty bottle back to Sam, who quickly replaced it with another.

Another biker came up to the bar, placing himself between Atwood and Counsel, practically knocking the FBI agent off his stool. "Yo, brother!" said the biker. "Is Doc gonna make the run?"

Atwood almost gasped at the mention of Walsh's alias.

"Yeah, he's gonna be there. It looked doubtful for a while, but he'll be here." A few seconds later both men melted into the crowd. Atwood left Sam two bucks and slipped out of the bar.

Atwood sat silently for a moment after returning to the jeep.

"Well?" Leverick sounded impatient.

"He wasn't there, but I heard them talking about him."

"What did they say?"

"It was just as we thought. He must have been laid up some place, injured from the crash. At least it's not too bad, because I heard them say that he was going on the Eureka Lake run."

"Oh, shit. We have to pull him. We have to find out where he is and pull him *now*. Let's issue a warrant for his arrest on a parole violation, push these assholes for information on his whereabouts, and yank him."

"No good. The run is only two days away, and these guys are too pumped up. We start harassing them about one of their members and we could have a major incident on our hands, further putting Martin at risk. I think we should wait for the run. With all the other clubs and civilians around Eureka Lake that weekend, we might be able to pull him without causing a problem. We have a better chance of catching him alone there. Besides, we'll have time to organize backup from the state troopers."

Leverick started the engine.

"Do you know how to ride a motorcycle, Richard?"

Atwood smiled confidently. "Fuckin' A, I do, Dalton."

Chapter 24

Earl "Crusher" Miller was the most feared Outcast ever to hold the position of president. He had begun the Black Heart Squad so that The Outcasts' killers would have something to aspire to. Members of this elite group had a black heart tattooed on their chests, with the words DEATH IS CERTAIN, LIFE ISN'T printed in black on a silver banner.

Twenty-five of the squad had answered Miller's summons. They were all crammed into the living room—on the floor, couches, tables, anywhere the bulky men could manage to sit or crouch. Miller sat upright on a reclining chair, holding a leash. The leash was attached to a leather dog collar worn by a young girl of no more than sixteen. The naked girl sat with her head between her knees, her hands folded on top of her head. Miller occasionally snapped the leash, causing her to wince painfully. Chuckles would break out among the bikers each time the pressure of the collar caused her to gasp.

"Before we get down to the meeting, brothers, let me tell you about Mary Lou. Mary Lou here has been a very bad little cunt. Haven't you, bitch?" He snapped the leash hard against her back. She nodded tearfully.

"Quit that whimpering before I smack the shit out of you!" Miller raised his hand. The girl cowered and lowered her head to her knees. "Mary Lou tried to run away this morning. Didn't you, cunt?" No response. "If Crusher hadn't come looking for his little sweetheart, she would have left for who knows where. Right?" He yanked the chain so violently that Mary Lou fell on her side, gasping for air. Again she said nothing. "I said *right*, cunt?"

"Right, yes!" She grabbed the collar and loosened it so she could breathe freely again. Miller removed a dagger from his boot. "Put your hand on the table."

"No . . . Crusher! Please . . . no!" she begged.

"Do it now, or every one of these brothers is going to smash your little face with his hammer. Now do it!" he growled. The girl place her opened hand on the white formica table. She bit hard on her bottom lip, shaking her head from side to side and silently crying, "No . . . no . . . no."

Miller stood up, still holding the leash. He placed the sharp blade on her pinky finger, just below the knuckle.

"You're Outcast property, cunt. Our colors, bikes, guns, dogs, and bitches are our property. We don't lose what's ours. God forgives, Outcasts don't."

Grunts of agreement could be heard from the group of men. Without warning Miller increased the pressure of the knife on her pinky. The finger popped off, like the stem of a carrot, and rolled onto the floor.

Miller released the chain, allowing the hysterical and screaming girl to scramble around the floor, trying to retrieve her lost finger. She grabbed the severed digit and scurried to the kitchen for ice and a dish rag. Miller turned to the group and held out his arms.

"Do I know how to treat a woman, or what?" The bikers laughed and cheered their leader while Mary Lou struggled to put on her shorts and T-shirt, her hand wrapped in a blood-soaked towel. She held a paper cup in her teeth where she had placed the finger.

"Here's ten bucks," said Miller. "Get yourself to a hospital. We got business to discuss." The frightened girl ran from the house.

"Lou, go with her." Miller shot a glance at Lou "Wired" Jackson, the youngest member of the killer squad. The slim, well-groomed biker complied and followed her out the door. "I'll let you know later what goes down here, man!" yelled Miller. Wired raised his hand in acknowledgment, then turned down the street, out of sight.

Miller grunted as he lifted his six-foot-five, three-hundred-twenty-pound frame out of his chair. His injured left eye was half-closed. Two years earlier, while riding home from the Des Moines clubhouse, he had gone over the high side on his chopper. His face had hit the pavement, shattering both cheekbones. The left side had never properly healed, leaving him little control over his facial muscles. His face would often twitch, his left eye fluttering opened and closed.

Miller stroked his long black beard as he paced back and forth. After a minute of expectant silence, he turned to his hand-picked squad of killers.

"I'm sure you all know that the hit on Frank David in Minnesota fucked up somehow. Our man in St. Paul says David's house is guarded twenty-four hours a day by Henchmen strikers." The Black Hearts listened attentively. The air was heavy with cigarette smoke and perspiration.

"Fuck 'em," said a burly, toothless biker wearing an old top hat and an eye patch over his right eye. "Let's kill the fucking strikers and his whole goddamn family." Some grunts could be heard as the bikers started to stir.

"Don't worry, brother," said Miller. "Anyone here

with a taste for Henchmen blood will have a chance for a meal. We got an opportunity to get over two hundred of those fuckers together this weekend and shoot their asses up but good."

"Crusher, man. If you're talking about Eureka Lake, that's fucking suicide. We can't just walk into a Henchmen camp," said John "Little John" Mackey, a short, muscular biker. "Hey, I'll take on those scumbags anytime, but, man, we'll be outnumbered almost ten-to-one."

Miller gave Little John a long, cold stare. "There were only twenty-five of them in Cleveland. We lost five times as many brothers as they did. I've been waiting years to give it back to them.

"Together, we've probably chilled over two hundred people. We are the elite of the elite. Most bikers only dream of becoming an Outcasts' Black Heart. They're not expecting twenty-five of the best. Believe me."

One of the Black Hearts jumped to his feet. "Let's go for it! Let's blow their sorry asses away! I don't give a shit if it's suicide! I'm not gonna miss an opportunity to kill that many Henchmen!" The rest of the group roared their approval.

"The fucking run starts tomorrow. How the hell do we get from Iowa to California?" asked Little John. He stood with his bulky, tattooed arms folded tightly.

"I'll let our brother from Reno explain it," said Miller. Matthew "Spider" Alexander rose from a squatting position. The clean-shaven biker was the newest Black Heart; he'd obtained his tattoo just three weeks earlier, for killing a Nevada judge who had a tendency to give maximum penalties to Reno bikers. Alexander had a spider-web tattoo that started under his chin and continued down to the black heart on his chest.

"I set everything up last week. We have a van. A big one. The windshield is fitted with bulletproof glass and the sides are armor-reinforced. Some dude from the military did the work for two ounces of crank. I chilled his ass the next day." The bikers started to laugh. A few applauded and whistled. "In addition to two up front, over twenty of us can cram into the back of the van. I'm gonna drive right through the middle of their fucking party and, brothers, we're gonna come out spraying."

"The plane leaves in four hours," added Miller. "No hardware. Bury your colors until we pick up the van. I'm asking every one of you to come. Anyone out?" No dissenting voice was heard. They were all aware of the club's fourteenth bylaw, which stated that any member who refused a request from a brother who was willing to partake in the activity himself risked the loss of his colors and his life.

The parking lot outside Mike's was blanketed with motorcycles. This was the traditional meeting place for several Henchmen chapters before a major run, and the lot was always buzzing with last-minute oil checks, tune-ups, and roll calls. Several weeks prior to the run, the road captains of the various chapters had to map out routes and coordinate with each other so that every member's departure and arrival time would be known. Once the road captain of the mother chapter had all the information, he would call ahead to the local police or sheriff's office of any town the club planned to pass through on the way to the run.

Counsel conferred with Crazy, who was busy writing on a clipboard. Counsel motioned for Little Vinney to join them as he came by.

"Hey, Vinney, come here, man." Counsel took off his sunglasses and wiped them on his shirt.

"What's up, Counsel? Crazy." Vinney was visibly excited. He was wearing a Kaiser helmet outfitted with a pair of bull's horns. For many members like Vinney, the run was a chance to show the citizens what being a biker is all about. The club got a kick out of freaking out passing motorists on the highway, who were shocked by the sight of over two hundred bikers riding two abreast through the streets. Pedestrians in the dozen or so towns that The Henchmen would pass through made it an annual affair, as a parade of Huns on wheels rumbled through their otherwise peaceful small town. Many of the children who gathered to watch the procession imagined themselves riding a motorcycle one day. Many of the men would look on with hatred—hatred for something they feared and didn't understand. Hatred for the part of them that wanted to break out and live free, riding on a big Harley and not caring about society and its rules and regulations.

"What's the status on the main crash truck?" asked Counsel. Crazy continued to write, occasionally looking around the lot to verify the presence of certain members.

"Left last night. Snake's chick and Pam drove. They probably got there about four this morning."

"Good. Crazy, did you talk with the police chief at Bridgepoint?"

"Yeah," he said, without looking up from his paperwork. "He says everything's cool. Most of the dudes involved in last year's hassle don't even live there anymore."

"Sounds like it's all smooth sailing," said Vinney, making a sailing motion with his huge, tattooed hand.

Vinney, as assistant road captain on this run, was in charge of securing the crash truck's arrival. Besides beer and drugs, the crash truck transported a variety of small-caliber weapons. By sending the crash trucks ahead of or behind the pack, they could easily slip through the various checkpoints that so often delayed the main contingent.

"Okay," said Counsel. "Let's get ready to ride. As soon as Doc and Fat Jack get here, we pull out."

Amy Walsh glanced down at the copy of *Roughriders* that lay open on the bed. Pictures of last year's motorcycle weekend in Laconia, New Hampshire, covered the pages. She checked every detail carefully. She wore a tight miniskirt of blue leather, a black-and-white tube top, and soft black-leather boots that came up over her knee. She applied lipstick and eye makeup exactly like the woman's in the picture. A pair of dark sunglasses and a small leather shoulder bag completed the look. Amy glanced in the mirror and said with a nervous sigh: "This is it. Time to find me a biker named Martin Walsh."

She left the house, map and suitcase in hand. She placed the suitcase in the backseat of the car and set out on her six-hour ride to Eureka Lake. She repeated in her mind the question that she had been asking for days: *What can be wrong? Why hasn't he called?*

The ride would seem endless.

By the time Fat Jack and I arrived, most of the bikers were lined up and ready to ride to Eureka Lake. Counsel steered his bike next to mine. I was making some last-minute adjustments to my carburetor before taking off.

"Here, Doc. Hold on to these." Counsel handed me a vest, a Henchmen belt buckle, and a gold Henchmen insignia pin.

"What's this?" I asked.

"They're Monk's. He must have left them at the

clubhouse early this morning. One of the prospects saw him leave around four-thirty."

"He quit?"

"Seems that way. We're gonna have a security meeting about him after the run."

Yeah, I'll bet you will, I thought. *Probably decide to kill the poor son of a bitch. But it's almost over for you, scumbag. First opportunity on this run, I'm gone and you're finished.*

"Why give them to me, then?" I asked.

"I don't know, really. You two seemed tight. I'm thinking maybe he'll try to contact you or something. Just sit on the stuff for a while, okay, Doc?"

"Sure, what the fuck." I rolled the items up in the vest and stuffed it in my rear saddlebags.

The Henchmen were ready to move out. The Los Angeles chapter would lead the pack, as was customary. Counsel rode to his position at the edge of the parking lot. Crazy pulled up next to him, in the traditional position of the road captain. Hank the Skank was directly behind Counsel. Next to him Snake, with his jet-black Harley. The rest of the chapter joined the formation, with me riding to the left and behind Iron Man. The sergeant-at-arms always rode at the rear of the full-color-wearing members. Prospects and honoraries rode behind him.

It took thirty minutes for all the chapters and other clubs to get into formation and join the run. The sea of bikers stretched for almost a quarter-mile. None of us would drive over fifty-five for the entire trip to Eureka Lake. Two miles behind the pack were three more crash trucks. These were intended to pick up members who had broken down or had been ordered off the road by the chapter's sergeant-at-arms. That killed my chances of just laying back and quietly disappearing.

Iron Man had had a leather strap custom-designed for him by one of the local motorcycle shops. An aluminum baseball bat sat inside, like a Samurai sword in its scabbard. It was Iron Man's job to make sure no one was too stoned to ride. If he noticed a member driving recklessly, he would pull up next to him and whack him on his arm or leg with the bat. He could even order him to pull over and wait for one of the trucks to arrive.

I did find riding my Harley for the long distance a welcome relief, after spending so many days cooped up in Fat Jack's house. The pain and confusion in my head subsided with the soothing rhythm of the highway. This was the first time I'd really felt right since I'd regained consciousness. I let myself become part of the great wave of thundering machines. I was going to make it through this operation. I was sure of it. A little *too* sure of it, as I would soon find out.

Chapter 25

A banner hung across Main Avenue. It read: EUREKA LAKE WELCOMES BIKERS. Men and women, young and old, crowded the sidewalks to view the arriving bikers. Leverick, Atwood, and Samuels had arrived early, to position themselves by a refreshment stand across from the entrance gate to the swap meet and camping field. The Eureka Lake run was the oldest and biggest of The Henchmen's events. The Elmwood chapter arrived a day early to set up the tables for the motorcycle parts and accessories. Their two burliest bikers, both Wild Bunch members, stood by the gates, ready to turn back any club that hadn't been invited by The Henchmen.

Animal Field, as the residents of Eureka Lake referred to the six-acre property, was rented by The Henchmen every year for three days. Their stated purpose: A "swap meet," for motorcycle enthusiasts to trade and purchase parts and accessories.

"Any sign of him?" asked Atwood, as he returned to the aluminum picnic table. He carried three hot dogs, two cokes, and a black coffee.

"Not yet," responded Samuels. "Only the Elmwood chapter and a club called 'The Proscritos' have yet to arrive. About fifty or so independents have checked in so far."

"Independents like us," said Leverick, as he tugged at his denim vest.

"Yeah, real hot-doggers." Atwood removed the lid from his coffee and took a sip. "I want to be ready to move in quickly if we have to," he said seriously. "Is every thing set with the backup?"

"Most definitely," said Leverick. "I'm in contact with the captain of the troopers." Leverick held a beeper-sized communicator in his hand. "There are almost a hundred troopers just on the other side of the hill. The twenty-man local force is also on call." He pointed north to a hill about two miles across the field. The Governor had reluctantly agreed to allow Atwood and Leverick to command the troopers, but only after a call from the FBI director himself had convinced him to cooperate. State troopers resent federal officers taking command of what they perceive to be a local problem.

"I just hope that if we do have a situation they come through, or our asses are cooked," said Samuels concernedly. "I don't see why we can't just set up a roadblock and arrest Martin on some hokey charge."

"Forget it," said Leverick. "Mark Nelson, the trooper captain in charge of motorcycle gangs, said he has an agreement with The Henchmen. After the riot in '75 over the roadblocks and searches, he agreed to leave them alone as long as the bikers contain themselves to Animal Field. They also had to agree that they wouldn't send anyone outside the grounds for extra beer or food, in groups larger than three."

"What makes you think Martin will be in one of those groups of three?" asked Samuels.

"Doesn't matter," said Atwood boldly. "Nelson agreed that if we fail to pick Martin up during the weekend, he'll authorize stopping the bikes on the way out. You see, he only agreed not to block them coming in."

Molly took a bite of her hot dog and nodded. Leverick stood up and placed his hand over his eyes to block the sun's rays.

"This could be them," he said, as he spotted a large contingent of bikers coming into view down Main Avenue. "It's definitely them. I can see Counsel at the head of the pack. No sign of Martin yet."

"He'll probably be riding next to the sergeant-at-arms at the rear," said Atwood. "Keep looking."

The bikers rode through the checkpoint in pairs. Leverick was the first to spot Martin Walsh.

"I see him. Christ, there's a *lot* of these guys here!" He looked down at Atwood, who was still nursing his coffee. "What now?"

"Now we wait. If Martin comes out, we grab him. My guess is he'll use the first opportunity he gets to look for us or get to a phone. He's got to figure that we can't be far behind him."

"We hope," said Samuels pessimistically. The three agents watched as more than a hundred bikers flowed into Animal Field.

By four o'clock that afternoon the number of arriving bikers had dwindled. There were still some stragglers coming in, but most of the spectators had gone about their business. Five members of the St. Paul chapter were making camp at the edge of the field.

"Hey, Jimbo, let's go, man!" said John Hollister. "I can't wait to see Dr. Death again. The mother chapter's setting up now at the other side of field, near The Watering Hole. We can grab a couple of beers and say hello."

"Take it easy, Johnny," said his older brother. "I know you're anxious to see the dude, but let's make fucking camp first. We're gonna be here for three days. Cool it, bro. We'll go over in a few." John Hollister shrugged and began to unfold his sleeping bag.

What can a few minutes matter? But won't Dr. Death be surprised!

I joined Iron Man and Counsel and walked over to "The Watering Hole," a makeshift bar with kegs of beer that would pump all weekend. After buying our beers, we walked over and sat on some chairs surrounding an old wooden pickle barrel. There were ten similar settings scattered within ten yards of the beer kegs. We quickly guzzled the first round and I volunteered to get some refills. I grabbed the three mugs and walked toward the beer taps. I needed to make my move soon. Besides the tension between Counsel and me after that Helmsford incident, there was a lot of tension among the California chapters over the San Pagano massacre. I had heard one of the bikers from Elmwood inquire of Iron Man, "Any more chapters get hit by The Outcasts, brother?" Something about his tone was accusatory. Or was it my imagination? I wasn't planning to hang out long enough to find out.

As I filled the last beer, I was startled to see three dollars being held under my nose. I had never understood the words "a chill ran up my spine" until I heard Amy's voice right then.

"I'll buy this round, Martin," she said.

I felt dizzy. The sight of her face brought back the pain in my head. For a moment I thought I might be hallucinating, that the knock on the head was causing me to see Amy when in fact there was no one there at all.

"Are you all right?" she asked. She put her hands on my face. This was no mirage. She was really here.

"Amy?" I looked over at Counsel and Iron Man, who were waiting impatiently for their refills. "What the hell are you doing here? You want to get us both killed?"

"Martin, I'm sorry. I *had* to come. You hadn't called in so long, and when I heard about those bikers getting killed I didn't know what to do."

"I'm fine. Look, you have to get the hell out of here. This is too dangerous." I could see Iron Man out of the corner of my eye. He stood up, funneled his hands around his mouth, and yelled, "Yo, Doc, bring the bitch here if you want, just bring the fucking beers!" He sat down and laughed with Counsel. Amy was crying. I handed her one of the beer mugs. "Carry this. Remember, my name is Doc. You just met me here at the beer stand. We'll volunteer to get another round and then run the hell out of here, okay? Can you do this?" She took a couple of deep breaths, looked over at the bikers, and swallowed hard. "Yes, Martin . . . Doc. I can do it. Let's go."

When we got back to the table I had Amy sit on my lap.

"Shit, man, the fucking beer must be piss-warm by now," said Counsel, as he looked Amy Walsh up and down. "Not bad, Doc. Never knew you were such a quick operator."

Iron Man guzzled down his beer.

"I'm going to get another one myself. I'd grow old waiting for you to fucking get it." Iron Man went back to the beer kegs to get a refill. I thought that maybe Amy and I should try to run for it. The Base I team couldn't be far. They might even be watching right now.

"Dalton! Quick! Look at this shit!" He handed Atwood a small pair of binoculars. The food stand was at least a hundred and fifty yards from The Watering Hole. The miniature pair of FBI-issued binoculars was as powerful as most of the full-sized models found in sporting goods stores.

"Is that who I think it is, sitting with Walsh and the two Henchmen?" asked Leverick recognizing Amy from a picture in Martin's file.

"Holy motherfucking shit! What the hell is *she* doing here? I think we might have to move in now."

"Should I call it in to Nelson?"

"Wait, there are two other men approaching them. I recognize one. The St. Paul chapter's V-P. I don't know the other guy. Molly—go down there and get her away from the group. Act like she's a friend who wandered away from her old man or something. Get her as far away as you can, and we'll give the order to move in."

Molly Samuels slung her leather bag over her shoulder. She walked through the entrance and past the Elmwood chapter sentries, who made lewd remarks but made no attempt to stop her. She made her way down toward the The Watering Hole. Atwood kept watching. Leverick made contact with Captain Nelson of the state troopers and placed him on alert.

"We got some visitors, Counsel," I said curiously. Counsel turned around.

"Hey, it's Jimbo from St. Paul! Well, fucking Jimbo! How are you, brother?" Counsel kissed and embraced the biker.

"This is my brother Johnny," said Jimbo.

"Johnny." Counsel shook his hand.

I was holding Amy's hand, squeezing it tightly.

The biker Counsel had called "Jimbo" continued, "Listen, man. I'm sorry to hear about the San Pagano chapter. Those fucking Outcasts should all die."

"We'll get our chance, brother. I got big plans," Counsel said acidly.

"Hey, man!" said Jimbo enthusiastically. "Johnny used to party with the Saints years back. He's dying to see Dr. Death again. Is he around?" An acute sense of dread blanketed me at that moment. Counsel slowly turned and shot me a cold look.

"That's him." Counsel pointed at me, then looked toward Johnny for his reaction.

"No fuckin' way. I'd know the motherfucker anywhere. I don't know who you got here, man, but it ain't the Dr. Death I know from Satan's Saints."

Counsel pushed over the barrel violently. I pushed Amy out of the way and jumped from the chair. Suddenly Molly Samuels appeared, grabbed Amy by the arm, and pulled her away from me and the bikers. *Thank God!* I thought. Leverick and Atwood weren't far behind. Amy protested as Samuels practically had to drag her away. "Martin, no!" she cried.

"Who the fuck *are* you, man?" growled Counsel, grabbing me by the lapels of my vest. I could feel the heat of Counsel's breath on my face. Counsel's eyes were wide with both anger and surprise. "I'm gonna fucking do you myself, you cocksucker. Counsel pulled out a nine-millimeter pistol and pointed it at my head. "Tell me how the fu—"

The screams from The Watering Hole stopped Counsel in mid-curse. He turned his head to look. So did I. People were scrambling to avoid a van plowing through the tables. Four people were run down by the vehicle before it came to a stop. The back of the van popped open and what I was sure were Outcasts started pouring out of the back, spraying machine-gun fire in all directions. They must have been on the far end of the campgound since early in the morning, waiting for the run to fill up with Henchmen so they could inflict a high number of casualties. I lunged at Counsel, who was still absorbed in the chaos, smashing my elbow into his face. He dropped the pistol and fell back over a chair. I picked up the gun and started to run toward the entrance. The bikers from St. Paul joined everyone else in scattering all over the grounds, retreating behind motorcycles, trucks, and anything else that would shield them from the onslaught. As I was running I looked over my shoulder and saw one of the St. Paul bikers fall. Iron Man was running for cover as well, about twenty feet to my right. I saw him duck behind a red van and out of sight. I could see that Molly Samuels had already gotten Amy through the gate. There was no time for me to run that far—I would be picked off by one of The Outcasts. I managed to get behind a cluster of pickup trucks and vans about fifty yards from the entrance.

I took up position behind a white pickup and shot an Outcast dead between the eyes as he approached the vehicle, spraying his Uzi in a wide arc. Several Henchmen had made it to their crash trucks and armed themselves. The Henchmen and the invading Outcasts exchanged a barrage of gunfire. The state police moved in from the north. A fleet of cruisers with lights flashing and sirens blaring entered the war zone. One trooper was felled as he exited his car. The others started shooting at bikers on both sides. Confusion, smoke, and death were everywhere. I cautiously looked out from behind the pickup to see if Counsel was still out there. He was nowhere to be seen.

Atwood and Leverick met up with Molly Samuels and Amy Walsh. "Take her to the police station off Main Avenue," ordered Atwood. "Nelson's men are moving in now, and we're going in after Martin." Samuels and Amy Walsh began to trot down the street. Atwood and Leverick managed to take cover inside the grounds, behind a row of bikes.

"You see any sign of Martin?" asked Atwood.

"No. I think I saw him run behind that group of

trucks, then I lost sight of him." Leverick's eyes widened with surprise. "Watch it!" he said. Atwood turned and fired. An Outcast fell dead beside them. Almost ten more minutes went by before the troopers managed to bring the situation under control. Fifty more police arrived on the scene as backup, and mass arrests were being made. Eighteen members of the Black Heart squad, including Crusher Miller, had been killed. Fifteen Henchmen, ten associates, and four women also lay dead. Iron Man had himself killed four Outcasts before taking cover behind the crash trucks.

I crawled on my hands and knees toward the front of the pickup truck. Slowly, I lifted my body and reached for the door handle.

"Leaving the run, brother?" said Counsel sarcastically, as he placed the barrel of a .38 behind my ear. Iron Man appeared around the front of the truck and lifted me to my feet. "I'll take that," he said, relieving me of the nine-millimeter. He stuck it in his belt. He entered the truck and moved to the passenger side. Counsel motioned with his gun for me to enter next. Counsel got in, placed the gun in his belt, and took off toward the gate with me trapped between them. Iron Man held a revolver to my head. Shots were fired at us as we left the grounds. The side-view mirror shattered as a bullet pierced it. Iron Man pressed the gun harder against my head.

"Fuck it," said Captain Nelson to one of his troopers, as they watched a pickup truck speed away. "It's probably no one important. We need the manpower down here." The troopers continued to round up bikers and confiscate their weapons. The Outcasts "suicide mission" had proved to be just that. Most members of the Black Heart Squad were now dead.

Chapter 26

Counsel raced the pickup down Main Avenue. He almost mowed down a group of pedestrians who were still lingering under the welcome banner. He made no attempt to slow down. They either jumped out of the way, or they got killed. Counsel's eyes were staring straight ahead. Wherever he was heading with such fierce concentration, it wasn't going to be good for me.

My worst nightmare was realized when Counsel slammed on the brakes and stopped in front of the now abandoned Eureka Lake police station. Molly Samuels and Amy were descending the huge stone steps. Counsel placed his gun behind my ear. "If you even breathe too hard, dipshit, I'll blow your fucking head off!" As soon as they were close to the pickup, Iron Man jumped from the truck and confronted them. Molly Samuels stepped in front of Amy and reached inside her bag for her revolver. Iron Man fired a round that ripped through her shoulder. Molly fell to the ground, and Amy screamed as Iron Man trained his gun on Molly's head and squeezed the trigger. He clicked the empty pistol three times. "Fuck it!" he said, as he threw the gun down.

"Grab the cunt and get the fuck inside, man!" ordered Counsel, his .38 still pressed against my head. I was paralyzed with fear. Fear not for myself, but for Amy. I had to make a move soon, but if I got myself shot she would die shortly thereafter. That was certain. Iron Man lifted Amy off her feet and shoved her hard onto my lap. He was barely inside himself when Counsel began to race down the avenue again. Iron Man produced another pistol, a .25 automatic, from a leg holster, and pressed this against my head. When we reached the edge of town, Counsel turned onto an old dirt road into the hills, where the club owned a small cabin.

"Counsel, listen. What the fuck does she have to do with this?" I asked, hoping against hope I could reason with him. One of my many conversations with Roger Wolfe flashed through my mind. "If you're suspected by your targets of being an operative, maintain your innocence till your last dying breath. As long as there's some doubt in their minds, you'll have a fighting chance. Integrity and brains, my boy. The key to survival."

"She called you 'Martin' back there," Counsel answered. "I heard her when the other bitch started to drag her away. Helmsford was right! You're the fucking man, a motherfucking agent!" We hit a bump. Amy's head hit the roof, hard. Iron Man laughed.

"Bullshit, man!" I protested. "I've proved myself already!"

"Then who the fuck are you? Why didn't Jimbo's brother recognize you?"

"Let's do the two of them," said Iron Man. "We don't need this shit."

Counsel pulled the vehicle within twenty feet of the cabin. Iron Man climbed out and held the door open for Amy and me to get out. Counsel followed, and trained his pistol on me once again.

"Don't get slick on me, Doc. Or 'Martin.' Or whoever the fuck you are. Keep your hands on your fucking head."

* * *

Atwood and Leverick checked the entire field for Walsh. They caught up with Mark Nelson at the Black Hearts' van.

"I can't figure the size of the balls on these crazy bastards. They pack twenty-some-odd men into a van and drive in to make a suicide hit. Christ, that's nuts," said Nelson.

"There's no sign of our man, Nelson. Are you sure no one has left the grounds?" asked Atwood.

"One pickup got away. We figured it was just some hot-dogger. Too much shit going on down here to chase 'em. We must have gotten our signals crossed here. We should have had that gate covered. Sorry, gentlemen."

Atwood and Leverick looked at each other. Without another word they moved rapidly toward the exit gate.

"Shit, Richard," said Dalton Leverick as the two men ran toward their motorcycles. "Counsel and Iron Man are unaccounted for, too. The three of them must have left together."

"Do you think they made him, Dalton?"

"Yes. I do."

The two agents mounted their bikes and exploded onto Main Avenue, heading toward the middle of the town. They could see the flashing lights of an ambulance, surrounded by a crowd. They dismounted ten feet from the crowd and jogged vigorously until they reached the scene. Samuels was being lifted into the ambulance by two paramedics.

"Hold it a moment!" ordered Atwood. A young police officer stepped in front of him. "Move aside, son. FBI." Atwood flashed his identification. He and Leverick climbed into the back and crouched next to Molly Samuels.

"Molly, what happened?" asked Leverick, as the vehicle accelerated. He held on to the roof to maintain his balance. Molly was alert, but she was in tremendous pain.

"They—" She winced. "They got Amy Walsh. Martin was with them." She sucked in her breath as the ambulance hit a bump in the road. "I think it was Iron Man Morgan who shot me. It happened . . . pretty quick."

"Did you see which way they went?" queried Atwood.

Samuels closed her eyes and winced in pain. "No . . . I couldn't." She closed her eyes again and lay back on the gurney.

"God help them now, Richard. Damn it!" Leverick punched the roof of the ambulance. "We never should have let him go in so deep! Never!"

"Don't count Martin out, Dalton," said Atwood. "He's got what it takes to survive."

They were walking us to the cabin. I hesitated, allowing Amy to move in front of me. I held back a little more, until Counsel was about two feet behind me.

"Get moving, man!" ordered Counsel. "Don't think I won't—"

I shot a powerful back-kick to his groin, which doubled him over. His pistol fell to the ground. I kicked him in the face and quickly picked up the weapon. I turned toward Iron Man, who was already swinging an eight-inch buck knife at my neck. *Christ,* I thought, *this guy produces weapons like a regular Rambo.* I instinctively raised my arm in defense. The knife slashed my forearm and I lost the gun. Iron Man took a second swipe at my neck. I ducked under his arm and threw a hard elbow strike to his rib cage. Iron

Man gasped for breath. I sent a flying kick to his chest, knocking the three-hundred-pound biker off his feet.

"Martin, look out!" warned Amy. I leaped onto Counsel, thwarting his effort to reach the gun. Amy quickly picked up the weapon and threw it into the woods. I hit Counsel across the chin with two thunderous right hands, sending him onto his back again. The pain in my forearm and the loss of blood were weakening me. I turned to check on Iron Man, and was met with a kick to the chest from the sergeant-at-arm's huge boot. I fell on my back, dazed. Counsel shook off my punches, hopped to his feet, and grabbed Amy by her neck.

"Who the fuck is he?" Counsel yelled. *"Tell me, cunt!"* He tightened his huge fingers around her neck. I could see she was only seconds away from passing out. Choking and gasping for air, Amy could hardly speak. "He's . . . my husband, Martin Walsh," she said tearfully.

"Well, you're gonna watch your husband die!" said Counsel, as he pushed Amy to her knees. Iron Man picked me up off the ground and further punished me with a knee kick to the stomach. He let me fall, doubled over in pain. A blow to the back of my head with a hammer fist forced my face to hit the ground violently.

Amy, I thought. *I* won't *die. . . . I* won't *let this happen. . . . Got to get up. . . . Got to.* From the deepest recesses of my very soul I found the strength to get to my feet. Iron Man was reaching down for his .25. It must have come loose from its holster during our scuffle. I wasn't going to give him the chance to finish me off with it. I sprang to my feet and jumped on his back, locking my good arm around his oversized neck. I grabbed under his nostrils and pulled half his nose off his face. He roared like a wounded bear. I then hit him with three successive chops to his throat, crushing his windpipe. He fell forward like a great oak. I stepped over his lifeless body to face Counsel, who knelt over Amy, the buck knife to her neck. My heart was pounding so hard I thought it would burst from my chest.

"It's between me and you, Counsel!" I shouted. I started to inch closer. "Let her go, man! Me and you! Let her go!"

"Fuck you, you lying cocksucker! I'll cut *both* your throats!" Counsel was sweating furiously. He was getting a crazy look about him, and I was scared shitless for Amy. My only chance was to appeal to his ego.

"Go ahead, man!" I goaded him. "Cut down a man's old lady because you're too pussy to face him! I would expect that from an Outcast, never a Henchman. Is that what you are, Counsel? A pussy wannabe with no balls?"

There was a long silence. I could almost hear my blood rushing through my veins. I was about three feet away now. Counsel was breathing heavy, like a pressure cooker about to explode. Suddenly he pushed Amy flat to the ground and lunged at me in a wild, screaming attack. I waited until the last possible second, then ducked to the side. Counsel lost his balance and twisted violently around, slashing air in hopes of making contact with his target. Before he could get his bearings I shot a powerful straight left hand to his temple. He released the knife, and I followed up with two more blows to his jaw and neck. I grabbed his long, wild hair and pulled his head back. I then shot a murderous palm-heel strike to his jaw, taking him off his feet. As I moved in, he managed to kick me in the groin. Pain shot through my entire body. Without hesitation he kicked again, this time at my face. I fell flat on my back. He dived on top of me and locked his huge hands firmly around my throat. I tried to push him away, but the gash in my right arm was taking its toll. I was running out of strength. Counsel's head was shaking, and his eyes bulged in rage. I couldn't breathe. I felt my windpipe collapsing, my life slipping away.

Suddenly, the crazy look in his eyes turned to one of shock, and his grip on my neck loosened. Spit dripped from his open mouth as he gasped for breath. As I pushed him off me, Amy's terrified face came into view. She had killed him. Using Iron Man's buck knife, she had saved my life. I held out my arms and she slowly came to my side. Shaken and terrified, we sat embracing each other, barely saying a word. I have never been so grateful to be alive as I was at that moment.

Epilogue

Thinking back, I can't say for sure whether I regret that assignment. It was the worst experience of my life, but we did manage to disband The Henchmen. Some of the chapters dug up their previous colors and, having no mother chapter to direct their activities, went back to drinking, riding, and raising hell.

Parkins was allowed to resign. He broke under pressure from Atwood's grilling, and admitted to "bad judgment" in not having supplied backup for the San Pagano incident. But he wouldn't admit to having tipped off Helmsford. I'll never manage to prove it, but I know it was him. At least we were able to bust Helmsford on his Henchmen involvement.

Atwood retired last month and moved to New Mexico. Molly took early retirement because of her badly injured shoulder. Dalton and I are still good friends, although it's no more than an occasional phone call. He now heads up the team at Quantico, where they keep tabs on serial killings. He travels around the country, working closely with local police departments.

I often think about Monk, Dog, and the other Henchmen I got to know and, in some ways, even to respect. They were a ruthless bunch, no doubt, but nobody took care of business like they did. I went into the assignment thinking it was a clear cut case of good versus evil. I was the hero—out to stop the evildoers at all costs. If I've learned anything, it's that good and evil exist only in the definitions agreed upon by the majority. A president can order the bombing of villages, causing the deaths of children, if the majority decides to call it "war." The Henchmen lived outside our society. Judged by their own agreed-upon standards, they were righteous. By our society's, they were not.

There isn't much danger to my new assignment as Group Supervisor. I head a team of white-collar investigators. I'm home every night at six-thirty, and have the weekends off. Amy and I have another boy, Anthony, now almost two. My life is happy, organized, and simple, right down to the six new suits—all blue—that hang together in my closet. Right next to my Henchmen colors.

Don't miss Martin Walsh's next
action-packed undercover assignment in

STRANGLEHOLD

by D. Edward Bungert

A string of brutal murders becomes a media heyday
when journalists name the sinister serial killer "The
Wrestlemaniac." To track the killer, F.B.I. Special
Agent Martin Walsh goes undercover once again—this
time in the hard-hitting world of professional wrestling. But Walsh soon discovers that his quarry is only
the tip of the iceberg: a soldier in an international
conspiracy of bloodshed and corruption that might
cost this undercover agent his life. For Walsh, the
stakes have never been higher—an opponent, more
deadly. Time is running out, and only Special Agent
Walsh can break the stranglehold.

Available in January 1994